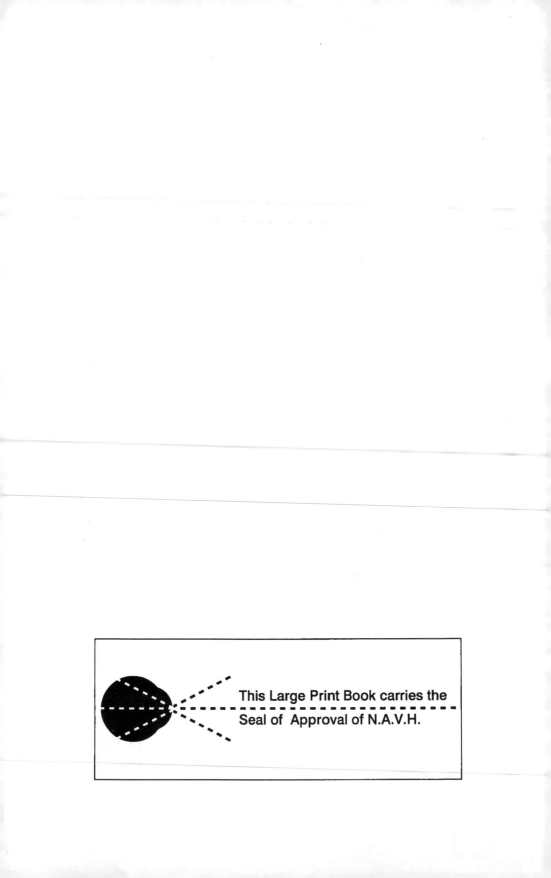

This Large Print Book carries the
Seal of Approval of N.A.V.H.

Wild Roses

Barbara Hazard

G.K. Hall & Co. • Thorndike, Maine

Published in 1999 by arrangement with Signet,
a division of Penguin Putnam Inc.

G.K. Hall Large Print Paperback Series.

The text of this Large Print edition is unabridged.
Other aspects of the book may vary from the original edition.

Set in 16 pt. Plantin by Minnie B. Raven.

Printed in the United States on permanent paper.

Library of Congress Cataloging in Publication Data

Hazard, Barbara.
   Wild roses / by Barbara Hazard.
      p.   cm.
   ISBN 0-7838-8666-7 (lg. print : sc : alk. paper)
   1. Large type books.   I. Title.
[PS3557.I34227W55   1999]
813′.54—dc21   99-15667

For Loree, with love

Chapter 1

My maid saw him first.

That was strange, come to think of it. I had spent so many hours watching for him in the months after Lord Blake died, I was so certain he was somewhere nearby. But I never saw him again after the morning I summoned him to the library at Trecarag Hall and told him he must leave. Till now. And in London too, where I had been sure I was safe.

I had gone shopping that morning to see if I could find a new hat I could take to the country with me when I went down to Oxfordshire with the Dowager Duchess of Lansmere. Bond Street was busy, crowded with people, horses, and carriages. It was noisy as well. When was it not? Newsmen ringing their bells, little girls crying their flowers, and men reciting casts and plots as they thrust playbills into unsuspecting hands. Above the din rose the indignant voices of two irate coachmen, arguing about who had the right of way.

At first I only shrugged when my maid said, "There's a man back there, ma'am. He's been following us, and he keeps staring at you."

"Pay him no mind, Franklin," I said, waiting

for the traffic to ease so we could cross the street. "You know how men often stare. Now then, I think we should try Madame Folly first. I do so like that green bonnet she made for me, don't you?"

"But ma'am, he's not staring at you that way," Franklin persisted.

It was then I turned slightly as if idly surveying the street. Yes, it was he all right, just as I remembered him. Tall and broad-shouldered with that distinctive nose that made all his other features seem insignificant. I pretended I didn't recognize him as my gaze went past him to focus on a shop window beyond. But I was aware of his deep bow even so, the way he swept his top hat from his blond hair, and I could not help but stiffen. For a moment, I panicked. I wanted to pick up my skirts and run as fast as I could, flag a hackney cab and put as much distance as possible between us. It took only a moment's reflection to realize that would do no good at all. He would only follow me straight back home. And even if he did not, it would be simplicity itself for him to find out where the late Lord Blake's town house was situated.

I forced myself to slow my hurried breathing. It wouldn't do to let Franklin know there was something wrong. The man meant nothing to her, for I had only engaged her after I left Cornwall. None of the servants I employed now knew anything about him, for I had let all Lord Blake's Cornish servants go. I wanted no one who had known about *him* anywhere near me.

I crossed the street and walked slowly toward the milliner's, looking into the shop windows as I went. Franklin walked beside me carrying my parcels. I saw she still looked puzzled, but excellent servant that she was, she said nothing further.

As we entered Madame Folly's, I was able to relax although I found it hard to concentrate even on the delightful confection of tulle and straw and forget-me-nots which Madame set reverently on my head. Franklin assured me it was the perfect hat for a summer spent in the country, and I nodded even though I had barely noticed it. I made arrangements for the milliner to send it on to Portman Square, and reluctantly left the shop.

"I'm suddenly feeling rather tired," I said as I smoothed my gloves, my eyes downcast. "Fetch a cab, Franklin. I'd like to go home."

As she nodded and moved to the curb, I looked around as casually as I could. Yes, he was still there across the street, staring into a shop window with his hands clasped behind his back, keeping an eye on the milliner's door that was reflected in the glass. Such an ordinary man he was. No one would remark him in spite of that nose — his height. He even looked like a gentleman, his clothes neat, and his starched cravat arranged to a nicety.

Hurry, Franklin, hurry! I ordered silently, afraid he would cross over and accost me. How

9

was I to behave if he did? What would I say? I wondered bleakly, very much aware there was nothing I *could* say.

I could feel panic gathering and threatening to overwhelm me, the beads of cold sweat on my spine, but fortunately Franklin beckoned just then. A hackney cab stood waiting at the curb and I hurried toward it. It seemed to take forever for it to reach Portman Square, although I knew it was only a matter of minutes. At last I hurried inside, leaving the maid to pay the cabbie. When the front door was shut behind me, I felt safer even though I knew that was an illusion.

I went through the dark hall to the drawing room while Franklin took the parcels upstairs. I could not sit down. Instead I paced up and down, thinking hard. When the door opened suddenly, I whirled, hand to my heart.

"Good gracious, Lucy, did I startle you?" Faith Abbott asked as she came in and went to a mirror to remove her hat. As she did so, she sighed. "I am sure I am the fondest of grandmamas, dear, surely you must agree that is so. But I swear if Forrestal doesn't stop singing the praises of his son and heir so constantly, I shall lose my mind."

I forced myself to concentrate and take my usual seat. "Perhaps if you were just to go to Lansmere House when the duke is out, ma'am?" I suggested.

"But then I would still have to endure Eugenia's conversation. I had no idea parenthood could turn two perfectly normal adults into such bores. Besides, I can see for myself how handsome the baby is, how sturdy and vigorous. Oh, Lucy, he smiled at me today! Yes, indeed, I'm positive it was a smile and not just gas, as Eugenia claimed."

I tried to pretend an interest I did not feel. Some of the boredom I tried to hide must have showed, however, for the dowager said, "But there I go, rambling on again, as bad as they are.

"Tell me, did you find a suitable hat? Not that the most horrid thing wouldn't look lovely on your head, my dear."

I waved away her compliment. "Yes, a white chipped straw with pale blue trimming. Franklin approved."

"Then I am sure it is ravishing. Your maid has impeccable taste."

"It is so good of you to invite me to Lansmere, ma'am. London in the summer is impossibly close and dull."

"Will you return here in the autumn, my dear?" the dowager asked.

"I'm not sure," I said, picking up my needle-point and setting a careful stitch. "My plans are uncertain."

"Surely a visit to Cornwall is in order, isn't it? I believe you told me once you have not returned to the estate since your husband died. It isn't wise to rely only on agents, no matter how trusted they may be."

"I shall never go there again," I said firmly.

The dowager was a darling, but she could be very persistent. So far I had been able to keep her in order by refusing to answer her most personal questions. She always accepted this in good spirit, even though I knew she longed to know everything about me. But I knew she behaved as she did because she was concerned for me, and I never took offense.

"Perhaps it would be wise to sell the place then, purchase another country home. To be sure, Cornwall is much too far from town to make an easy journey, but there are some lovely places in Kent or in Oxfordshire, near me. Perhaps we might look about this summer while we are there? What do you say?"

"I'll consider it, ma'am," I told her, measuring another strand of nile green.

"I do think we can be off by the end of next week, if that is not rushing you, Lucy," she said after a moment. "I have some engagements, but I can easily cancel if you would like to go sooner."

I would like that very much indeed, I thought, but I only said, "No, no, ma'am, do not do so on my account. There is the theater Saturday night, remember? And I am still waiting for the dressmaker to finish two gowns."

I put down my handwork and pressed my hand to my forehead. Suddenly I felt inexplicably weary. Tired of the pretense, tired of idle chatter — tired. "I am afraid I have the headache," I said slowly, massaging my forehead. "I think I had better go and lie down before it becomes any worse."

I did not look at Faith Abbot, but I was aware of her frown, how she sat forward in her chair and held out her hand to me.

"Lucy, I would not bother you when you are feeling ill," she said. "But I beg you to see another doctor before we leave. These headaches of yours, the way you so often seem exhausted — it is not right for a young woman your age. And I can tell you are not happy. Surely you do not still mourn your husband. How could you? It has been four years since he died, and he was sixty to your seventeen. But there!" she added, as I rose and turned away so she could not see my face. "I shall let you go, my dear. Have a good rest."

I thanked her and went to the door. The headache I had claimed to escape her was fast becoming a reality.

Once in my room, I let Franklin help me undress and put on a loose wrap, and I swallowed the cordial she brought me before I lay down on my bed with a cool cloth on my forehead. But the moment the maid left the room and closed the door behind her, I was on my feet again. The cloth fell unheeded to the carpet as I went to the window. Moving the draperies a little, I peered down into the square. It was quieter there than it had been in Bond Street, and there were fewer people about. In the garden in the center of the square, a small boy played with a hoop, watched by his nanny. An older woman I had seen a few times and believed to be a Mrs. King from three doors away, sat on a sunny bench with her companion, a thin, drooping girl who appeared to be reading to her from a book she held. At the end of the square a footman ran off on an errand, while another walked some lady's lapdog. Across the way a housemaid shook a duster from one of the upper windows of Lord and Lady Bradford's house. All very innocent. Very ordinary. And there was no sign of him. None at all.

I took a deep breath. I hadn't noticed I'd been holding it until then. Stooping, I picked up the cloth and went back to bed. I knew it was ridiculous to feel reassured simply because I did not see him there, looking up at the windows. He would come soon enough. Perhaps he already knew where I lived. Perhaps he had watched me and the maid drive off to the shops this morning, and followed us.

I stretched out on the bed and closed my eyes. Sleep had often become my refuge since my husband's death. Some days I didn't get up at all, just dozed the hours away, eating and drinking little. And some days I couldn't seem to stop crying, for no reason at all. I knew Franklin thought it strange, but she would never say so. I told myself I was very lucky to have such a discreet maid.

I sighed and put my arm over my eyes to block out the light. I supposed I would have to see the doctor the dowager was recommending; otherwise I would have no peace. But I didn't think there was anything he could do for me. I was not physically ill, indeed, I had always been healthy.

And I certainly had no intention of confiding in him, or anyone. No, never that, I promised myself as I drifted into an uneasy slumber.

It was late afternoon when I woke. I was very thirsty. My mouth felt thick and dry. I went to the dressing room and poured a glass of water before I went to the windows again.

For a moment, I did not see him. Then my eyes sought the opposite side of the square. He was there, in earnest conversation with a liveried coachman waiting in an open landau to drive his ladies in Hyde Park. The sun shone brightly still; I had to blink until my eyes became accustomed to the light. When he looked toward my house, I dropped the drapery quickly, although I knew it was unlikely he could see much from that distance. It was then I noticed how cramped my fingers were, I had clutched the material so tightly.

Putting both hands to my head, I went to sit down on the side of the bed again. What was I to do? How was I to handle this, for handle it I must.

Think, Lucy, I ordered myself, think! Of course he would speak to me somehow. He wanted something. He had to want something, or he would not have bothered to come all the way to London.

It had to be money. True, it was only the end of June, but it was possible he had gone through the money I had sent him the first of the year as I always did. I had worried about that money right from the start. It seemed to leave me open to all kinds of danger. But I had come to see it as a necessary evil. At least it had kept him from shouting his ghastly revelations to the skies, something I had told myself I could never have borne. And I had felt safe, as long as I never went to Trecarag Hall ever again. I should not have forgotten that tiresome as the journey was between Cornwall and the capital, it was not impossible. And as Lady Blake, there was no way I could hide.

Fortunately I had no engagement that evening. I ate dinner with the dowager and managed to acquit myself well, for although she asked about my headache, she did not refer to it again. After her customary glass of brandy at the end of the meal, she left for an evening of whist at a friend's house. I was glad to be alone, and I told the butler I was not at home to anyone who might call before I went to the library.

I was determined to plan some sort of strategy to see me through the following days. He knows where you are now, but he can't get at you, I told myself. As long as you remain within doors, he can't get near you. Of course that was a problem in itself. I could not constantly claim a headache or some other vague ailment. The dowager would summon the doctor to call in a twinkling if I did, and what good would that do? No, I would have to go about as usual to those engagements I had already accepted. I thought hard for a moment. Yes, there was a soiree at the Duke of

Severn's in two days' time. I managed a weak smile. That was one place I would be completely safe. The duke was of the old school, very conscious of his worth. No mere commoner would ever be able to gain admittance to his home and his presence. Then there was a Venetian breakfast on Tuesday next, to be followed by a drive in the park. That would be more dangerous. Anyone could use the public parks and frequently did. Still, unless he threw himself in front of the team, he could hardly accost me there. As long as we kept moving, I reminded myself, remembering how often the dowager stopped to greet friends and converse with them. Perhaps it would be wise to excuse myself from that excursion. On Thursday I had a last fitting on those gowns I had told her about, and oh! — there was the theater, another potentially dangerous place. I knew it was entirely possible he had gained the confidence of one of my servants and so would know where I was going to be and when. He could be personable when he chose to be, easy and confident. The perfect gentleman.

Oh, why had I told the dowager there was no need for us to leave town early? *Why?*

I poured myself a small glass of brandy. And then there was the doctor. I would have to make arrangements to have him call first thing, just in case Faith Abbott mentioned that early start again.

Would *he* come down to Lansmere Park, I wondered. It was not that far from town. But unless he had made the acquaintance of one of the maids, how would he know where I had gone? And it would be harder for him to get near me in the country. He would stand out there as the stranger he did not appear in town.

I sipped the mellow liqueur slowly, thinking hard. It was then I realized that all this conjecture was doing me no good at all. I would have to talk to him eventually, to find out what he wanted, and I must be prepared to deal with his demands even though just the thought of speaking to him made me feel ill. But if I did not there was a good chance he would see to it the entire world learned the secret I had struggled so desperately to keep hidden. And if that ever came to pass, I knew I would not be able to stand the shame and the ostracism I would be sure to face.

The *ton* might be capricious, even careless on occasion, but it could also be cruel when one of its members strayed from the correct behavior that was expected of anyone of high birth or degree. And while men were given greater lenience and allowed all sorts of peccadilloes, that did not hold true for women. No, women were held to a higher standard and censured much more severely if they deviated from the correct form. Since I could not see myself putting a pistol to my head or taking poison no matter how horrible the situation, I would have to change my name, disappear to some remote village, and live a life of quiet obscurity. Alone.

It did not sound at all enticing.

Chapter 2

A Dr. Radcliff came to call as requested two days later. At the dowager's urging, I had seen one of his colleagues when I first arrived in town, and I did not expect this Dr. Radcliff to be of any more assistance than he had been. Franklin remained beside me while he examined me, but I dismissed her after she had helped me dress so I alone could hear what he had to say.

"You appear in perfect health, m'lady," he announced when we were seated in the drawing room and he was sipping a glass of wine. "I could find no reason for these strange headaches you say you have. You are how old?"

"I turned twenty-one in January."

He did not smile at me. Dr. Radcliffe was a middle-aged man, rather portly and with great dignity. He wore a pair of wire-rimmed eyeglasses that kept slipping down his surprisingly thin nose and he was forever peering over them, or impatiently pushing them back into place.

"You are young, m'lady. I understand you lost your husband some time ago?"

"He died in the summer of 1811."

"Had you had these headaches during your

married life, ma'am?" he asked, bending toward me a little.

"Sometimes," I invented. "Not often."

He frowned. "Well, ma'am, you will not care to hear my diagnosis perhaps, but I will give it to you just the same," he said sternly. "You do not need a tonic or a cordial, nor any herbal concoction. You have gone against nature's plan for the weaker sex, and you are suffering as a consequence. You do not have enough to do. In short, you are bored. It is not right for a young woman your age to live alone and idle. You need a husband, and the sooner you get one, the sooner you will be well. A husband, ma'am, to care for and comfort, and a great number of babies to keep you occupied. Yes, that's what you need! Women were put on this earth to be helpmates to men. When they do not fulfill their divine assignment, they become ill. You may trust my judgment. I have seen conditions such as yours many times."

He sat back looking satisfied and I thanked him as kindly as I could and said I was sure he must be right. Only then did he smile at me. After he had bowed himself away, I shook my head. A husband was the last thing in the world I wanted. Not again. *Never* again.

I had not seen the man who was following me for two days. True, I had remained at home pretending illness, secure the dowager would not protest since I had summoned the doctor as she had suggested.

Many times I had gone to the windows to look

for him, but he was not there.

Oh, let me dispense with this subterfuge! I know his name as well as I know my own, though I admit I hate to say it. He is Jaspar Hayes. There now, see? I am barely trembling.

Of course, it would have been difficult for Hayes to loiter about constantly. To do so would call attention to himself, and perhaps he didn't want that. Not yet, anyway. Still, every time I heard the knocker, I started. My butler had strict orders not to admit any strange men, so I called myself every kind of fool when I jumped as I did, but I did not seem to be able to stop it.

Was Hayes toying with me, the way a cat toys with a mouse? Had he deliberately made sure I saw him that morning on Bond Street, and then gone away to let me fret, as I am sure he knew I was doing, until such time as he decided to make the next move? I wouldn't put it past him. He had a mean streak, although mostly he kept it carefully hidden. And I remembered how he had acted that morning in the library at Trecarag four years ago. He had been furious with me, and I had been frightened although I told myself I must not show it, or give him any other advantage. The funeral had been held the day before, and Hayes had appointed himself chief mourner. I had said nothing then. The funeral had been poorly attended. There were no close relatives, even if they could have come such a great distance. But I still remembered Hayes's face when I told him he must leave the Hall and never return. He had railed at me, called me the most awful names, at the top of his voice, too, but I had held firm. I had even threatened him with the law if he did not do as I bade. I reminded him I was mistress of Trecarag now, and as such, the only one to make decisions concerning it. And no, he was not going to live there, pretending he was master. When he would have come to me, to beat me into submission no doubt, I took a pistol from a desk drawer and assured him I would use it if I had to.

"The servants may not know anything, but I am sure they have their suspicions," I had said as coldly as I could. "I'll say you attacked me, and I fired at you in self-defense. Don't think I won't, sir."

At that, he had shrugged and held up his hands in submission, but his blazing eyes made me keep that pistol handy. Now I was reminded I had better get it from my trunk where I had stored it, then clean and load it. I might well need it.

I had given Hayes money, more money than he had ever seen before, I'm sure, and I promised there would be more on the first of January every year if he made himself scarce and did not bother me again. For a moment then I had wondered if he would take it. I could see him weighing the gold against his desire. Fortunately, the gold won.

A knock on the door interrupted my musings. When the dowager came in, I was ready for her.

"What did the doctor say, Lucy?" she asked, her old face concerned.

"He is having a tonic made up for me, ma'am," I lied. I could hardly tell her the doctor's prescription for my well-being, for I knew she would start to go through her list of eligible males immediately and that would never do. I'd had enough trouble with her matchmaking already this Season.

"What did he think was the problem?" she persisted.

"He had no idea, ma'am. In fact, he says there is nothing much the matter with me. We must hope a summer in the country will help. I am sure it will, and by autumn I'll be in prime twig."

Faith Abbott sat down, still looking puzzled. "It's true you're blooming, but then you always are, Lucy," she said at last. "But still, I can tell you are sad about something — distressed, even. I wish there was something I could do to help you, indeed I do."

I rose and went to kneel and give her a hug. "You have been much too good to me already, ma'am," I told her, swallowing a large lump in my throat. It had been a long time since anyone really cared about me the way the duchess did. I knew I had been fortunate when she wrote shortly after Lord Blake died and invited me to Lansmere. Lord Blake had been a distant relative of her husband's, and so, as she told me, that made us family. I was glad of it. I had cast off my own family after my wedding and I had not seen them from that day to this. Don't think it is easy to stand alone in the world. It isn't easy at all, no matter how much money you have. I know that for a fact.

"Now there, we must stop this or we'll both be watering pots," Faith Abbott said briskly, hugging me once again before she drew back. "What are you wearing to the duke's soiree this evening? The violet silk, I hope. I think it is my favorite of all your gowns. It deepens the blue of your eyes."

"I had thought the rose muslin, but of course for the Duke of Severn, perhaps the violet would be more appropriate," I told her, glad of the turn the conversation had taken. A moment later I almost gasped aloud.

"I say, Lucy, have you seen the man who keeps hanging about watching the house?" the dowager asked, going to the window and boldly holding the draperies aside. "Yes, there he is now across the square, lounging against the palings of the garden and staring right at me."

"I make it a point never to pay any attention to such men, Your Grace," I said as evenly as I could. "No doubt he will tire of his vigilance soon enough."

"I wonder who he is?" she persisted, bending closer to the window to peer out. "I am almost sure we do not know him, yet there is something familiar about him. It bothers me that I cannot put my finger on what that could be. Mmmm — his height, perhaps?"

Alarmed now, I rose and went to her. Putting

my hands on her shoulders, I turned her about and marched her back to her chair. "Please, ma'am," I said, trying for a light tone, "I am sure he could see you there, and much better not to encourage him in any way, don't you agree? Well, we are off to Lansmere next week and we'll never have to see him again."

"Yes, dear, but still I have to wonder what he wants. Besides you, of course." She laughed then and I made myself smile. "It has been a great many years since I had any illusions that men wanted *me!* No, he is staring at the house because you are inside. I've a good mind to go out there and ask him what he thinks he's about, and find out his name in the bargain."

"No, no, I beg you will do no such thing," I told her, clasping my hands together so she would not notice they were trembling. "It would give him a distinction I am sure he does not deserve.

"I wonder who will be at the soiree tonight? I do like the Duchess of Severn, don't you, ma'am? She is so kind."

As I had hoped, the dowager was diverted. "Yes, the duke was lucky to find her all those years after his first wife's death in childbirth. And they are happy, which is most unfashionable. Still, it is heartwarming to see, nevertheless. And to think he has another child now, and at his age, too, for he's well into his forties, you know."

She chuckled a little. "The duchess is much

younger. Still, he did have those three sons as well as the twin girls who made their come-out to such acclaim a few seasons ago. And now, here is another little girl."

Uncomfortable, I made a noncommittal sound but that only encouraged her and she went on, "But why am I surprised? Large families have always been the norm, due, no doubt, because many children do not survive to maturity. Isn't that sad? Every time I see my darling grandson I pray he will be spared."

"We must certainly hope so," I said quickly, aware I had made no contribution to the conversation for some time.

"Yes, especially since his mother has no intention of breeding again if she can help it. I heard her say so to the doctor when he came to call the other day. I don't know why she is so adamant. She had an easy birth for all it took place in a carriage."

"I believe some women do not care for childbearing," I said, my eyes steady on my needlepoint.

The dowager snorted. "Care for it? I should say not! Nasty, painful business it is, and dangerous as well. But the results justify the means, wouldn't you say?"

I was not required to comment, which was just as well, for Faith Abbott was gathering up her belongings before going to her room for her usual rest. I had to smile a little. She had often declared that of course she never slept during the day, unlike other old ladies. But I had seen her drop off right here in the drawing room, her chin on her chest, her eyes closed, and an occasional soft snore issuing from the depths of the chair she was sitting in. Of course I never mentioned that.

Once alone again, I went to the window to see if Hayes was still hanging about. To my relief, he was nowhere in sight. As I went up to my room feeling relieved, it occurred to me that he might very well be standing at the back door instead, questioning one of the maids, and I shivered.

We arrived in Berkeley Square at the Duke of Severn's impressive town house very near the appointed time that evening. There was a line of carriages waiting their turn to pull up to the steps, over which a red carpet had been laid all the way to the street. An awning had also been erected to protect the guests. This evening such precautions were unnecessary for the day had been fine and the night sky had a host of stars. The warm temperature and the scent of the flowers that filled huge urns flanking the doorway was enchanting. I am not at all romantic, but Faith Abbott sighed in delight.

At last we left the carriage and made our way inside and up the stairs to where the duke and duchess stood to greet their guests. The duke, a singular man with strong opinions, never invited a crowd to his parties. I had attended some before and can attest to their superiority. Still, most hostesses preferred to fill their rooms with as many of the haute ton as they could persuade to come, and if some frail young lady or an elderly gentleman fainted and had to be carried outside to be revived, so much the better. A crush was a sign of popularity.

I glanced around casually as we entered the first drawing room. There were several people present I was slightly acquainted with, and I smiled and nodded as we moved forward. The dowager stopped to greet a friend, and I found my gaze drawn to a gentleman standing over against the wall. He was staring at me intently, but I was used to that. It was only when he raised his quizzing glass for an even more detailed perusal that I began to feel a little annoyed. Turning my back to him, I moved away. A string quartet was playing in one corner of the room, and nearby, the present Duchess of Lansmere was holding court. I went to join that court, although I am not especially fond of Eugenia Abbott, and at this time after the recent birth of her son, I found her tedious.

"There you are, Lady Blake," she said with an arch smile. "Now how shall I punish you? You have quite neglected me and my darling wee Reginald. Indeed, you have not come to call for over a week."

"Why, I beg your pardon, Your Grace," I said. "I feared to weary you by adding to the throng of callers you have had."

The duchess laughed gaily, well pleased with

my answer, and her husband said, "There will be plenty of time for Lady Blake to admire the baby, my love. Have you forgotten she is to come down to Lansmere with Mother for the rest of the summer?"

I thought to ask a young lady next to me if she were going to Brighton, for I was not at all comfortable having my plans bruited about in such a way. Miss Haven sniffed as she said her family was for Tunbridge Wells as soon as the Prince left London. She didn't sound a bit happy about it, either. Her brother, a young man terribly impressed with himself, asked me if I had enjoyed the races at Ascot this year. I gave a vague reply. Turning slightly to see where the dowager was, I became aware of a liveried servant standing at my elbow with a tray.

"Champagne, m'lady?" he asked, and it was all I could do not to faint with the shock. Hayes was here! Right here in the Duke of Severn's drawing room, the most exclusive, correct private home in London. My head was spinning and I am sure I would have fallen if a hand had not grasped my arm just then.

"You are feeling unwell, ma'am?" a deep voice asked softly. "Allow me to escort you from the room."

I looked around, but Jaspar Hayes had disappeared. There were several tall footmen serving drinks, and in their livery and with the white wigs they wore, it was impossible to tell one from the other. But how had he managed to gain admittance here, even dressed as a servant? I wondered. I knew people often augmented their household staff with servants hired for the occasion, but surely Severn, high stickler that he was, would not have countenanced such a man as Hayes!

Then I told myself I was being ridiculous. How could the duke possibly know the man's background? He was personable; neat and clean as well, with good manners when he chose to use them. He would be considered unexceptional by Severn or his agent.

"Here is a sofa, ma'am. Please be seated."

I sank down without even looking at my rescuer. As he sat down beside me, I fumbled in my reticule for my handkerchief. I could feel the cold sweat on my back, and I was sure my face was damp as well. Desperately, I swallowed the bile that was rising in my throat.

"Take this," my escort said, handing me a snowy white square of linen. I put it to my face gratefully, wishing I could hide behind its ample folds for the remainder of the evening.

"What overset you, ma'am? Are you ill?" he continued.

"No, no. I only felt a sudden weakness," I managed to say. "Thank you for your assistance, sir. It was most timely."

I handed him his handkerchief as I spoke, and looked at him directly for the first time. Somehow I was not surprised to discover he was the gentleman I had seen when I first entered the drawing room, standing against the wall, staring at me.

"I was glad to be of service," he said smoothly in a deep pleasant bass. "But we have not met. I am Gareth Powell. Completely at your service, ma'am."

Before I could speak, the Dowager Duchess of Lansmere arrived in a whirl of skirts. To my surprise, she ignored me to throw herself into Mr. Powell's arms as he rose to bow to her. "Gareth, my dear! Whenever did you arrive in town?" she asked. "Oh, do give me a kiss, dear boy!"

He responded with a warm smile, and the face I had thought rather harsh and forbidding, changed completely. "Your Grace," he said, bending again to kiss her on both cheeks. "I came up a week ago, and no, you are not going to part my hair because I haven't called. For one thing, when I went to Lansmere House no one mentioned you were in London."

"That is because I am staying with Lucy, er, Lady Blake, I mean. Lucy, have you met my godson?"

"Indeed," I replied, wondering if he would tell her how I had almost fainted, and hoping he would not.

The dowager shook her finger at him. "But of course you have met him. What was I thinking?" she said. "I imagine it took him all of three minutes to decide you were the loveliest woman at the party and make his way to your side. Confess, now, Gareth. Wasn't that the way of it?"

"You know me entirely too well, ma'am," he said easily. "Come, sit down here and let me get us champagne. It has been a long time since we've spoken, ma'am, and I would know what you have been up to."

He left us before the dowager could become indignant and tell him that of course she had not been up to anything! Feeling a little calmer, I took a few deep breaths before I looked around the hall. There were several people there, admiring the oil paintings and chatting. Immobile, at attention along the walls were two footmen in the duke's livery. To my infinite relief, neither was Jaspar Hayes. But even though I could not see him, I knew he was there. Somewhere. Just out of sight. Waiting until he could get near me again. The dowager began to tell me some gossip she had heard, and I was required to do nothing more than nod occasionally, and smile when she chuckled.

Mr. Powell came back with a footman bearing a tray. He was not Hayes, either, but I was not comforted by that. Instead, I wished I might run down the stairs and out into the soft spring night, run until I reached home again. *And what would you do then?* I asked myself scornfully. *Hide under the bed? Jaspar Hayes is not a ghost or a bugbear. He is real and soon you must face him. He has shown you tonight he can get as close to you as he wants, whenever he wants to, and there is nothing you can do to stop him.*

"Lucy, didn't you hear me?" Faith Abbott demanded, and I put Hayes from my mind.

"I beg your pardon, ma'am. I was woolgathering again. You said . . . ?"

"I was only remarking it would be grand if Gareth could come and stay at the dower house this summer. We shall be very dull, just the two of us, but I am sure he will liven things up considerably. Please add your entreaties to mine, Lucy, do! I know it would be difficult for him to deny *you*."

Chapter 3

Oh, dear, I thought, she's matchmaking again. But I could not say anything, not with Mr. Powell looking at me so expectantly, as if he knew very well the fix I found myself in.

"But of course he must come if you wish it, ma'am," I said evenly. "Unless he feels it would be too tame entirely. If you remember, you and I spoke of some extensive gardening you hope to accomplish — hardly a gentleman's pursuit, gardening, now is it? And then we may look about for a suitable place for me, in case I decide to sell the estate in Cornwall."

"I do assure you I am very fond of gardening, ma'am," Mr. Powell said. "As for inspecting property, why, I should be delighted to assist you. I have only recently acquired a home near Chipping Norton —"

"Gareth, never tell me you have Viscount Clough's place now," the dowager interrupted. "How grand, for you will be within a half day's drive! Of course, I suppose it was too bad he gambled it away, but there. One man's loss is another man's gain."

"You won the estate gambling, sir?" I asked, wondering at my boldness and not even trying to hide the revulsion in my voice.

He stared back at me calmly. Not a flicker of emotion showed on his face. "No, I did not, madam," he said. "I bought it from the man who won it at play. He had no need for it, and I did.

"But I hear the orchestra tuning up in the ball-room upstairs. Might I beg you for the first set, m'lady?"

"Yes, do run along, Lucy," Faith Abbott said, making shooing motions with her hands. "I must find Lady Gately and tell her the *on dit* I just heard. *You* know . . ."

She winked at me as she rose. There was nothing left for me to do but agree to Mr. Powell's invitation. To tell the truth I was not at all loath to do so. On his arm and in his company, Hayes would have to keep his distance. As we went up the stairs, Mr. Powell said, "Would it distress you if I came and stayed at Lansmere, Lady Blake? I would not do so for the world if that is the case, no matter how my godmother pleads."

For a moment I wanted to applaud his sensitivity, that is I did until it occurred to me he had backed me into a fine corner. If I said it would bother me, I would sound impossibly vulgar, and if I said it would not, he as good as had my permission and approbation. He was clever, this Mr. Gareth Powell. Very clever.

"Why would it distress me?" I countered. "Still, I do wonder why you would feel it necessary to stay at Lansmere when your new estate is just a short distance away. And surely there must be a great deal for you to do there before the winter storms arrive."

"As you say, m'lady," he agreed, his voice so cordial it put me on my guard. "That is why I intend to accept Her Grace's kind offer. I am having the entire place redone — a new wing built as well as new wall coverings and paint, even new furniture. To tell you the truth, I came up to town to seek out an invitation so I might avoid the chaos that is sure to ensue. And the smell of fresh paint is so unpleasant, isn't it?"

We had reached the ballroom then, and he led me forward to take our places in the set that was forming. Before he bowed, he said, "And perhaps while I am there I will be able to discover what is frightening you so badly, ma'am. No, no, don't bother to deny it! You were as white as the morning mist when I first approached you in the drawing room, in fact, you were terrified."

I could think of nothing to say to him in rebuttal. Instead I curtsied and tried to look puzzled — confused. I do not think I succeeded, however, and I prayed he would not discover how damp my palms were inside my long white kid gloves.

It seemed an age before the set was over and I could leave him at last. Fortunately, a gentleman of my acquaintance asked for the next set, and took me to visit with his sister until the musicians returned to the gallery. Still, I noticed Gareth Powell did not leave the ballroom, nor did he ask any other lady to dance. That was perhaps just as well. Although he knew the steps perfectly, Mr. Powell was not an easy, graceful dancer. I wondered why that had not annoyed me. Indeed, I had found it oddly endearing instead.

At one point during that next set, I saw Jaspar Hayes again. He was standing in the doorway leading to the supper room, scanning the dancers. I tried to look away before he saw me, but I was not quick enough. Horrified, I saw him smile at me and wring his hands in satisfaction. It was then I missed my step and almost tripped my partner. His fervent apologies for my clumsiness occupied several minutes of our time, and when I looked up again, Jaspar Hayes was gone.

It was very late when we returned to Portman Square, in fact dawn was not far away. I had spent what seemed to be the entire evening looking out for Hayes, although I never saw him again, not when I was dancing, eating supper, or conversing with the other guests. Faith Abbott was full of conversation during the short drive home. It was now established that Gareth Powell would come to the dower house at Lansmere. From there he would be able to ride over to his own property often, to inspect the work being done. In one way I was sorry he would be with us. He saw entirely too much for my comfort. On the other hand, it was comforting to know there would be a man about for protection. I did not think Hayes would hesitate to invade the dowager's home, staffed as it was with mostly elderly servants. But perhaps the masculine Mr. Powell would give him pause.

For I knew now Hayes would find me at Lansmere. It was obvious he had made friends with one of my servants, for how else could he have known I was to attend the Duke of Severn's soiree? And far enough ahead of time, too, that he could get himself hired as one of the additional staff? And if that had not been enough, he had been at my elbow this evening when Lansmere had mentioned my visit to his mother's. Yes, he would come to Oxfordshire, that was one thing I could be certain of. For a while that night — or what remained of the rest of it, for I could not sleep in spite of my exhaustion — I considered canceling my arrangement with Faith Abbott, and going off somewhere by myself. Of course I would have to be very careful, keeping my plans secret almost till the last moment, and even then apprising no one of my destination. I toyed with the idea of a visit to Land's End or even northern Scotland before I gave up the scheme. I could escape Hayes that way, but I would have to return to civilization eventually. And he would find me then. I knew he would find me.

The first rays of the sun were lighting the sky when it occurred to me how much easier my life would be if Jaspar Hayes were to have a serious accident. If he fell from his horse, for example, or ran afoul of robbers some dark night — even met his end in a duel.

I shook my head. For all his pretense, Hayes was not a gentleman, and so could not engage in duels.

And I knew none of the dire accidents I pictured were likely to beset the man, and to even be thinking of some deadly disease carrying him off was ludicrous. He was young and strong and healthy. My salvation did not lie in that direction.

I did not see Jaspar Hayes again during the time we remained in London, not in the square or anywhere else. Our visit to the theater the evening following the soiree was completely uneventful. True, I spent most of the time studying the people who were attending the play rather than watching the stage, but for all my careful perusal, I could see no sign of the man. The Venetian breakfast on Tuesday was not marred by his presence either, although you may be sure I looked all the servants over carefully. I have never understood why an entertainment called a breakfast should be held in midafternoon, but such are the incomprehensible ways of society.

Encouraged by Hayes's absence that day, I went on with the dowager and two elderly gentlemen of her acquaintance, for a drive in the park. We saw Gareth Powell strolling with a party, but nothing more noteworthy than that. Faith Abbott was very interested in the ladies accompanying her godson. I was sure he would get no rest until he had explained everything to her satisfaction.

By this time, I never went anywhere without my pistol in my reticule, and I kept that reticule close to me even inside the house. I am not a bad shot. My older brother taught me how to aim and fire, as well as clean and load the gun. I did not think I would hesitate if Hayes gave me the opportunity. Indeed, sometimes I wished he would invade the house so I could shoot him as a housebreaker and have done with this nightmare.

Franklin was busy packing for the summer, and two days before we were to leave, I asked my man of business to call on me. I had decided that no matter what happened, I would not come back to this house. I had never liked it, dreary and old-fashioned as it was. I had lived here with Lord Blake when we were first married. It held no happy memories for me.

Mr. Kittering was agreeable when I told him my plans, and promised to see to everything for me, including selling the furnishings. I was determined I would carry nothing away with me, not a single demitasse spoon.

"Of course the servants must go as well," I concluded.

He looked at me askance then. "But, m'lady," he said, "some of them are elderly. They will have trouble finding new positions."

"Pension them off, then," I told him. "The younger ones must be turned away with only the year's wages."

In my mind I was remembering the servant

who had betrayed me to Jaspar Hayes, and although I knew it was unfair to the others, I did not care.

"Would you like me to look about for another London house, ma'am?" Mr. Kittering asked. His voice sounded stiff and showed his disapproval. I didn't care about that, either.

"Not at the moment. My plans are uncertain at this time. Oh, I may also be selling Trecarag in Cornwall. I shall keep you informed of my decision regarding it."

He bowed, but the look on his face showed that this wanton disposal of perfectly good property did not suit him at all. We parted formally, but when he was gone, I felt as if a weight had been lifted from my shoulders. No more Portman Square, I whispered as I skipped a little going to the library door. Never again would I have to come home to this stuffy hall, that ugly dark wood staircase. And in two days' time I would never have to eat my dinner again under that ghastly oil painting of two dead stags whose only saving grace was that it was so coated with the grime of the years, its subject was almost impossible to decipher.

After a final fitting, my gowns were delivered, and early on a bright July morning, the dowager and I climbed into her massive traveling coach and set out for Oxfordshire. Our maids followed in my own carriage. Both vehicles were heavily laden with all manner of trunks and boxes and such supplies as we would find difficult to acquire in the country.

I looked around the square, quiet now at six in the morning. There was no one about, most certainly not Jaspar Hayes. I had not expected to see him. As the carriage turned at the end of the square, I looked back at Blake House and silently bade it good riddance.

I had discovered on our journeys together that Faith Abbott was not a good traveler. The motion of the carriage made her queasy, and after an hour or so, she could find no comfortable place to put her old bones, as she described it. Still, she did not insist on stopping often, for she told me it was better to do the thing all at once and be miserable for a short time, than prolong it and be miserable forever.

Accordingly, we reached Lansmere very late that evening. The duke and duchess were still in town although we expected them in a week's time. Mr. Powell would also come to us then, for he had some unfinished business in London. The dowager went immediately to her rooms, tossing an apology for deserting me over her shoulder as her maid helped her up the stairs. I wished her a good night and had a lonely repast in the dining room. Later, I found Franklin had unpacked what I would need for the night, and when I climbed into bed at last, I slept more soundly than I had done since encountering Jaspar Hayes in London.

The next day was gray with intermittent showers, but I was busy getting settled and helping Her Grace take up the reins of her household once again.

The dower house at Lansmere — how should I describe it? It was so warm and gracious, so very unlike the home of the Dukes of Lansmere which was all hard red brick, symmetry and severity. I never saw Lansmere Park without shuddering a little, and I certainly did not envy anyone who had to live in it. But the dower house was another matter entirely. It was only two stories high and it had been extensively renovated over the years. One Lansmere dowager had put on a wing that curved in a delightful way around one side of the formal gardens. Another had built a pretty gazebo at the end of a winding path through the woods. The path followed a brook and there were several small pools complete with water lilies and carp. Floor-length windows on the back of the house opened to a bright terrace with a pergola at one end. The whole five acres of grounds were enclosed in high brick walls, some of them softened by climbing vines.

Faith Abbott had put her own stamp on the house with handsome furniture and pretty silk draperies and upholstery. There was an airiness to the place, a lightness that lifted the spirits and welcomed the visitor. The soft pastels she favored were offset by the jewel-like tones of the occasional contemporary painting. I recognized a Gainsborough and a Turner.

I had been given my usual small suite on a corner of the second floor — a bedroom, sitting room, and dressing room. There was even a balcony with a long chair set out if I wanted to be alone to read or sketch.

At dinner that evening, I found the dowager completely recovered from the ordeal of traveling, and we spent a happy hour enjoying roast lamb, new peas, aspics, and an excellent Dover sole before our sweet of strawberries and clotted cream. The dowager told me the strawberries grew in a kitchen garden behind the servants' wing. They were delicious.

Later we sat before a small cozy fire in the drawing room and discussed the gardens. I was anxious to explore them; I hoped it would be fair tomorrow. All my visits to the dower house had occurred in either late autumn or the winter months. I had only a vague idea what the gardens might look like when they were not dreaming deep under the snow.

"I thought I might enlarge the rose garden next year," Faith Abbott said. "You must help me decide how best to do that so I may set the gardeners to preparing the ground."

She shook her head ruefully. "Dear me, I hope I won't have the usual argument with Fleming. My head gardener," she explained. "He is rather set in his ways, opinionated even, as most men are apt to be. Anything new or different upsets him."

I must have looked a question for she chuckled and said, "He comes around, of course, after massive coaxing. The time I had with the dahlia bed! Then there was the mixed tulip display I wanted on either side of the drive. But fortunately he adores roses. It shouldn't be too difficult."

"As do I," I said. "When I was a young girl I used to imagine I would someday have a garden that would be exclusively roses. All kinds of them — climbing roses, rose trees, even the wild ones that grow along the hedgerows of country lanes. There was one wild rose at Trecarag that I adored. It was the palest pink and it had such a sweet yet spicy aroma. I have never seen it growing anywhere else."

"Fleming would never countenance wild roses," the dowager said regretfully. "He would consider them beneath my touch. I tell you, Lucy, my servants one and all are vigilant in preserving my dignity and standing in the world. But I suppose I do forget I am a dowager duchess more often than not."

She made a little face at me and I smiled. No, Faith Abbott did not consider her worth, or desire the pomp and obeisance she might well have claimed. It occurred to me she would have been just as happy as a squire's wife, if that had been her lot in life. Still, she was the kindest woman I had ever known, and the jolliest, and I was proud to call her friend. Despite the disparity in our ages, I knew I would never have a better one.

We went early to bed. The sound of the rain and the fresh country air had made me sleepy and I was looking forward to my big four-poster with its featherbed and soft pillows.

I did not bother to call Franklin. She had been busy all day unpacking and I had sent her off to bed earlier. It was a struggle to get out of my gown unassisted, but I managed, and if I did not brush my hair as long as she was wont to do, I made a creditable job of it.

After tying it back with a ribbon and putting on some of the face cream Franklin insisted I use, I went yawning into the bedroom, holding a candle high to light my way. It was then I smelled something that stopped me in mid-stride. No, I told myself, No, it isn't possible. It is only that I have been speaking of the wild roses at Trecarag that makes me think I can smell them now. Still, a hint of that piquant aroma persisted, and I lifted the candle higher. My hand began to tremble and the candle cast strange moving shadows over the walls, the dressing table, the bed.

The bed! I put my other hand to my mouth to keep from crying out as I forced myself to approach it with slow, reluctant steps. It had been turned down, the satin coverlet removed. I could not tell if Franklin had done so or someone else.

I edged closer. The sweet scent was stronger now, although not overpowering. It was then I saw the two pink rosebuds that lay on one of my pillows and I began to shake so badly I had to put the candle down lest I drop it.

The rosebuds' stems had been tightly entwined and tied that way with a piece of string.

Near them, on the white linen case there was a single drop of blood. It was still red, still glistening even, as if it had been put there only moments before, perhaps while I sat in the dressing room brushing my hair. I shuddered, my hands fists pressed against my mouth. Jaspar Hayes had been here in my room. It had to have been him. Who else before tonight knew of my affection for these particular roses? And the symbolism of the entwined stems, that drop of blood . . . It was him, all right, and it was horrible.

I made myself pick the roses up, made myself open the doors to the balcony so I could throw them away. In my haste to be rid of them, I did not even consider he might well be standing in the garden beneath, watching me. But as I closed and latched the doors and drew the curtains securely across them, that did occur to me and I remembered my pistol.

I had not thought it necessary to keep it handy in the dower house, but now I went to the wardrobe and took it out of the bandbox where I had hidden it earlier. I put it carefully down on a table before I stripped the stained case from the pillow and took it to the dressing room to wash the blood away. When I was finished I did not get into bed. Instead, I wrapped myself in a light blanket and curled up on the chaise, my pistol close to hand.

Chapter 4

I did not sleep. Instead, I lay there staring up at the dark ceiling and listening to the rain. If anyone should ask me, I would be able to tell them exactly when that rain stopped, just before dawn. There would be no impediment to exploring the gardens today, if I could find the heart to do so.

He was here. Well, that was no surprise. I had expected he would come to Lansmere, although I had hoped for a few normal days as a respite. Still, even though I had never belittled his abilities, I was stunned at the ease with which he had made his way into the house, found my rooms, and invaded them. The high brick walls around the grounds had not deterred him, nor had the locked doors and windows kept him out. It was then I recalled the tall tree outside my balcony. Perhaps he had climbed that tree to gain entry. It would be no feat for a vigorous, determined man, and he was certainly that.

For a while, in the darkest reaches of the night, I toyed with the idea of sitting in the dark tomorrow night — or as many nights as it took — pistol in hand, aimed at the balcony door. But how I was to explain such behavior to the dowager, to say nothing of the nearest justice who would come to investigate the shooting death, I did not know. Once again I wondered what Hayes wanted. If it were money, surely it would have been easier to demand it, rather than go through this elaborate charade he had set up.

I shivered in spite of the blanket, the warm summer air. Could it be he enjoyed taunting me, torturing me this way? But someone who felt that way could not be sane. And whatever else I might have to say about Mr. Jaspar Hayes, I did not question his sanity. Unless he had changed radically, that is. Unless in the four years since I had last seen him, the injustice he felt had driven him tumbling over the edge to madness. To think I might be in danger from a madman was so horrifying I reached out to make sure my pistol was still handy.

Toward morning, I gave up trying to sleep and went to the balcony door again. I was confident Jaspar Hayes was not there now, for no man, not even a gibbering idiot, would have stood about all night in the heavy downpour.

When I opened the balcony doors and stepped outside, the garden lay wet and dripping below me. The flagstone paths shone blackly and the drenched scent of the flowers was heavy in the morning air. A little breeze wafted that scent toward me. At any other time I would have closed my eyes in delight, to savor it more fully. Now I only inspected the nearest tree. Yes, one of its sturdy branches was close to the wrought iron palings of the balcony. I sighed and leaned against the doorjamb to think.

But after worrying over everything I knew, I could come to no conclusion. The next move in this game was up to Jaspar Hayes. There was nothing I could do except wait, and hopefully react to that move in a way that would give me the advantage. For a change, I thought grimly.

I made myself go to bed then, aware Franklin would wonder if it were not slept in. But just knowing he had touched the bed, perhaps even smoothed the linen sheets before he put that disreputable reminder down, made it impossible for me to sleep easily.

I rang for the maid around nine-thirty and when she came, ordered breakfast in bed. I felt slow and heavy, and I did not care to face the dowager until I had myself more in hand. When I finally came downstairs an hour later, the butler told me Her Grace was out in the gardens. As I strolled down the terrace steps to join her, I saw her in the distance, conferring with a tall, sturdy man near some rose beds. I was sure he must be this Fleming she had told me about. Although he held his cap in both hands correctly, he appeared to be arguing with Her Grace, and remembering the wild roses I had thrown away the night before, I went to find them. There was no sign of them under the balcony although I searched diligently and even investigated the shrubbery. Had Hayes removed them or had some gardener found them? There was no way to know. I walked

50

slowly down a path nearby. My sandals and the bottom of my muslin morning gown were wet now. Ahead of me in the wall I saw a wide wrought iron gate. Obviously it had been placed there so the gardeners could wheel their barrows of clippings and debris into the uncultivated land beyond. As I went nearer, my breath caught in my throat, for there in the damp earth before it, was the clear print of a boot. Not the kind of sturdy boot that workmen wore, either. No, this boot had an elegant pointed toe and a distinct narrow heel. At least I had solved the problem of how Hayes had got into the grounds, I thought bleakly. The gate had no lock, only an old iron latch. Anyone could reach through the bars and release that latch. Thoughtfully, I smoothed the bootprint away with the toe of my sandal. If I left it, it might cause awkward questions. And Hayes was not after Faith Abbott. I did not want her to become alarmed.

"There you are, Lucy," her cheerful voice called, and I turned and tried to smile. "Do come and meet the magician who makes the gardens so beautiful."

I suspected from the dour expression her companion wore, he was well aware this blatant flattery was intended to soften the rigid attitude he had obviously taken about enlarging the rose beds.

After introductions had been made and the man had touched his forelock, he said as if I had not appeared at all, "Call me a magician if ye likes, Your Grace, but I tell ye we've enough roses. To be uprooting them delphiniums and campanulas is pure murder, it is."

"Well, we shall see," Faith Abbott said calmly. "Do say you will at least consider it, Fleming. I adore roses, and there are several new varieties I am anxious to try. Besides, we can always put the other flowers in another bed somewhere. But you will know best about that, of course.

"Lucy, dear, I trust you slept well?" she asked as she turned away and took my arm. I could hear Fleming mumbling to himself behind us as we moved away. From the quiver at the corner of the dowager's mouth, I could tell she had heard him too.

"He'll come about, you'll see," she said in a whisper. "But truly, are you feeling well? You look very tired this morning."

"I'm afraid I enjoyed my dinner too much last evening," I said as lightly as I could. "I had trouble dropping off. But come, let us not waste a moment of this glorious day on my ailments. Ma'am, that bed of lilies and lobelia is exquisite. And I do like the sweet alyssum that edges it. Tell me, what is the tall blue flower over there called?"

We stayed in the garden admiring it and making plans until thirst drove us to the terrace where a light repast had been set out for us. I was not particularly hungry after my late breakfast, but the dowager set to with a will, confiding she had been up at first light. "There is something about the country that invigorates me," she confided, taking another bite of salmon mousse with cucumber sauce. "Strange, that, isn't it? It is so quiet and sleepy here — so busy and strident in town. Yet here I feel energetic, and in London, lethargic. Now, why is that, do you suppose?"

I sipped some lemonade. "But you are not attending evening parties that last till three in the morning here," I pointed out. "And of course the air is purer. Only consider the clouds of smoke from London's chimneys."

Before the dowager could reply, the butler presented a calling card on his silver salver. Her face lit up in her wonderful smile and she said, "Oh, do show Mrs. Grey out here at once, Wells! It has been such an age since I have seen her."

As he went to do her bidding, she said, "You will like Alicia, Lucy. She is a few years older than you are, and she lives nearby. But perhaps you met her this past Christmas at the Park?"

Then she shook her head. "No, of course you didn't, for Alicia was on the Continent until May. Her husband was on some sort of diplomatic mission there. All very secretive, y'know. I don't even know which country they visited. Ah, men and their little games. Alicia!" she added as a tall, handsome young woman came smiling to join us. She was wearing a severely cut habit of beige twill, and she swung her riding hat in one gloved hand. Her chestnut hair gleamed in the bright sunlight. I admired her self-possession. She was so confident, and as neat as a porcelain figurine on the dowager's mantelpiece.

We were introduced and Mrs. Grey was persuaded to join us for the remainder of our nuncheon. As Wells set another place, she smiled at both of us. "I won't say no, ma'am," she said in a gruff alto that was oddly endearing. "I've been riding for some time and I had breakfast at dawn. Yes, thank you, Wells. Some of the salmon mousse and certainly the fruit salad. Lemonade would be delightful."

"How was your stay abroad?" Faith Abbott asked as she passed a basket of rolls. "Or shouldn't I mention it above a whisper?"

"It went very well. The Foreign Office is pleased. But I do not think I would care to live in Russia. It is so vast and empty, so cold and — and so *Russian*."

As we laughed, she wrinkled her nose and added, "Jack has to go back in the fall. I've begged off. Another winter in that frigid land is more than any wife should have to endure, care for her husband though she may.

"But what of you, ma'am? What have you been up to since I have been away?"

"I do not know, do you, Lucy, why all my acquaintance seems to assume I have been 'up to something,'" the dowager complained. "I've not been up to anything. Just enjoying the London Season, and, oh, setting a young bride and her husband straight."

Mrs. Grey almost choked on a sip of lemonade. "I can just imagine it," she said when she could speak. "I am sure all is well with them now?"

"Yes, it must be for we haven't heard a whisper in weeks, have we, Lucy?" Her Grace said serenely, causing her guest to chuckle again.

"But Alicia, we are having Gareth Powell to stay. He comes next week. I hope you and Jack will dine with us some evening," she went on. "And have you heard I have a grandson now? He was born in London just recently."

Quietly, I narrowed my eyes against the glare and let my mind wander while Faith Abbott told of the birth in a carriage in Hyde Park, and all the child's marvelous qualities. This might be news to Mrs. Grey, but I had heard it too many times already.

I must have dozed off for a moment, for I was startled when the dowager said, "Lucy, I swear you are about to fall out of your chair, my dear. Are you so sleepy then?"

I smiled at both ladies. "I'm afraid the warm sun has made me drowsy, ma'am. Do forgive me."

"It is hard to become accustomed when you first arrive in the country," Mrs. Grey said easily. "By next week I'm sure you will do better. Tell me, do you ride? I am always looking for a companion. So few ladies in the vicinity ride for pleasure. And my husband does not ride at all."

I must have looked confused since most Englishmen were astride every chance they got, for she added in a matter-of-fact voice, "He has been crippled since birth."

She refused my stammered sympathy and smiled when I admitted I did enjoy a good canter. Plans were made then for me to join Alicia Grey in four days' time.

As we strolled with her around the side of the house down to the stable, I thought how happy and content I could be here if only Jaspar Hayes was still far, far away in Cornwall. And then I saw that even though I might forget him when I was busy with other things, as soon as that activity ceased, he invaded my mind again. He was like a persistent gnat you could not get rid of, but he was infinitely more dangerous.

As I stood beside Her Grace and watched Mrs. Grey trot away on a handsome roan mare, I wondered where Jaspar Hayes was staying. Surely not in Lansmere Village at the inn. He would not dare come that close, would he? I wondered if there was any way I could find out — discreetly, of course. Somehow I felt the more I knew about the man and his habits, the better it would be for me. And perhaps if I had his direction, I could write him a letter asking him what he wanted and arranging to meet him somewhere alone. I remembered now how proud he had always been of his ability to read and write and how he had sneered at many of the servants at Trecarag because they did not have his education.

I knew it would be easy to walk to the village and make some inquiries. It was only a mile or so away. But asking questions might call attention to me. A widow inquiring for a particular gentleman must always be suspect. And in the country, as in town, gossip was an activity everyone indulged in with glee.

Of course I could ask Franklin to find out if any strangers were staying at the inn, but I hesitated to involve her in my terrible predicament. I felt the less she — or anyone — knew, the better. But perhaps when I went riding with Mrs. Grey I could suggest we stop at the inn for tea, then get her to tell me about the village, the shops, the inn itself. From there it would be easy to wonder casually if the inn had much custom when the family was away from the Park. Or something like that, I thought savagely. Oh, how despicable it was, all this plotting and conniving! To think I had come to this.

To my great relief, no more rosebuds were delivered to my room late at night, nor was there any sign of Jaspar Hayes either on the grounds of the dower house or abroad, whenever Faith Abbott and I went for a drive around the countryside. She had a number of acquaintance in the neighborhood, of course, and she delighted in calling on them and begging they accept a bouquet from the gardens, or some special treat made in her kitchen. Not all of these friends were noble, either. She seemed particularly fond of an elderly man, so bent with rheumatism he could not straighten up. We spent two afternoons in his little cottage and the dowager discussed old times with him. Mr. Jeffers had been the head groom at Lansmere Park when she came there as a young bride, and he had quickly become her champion and one of her favorite retainers. I found it fascinating to listen to them, for the past, as far back as 1775, was as vivid in their minds as last year.

Fortunately, the day I was to ride with Alicia Grey dawned fair. I was already mounted when she rode up the gravel drive to meet me. We trotted the horses until we reached open country, then we began to canter. It was invigorating. I had not had such a good ride for a long time although I knew I would be sore tomorrow.

We rode mainly within the Park's grounds. There were several bridle paths there, and excellent vistas, but despite them the cold, huge mansion in the background did not inspire me to admiration.

As we pulled up to rest the horses, Alicia Grey pointed to it and shuddered. It appeared she felt exactly as I did about the place. I had given up the idea of questioning her about the village inn for it had occurred to me another piece of information was much more pertinent.

Where had Jaspar Hayes found those rosebuds? I had only seen them growing in Cornwall, yet they had been fresh when I found them on my pillow. Obviously they grew somewhere in the vicinity. If I could discover where, it might give me a clue to Hayes's whereabouts.

Now I said casually, "I wonder if you know if a

certain wild rose grows here in Oxfordshire? There was one in Cornwall where I lived with my late husband I just adored. The dowager was asking me about it. It was the palest pink, and it had a luscious aroma."

Alicia Grey thought for a moment. At last she said, "I can't help you, I'm afraid. I'm not a gardener myself. But I don't believe I've seen such a rose." She laughed then. "Better you tell Her Grace to forget it. That head gardener of hers will never countenance any plebeians in his garden, never."

I smiled but I was disappointed.

"You know Jack and I are to come to you tomorrow night for dinner?" she added. "I did suggest you and the dowager honor us, but she would have none of that. I wrote to her to tell her Jack's older brother would be with us. He is Bradford Grey, Viscount Epstead. Perhaps you are acquainted with him? He is often on the social scene in London."

I shook my head. "No, we have not met. Lord Blake and I spent most of our married life at his estate in Cornwall. We were only in London for the first winter of our marriage."

"I was sorry to hear of his demise. You have my sympathy," Alicia Grey said in her gruff deep voice. "I cannot imagine living without Jack. You must find it difficult."

Something made me want to be honest with her, and I said, "No, it isn't difficult. I didn't love Lord Blake. He was sixty, and I, seventeen. The marriage was arranged by my father."

"Oh, my dear, I am so sorry," my companion said, stretching out a hand to me. "How I hate these arranged marriages! They are obscene, and I have often said so. But what were your parents thinking of?"

I shrugged. "They considered it an excellent match, and the bride price the viscount was willing to part with allowed my father to put a new roof on the old family house, as well as purchase several hunters. My mother looked forward to fashionable gowns and, of course, those seasons in London necessary to present my younger sisters. I do not see my family anymore, not since I discovered that that was all I was worth to them."

"And who shall blame you?" Alicia said. I wondered why I had been so open with her. I had never spoken of my family honestly before, not even to the dowager duchess. But there was something about this tall, handsome wife of a diplomat that made me want to confide in her and trust her. If others felt as I did, there could be no doubt she must be a considerable asset to her husband in his work.

We parted later with a smile. I sensed Alicia Grey liked me as much as I liked her. My heart felt lighter just knowing I had made a friend, even if I could not confide my most immediate, pressing troubles to her.

The Grey party came promptly to dinner the following evening, so promptly I was still above stairs. When I hurried down, I felt somewhat flustered, and silently I cursed what I was sure must be a heightened complexion. It did not seem to bother anyone but me, however. In fact, Viscount Epstead took one look at me, clasped his hands over his heart, and said immediately, "Stricken by Cupid's arrow in a moment! Who would ever have thought it? Jack? Alicia? I say, it was very bad of you not to warn me Lady Blake was so beautiful. Then I would have been on my guard.

"Good evening, ma'am. When and where should you like to be married?"

I looked around in confusion. The dowager was trying hard to look disapproving and failing miserably. Alicia had covered her lips with her handkerchief, but I could see her shoulders were quivering. Only Mr. Jack Grey looked properly disgusted where he sat in a comfortable chair, leaning on his cane.

"For heavens sake, Brad," he said in disgust. "Where are your manners? The lady will think you insane."

The viscount never took his eyes from me. He was a blond man of medium height, nearer thirty than twenty, which made his pronouncements all the more incomprehensible. "I assure you, ma'am, I spoke the truth. Granted, Jack is the diplomat in the family, but I have always believed honesty is the best policy. And, oh yes, I learned to cut to the chase at an early age. Have you come down to the country to escape your multitude of beaux? Of course you have! My compliments."

"Really, sir, you should be ashamed of yourself," Faith Abbott said finally. I noticed her voice shook only a little. "Never mind him, Lucy. I am told he is harmless. Come and sit here, my dear, and we'll ignore him."

Of course that proved impossible, for he was the type of person you could not snub. Taken to task, he merely ignored the lecture and held to his original course.

We were barely seated at the table before I found myself wanting badly to laugh. It was a merry dinner we all shared, and when the viscount begged me to let him take me for a drive the following afternoon, I agreed with a smile. He was such a nice sunny *open* person, even if he was absurd. And I had not laughed so often or so thoroughly for a long time. I sensed Her Grace was right. There was no harm in Bradford Grey. I could trust him as I knew I could trust his brother. Jack Grey was far more serious than his madcap sibling, perhaps due to his crippled leg. That was unfortunate, I thought as I went up to bed at last. Surely he was the better man to hold the title, even though it had gone, as was customary, to the firstborn son. I wondered if the late viscount had ever despaired that it must be so, for I could not imagine Lord Epstead a serious child. Far from it, in fact. Indeed, I was sure his nanny and his tutors must have often wrung their hands in frustration, trying to deal with him. I was equally sure they had enjoyed many a hearty laugh as well, once they were alone.

I do not know what woke me much later. The room was dark and there wasn't a sound, even though I strained to hear something other than the pounding of my heart.

I drew a slow, cautious breath. It was then I smelled the roses again. The scent of them was stronger this time, much stronger. Reluctantly, carefully, I took my hand from under the covers to feel around. Yes, there were petals spread there. Investigating as far as I could reach, I discovered there must have been hundreds of them, heaped all over the bed.

Dear God, I thought, Jaspar Hayes had been in my room while I slept! Perhaps he had even stood by the side of the bed and stared down at me before he did what he had come for.

I caught my breath. Was it possible he was still here? I wondered. Over by the fireplace perhaps? Lurking near the wardrobe? Or was he leaning against the chaise lounge, waiting for me to react? Waiting to come to me? I stifled a whimper.

Narrowing my eyes, I tried to pierce the blackness without moving my head, but I could see nothing. Still I did not move for what seemed an endless time. Then a sudden flutter drew my eyes to the balcony doors. In the faint starlight I saw they were wide open, and as I watched, the curtains there billowed in the breeze. The scent of the roses that breeze scattered was so strong I felt sick.

It was then I heard the sound of laughter coming from somewhere below in the garden. That laughter broke the spell. I threw back the covers and rushed to the balcony doors to slam and then lock them and draw the curtains tight across. What a ridiculous thing it was to do, to trust in such a fragile barrier. Hayes could breach it in a moment.

The laughter came again clearly. It was harsh and taunting, knowing even, as if he knew what I was thinking and agreed with me.

My legs gave under me then and I sank to the floor, trembling uncontrollably.

Chapter 5

The next afternoon Viscount Epstead arrived for our drive quite half an hour early. Since I was not ready, he spent the time in the dowager's company. I could hear them laughing together when I came down at last. It sounded as if they were in complete accord, and so lighthearted and gay, I envied them. What would it be like to be able to be like that? I wondered as I pinned a smile on my face before I joined them.

The viscount rose at once and bowed. As he did so, he said, "No, I was not mistaken after all. I cannot tell you how relieved I am, ma'am! Why, I spent the better part of the night worrying you were not the paragon I had imagined. By dawn, I was convinced that in the bright light of day I would find only a fairly agreeable-looking girl with more than one glaring fault that had somehow escaped me in last night's candlelight. My compliments, ma'am. You are exquisite."

Faith Abbott had resorted to her handkerchief, she was chuckling so hard. "I wonder if it is safe for you to drive with him, Lucy," she said at last as I rose from my curtsy. I was a little breathless at the intent I could see in the viscount's eyes. "He is certainly ardent, isn't he?" she added.

"Then I shall endeavor to cool that ardor, Your Grace," I told her. "But didn't you say he is considered harmless?"

"I find I take offense at that remark," Epstead said as he shook his head. "It makes me seem so — so insignificant, does it not? Rather like a cup of lukewarm chamomile tea.

"But we shall see, won't we? Give you good afternoon, Your Grace, and every bountiful blessing for bringing this lovely creature to Oxfordshire."

As we went to the front door, I discovered I had to hurry my steps to keep up with him. He took long strides for a man of his height and he did not dawdle.

Waving away the groom, he lifted me to the phaeton's perch himself. As he went around to his own place, he called, "Wait for me here, Harry. I've no doubt you'll find the duchess's kitchen all right and beg the cook to feed you. What a bad name you are giving me! People must say I starve my servants.

"All right, let 'em go!"

As we went smartly down the graveled drive, he said, "Harry is deceiving. He's as slim as a jockey, yet he eats like a bird."

"A bird, sir? Surely you mean a horse, or possibly a pig. Birds don't eat much."

"Now there you are wrong, ma'am. Just consider. Outside of a few melodious warbles at dawn and some sleepy notes at dusk, what else do birds do but eat? I've never seen one unoccupied or just hopping about, have you? And their young are voracious."

I had to admit he had a point. I was about to remark on his team, a matched pair of blacks, when he said, "Yes, yes, they are handsome, I agree. And sweet goers with not an ounce of vice in 'em. And that is all the time we are going to waste on my horses. We've more important things to discuss."

"How on earth did you know I was about to comment on them?" I asked in amazement.

He laughed, and the gates safely negotiated settled the team to a canter before he looked sideway at me for a moment. I could not help feeling flattered, his gaze was so warm.

"Most women do mention them first. I suspect their mothers taught them that is the way to a man's heart, for most of us prize our stables above all else. I am not such a ninny however. A horse is only a horse, while a companion like you is incomparable. Tell me, why have we never met before this?"

I looked straight ahead as I said, "I don't find it all that surprising. I lived all my life in Dorset until I married when I was seventeen. Lord Blake died less than a year later. Since then I have lived secluded."

"I don't wonder at it," he said cheerfully. "Knew the viscount. He was one of my father's older cronies. Being married to him would send anyone in search of seclusion. That awful laugh of his! But tell me, what were your parents thinking of to pair such as you with him? His wealth? His name?"

"I've no intention of discussing my marriage with you, sir," I said stiffly, still looking straight ahead as the road wound away behind us and new scenery came into view to be admired.

I would not have spoken so sharply except I was very tired. After discovering the rose petals in my room, I had spent a good half hour collecting them. I woke again at dawn to finish the job before Franklin could come in and find them. I was glad I had taken that extra precaution. There were still petals on the floor, on the chairs, and even one on the dressing table. Several had drifted under the bed. I shivered, remembering how bruised they had been. Bruised deliberately, I was sure, to send me a message. I had stuffed them into a large reticule I rarely used, then hid it in the back of the wardrobe until such time I could dispose of the petals without anyone seeing me do it and questioning me.

"May I hope the shadows I see in your eyes come from a sleepless night?" my escort inquired. I hoped he could not hear the involuntary gasp I stifled immediately. "I mean, because you could not rest for thinking of me, ma'am?" he went on. "I will admit my own rest was troubled."

I took a deep breath. "M'lord, please," I said.

"Please do not continue to speak to me this way. It is not at all becoming. Why, you don't even know me."

"That is a hit, ma'am. Of course I don't. But then, no man knows a woman until they are married. Believe me, I was not in jest last evening. I meant everything I said to you."

"You're not serious," I said in disbelief. "We are strangers."

"Only for a few more days," he persisted. "Then I guarantee I shall know you as well as you know yourself. And although I sense you are about to say love at first sight is impossible, allow me to contradict you. As I have just discovered, it is entirely possible. And I do intend to marry you, you know, just as soon as I can."

"Then you are facing disappointment," I told him, looking at him for a fleeting second. His profile was straight and true and his jaw surprisingly firm. Under the tall black hat he wore tilted at such a dashing angle, his hair gleamed golden in the sunlight. He was everything I had ever dreamed of marrying someday — when I was a girl, a thousand years ago.

"I am not going to marry again, not ever," I told him.

"Now, now," he said in the soothing voice one used to calm a child. It angered me a little. "No doubt Blake was a nasty pill to swallow — well, stands to reason, don't it? He was hardly any maiden's young dream. But he is gone now and you may please yourself. Or allow me the privilege of doing it for you."

For a moment I wondered if the viscount had supernatural powers. How could it be he seemed able to guess what I was thinking, and then remark on it? Was he clairvoyant?

Before I could repeat my intention of never marrying again, he changed the subject. Nodding his head at Lansmere Hall which could be seen in the distance, he said, "The duke and duchess and the heir himself are to return today. I must admit I admire their sangfroid, coming back so willingly to that dismal pile of ugly brick. Hopefully his future seat will not scar little Reginald for life."

Happy to discuss anything impersonal, I said, "I quite agree with you. I have always disliked Lansmere Park. I was there this past Christmas for almost two months, and it was difficult not to be depressed the entire time."

"Well, dear Eugenia might have had something to do with that. She was always a staid young woman, but achieving the exalted heights of duchesshood seems to have cast her even further into stiff propriety. I have not been invited to the Park since the first year of their marriage although Forrestal and I were great chums at one time."

I could not help smiling a little. Just imagining the irreverent Viscount Epstead who said exactly what was on his mind no matter how inappropriate, in company with Eunice Abbott was laughable.

"I don't think I'll ask what it was you said or did that caused your banishment," I told him.

"It wouldn't matter if you did," he replied in a gloomy voice. "I've not the faintest idea. Forrestal wouldn't tell me when he announced it would be better for us to meet in London at our clubs in future. I've often wondered since. Was it my remark about setting the mansion on fire and then rebuilding, do you suppose? I did not suspect dear Eunice was so fond of the place. How could I? Or perhaps she objected to my pleasantries. But everyone else in the party laughed at them, indeed they did. And I hardly think my suggesting a rousing game of hide-and-seek in pairs one dreary afternoon would be enough to cause my exile, do you?"

By this time I was laughing and he turned slightly to smile down at me. "That's better," he said in an encouraging voice. "You were getting much too serious yourself, you know. Almost like the Duchess of Lansmere in fact, and that would never do. Not for my future bride, it wouldn't."

He must have sensed how I stiffened, for he said nothing further. Indeed, for the rest of our drive he only spoke of innocuous things. He was bright and amusing and lively, but even so I found there was a great deal more to him than I had first imagined. He was well informed on current events in both Parliament and at Court, and some of his comments about the state of the world were both succinct and knowledgeable.

An unusual gentleman, Bradford Grey, Viscount Epstead.

When we returned to the dower house, the sun was beginning to cast long shadows across the lawns. I had not realized it was so late, so well-entertained as I had been.

To my surprise, the viscount did not bid me good day. Instead he came around and as he lifted me down while his groom stood grinning impartially at us both, he said, "Do you know, I forgot a message I was supposed to deliver to the dowager from Alicia. Shall we go and see where she is?"

I smiled at this obvious ploy. The hall was empty of servants, although I could hear feet in the upstairs hall, and the butler murmuring to a footman in the sitting room. Quite at home, Bradford Grey looked briefly into the other rooms before he led me toward the terrace.

"I wouldn't wager a ha'penny that we'll not find her in the gardens," he said as he held the terrace door for me. "She is so fond of them, isn't she?"

As we went out into the sunlight again, I heard Faith Abbott laugh, and a deep answering laugh as well. Surely I did not imagine the way Viscount Epstead stiffened, nor did I miss the quick frown that creased his forehead.

"So, Gareth Powell is here, I see," he said under his breath as the dowager caught sight of us and beckoned us to her side. "I might have known. Man's an opportunist. Always has been."

The maligned Mr. Powell rose to bow as we neared the table where he sat with the dowager duchess, enjoying a glass of wine. He looked as if he had only just arrived. Remembering the duke and duchess and their entourage were supposed to come today, I wondered if he had traveled with them.

Viscount Epstead was easily persuaded to remain and we took our places at the table. It was covered with a pale green cloth. A bowl of mixed flowers adorned the center. Beside the wine and a tray of glasses, a pierced silver plate held little cakes and some frosted grapes. It was a charming scene on a warm summer afternoon — very homelike, very welcoming.

Behind us in the garden, Fleming and two of his underlings worked on one of the beds. The garden looked superb, a riot of color except for one border full of drifts of shining white cosmos set against a dark yew hedge. No wonder Faith Abbott spent so much time here, I thought. I could see from the grass stains on her old muslin gown, and the weeds in the basket at her feet, she too had been on her knees working this afternoon.

It did not take long for the viscount to discover that far from being the casual caller he was himself, Gareth Powell had come to stay with us for the remainder of the summer. Although his face revealed nothing, I sensed the news irritated him. As the dowager told him of Powell's new home at Chipping Norton, I wondered at the antipathy I could feel between these two men. Although they were both polite to a fault, I was sure their dislike for each other was of long standing. I pondered what the reason for it could possibly be.

"I was most remiss earlier, Your Grace," the viscount said. "Alicia charged me to bring you a message, but when I arrived to take Lady Blake driving, it completely slipped my mind. You see," he added, turning toward me with a smile, "you see what just the sight of you does to a man?"

"What was the message?" Faith Abbott asked when he continued to smile at me, almost as if he had forgotten our companions. Gareth Powell did not look a bit pleased. In fact, from the fleeting glance I had, I could see he was angry. But perhaps I was reading too much into his expression. Certainly when next I looked at him, he only appeared to be grimly amused.

"She wants you and Lady Blake to come to a fete she is giving for the neighboring gentry next Thursday week," the viscount said. "It is to be a garden party and I expect she wants your advice, Your Grace, since she intends to remain here when Jack next leaves on his diplomatic chores. Oh, I do beg your pardon, sir. You must come as well."

"I intend to spend quite a lot of time at my new home this summer, overseeing the workmen," Powell said coolly. "I will not be here next Thursday."

"But of course. I quite understand. The renovations must be your primary concern. I don't think you will be missing anything, fetes hardly being your cup of tea, eh?"

Gareth Powell put his empty glass down and rose. "If you will excuse me, Your Grace, m'lady? I must see to my unpacking and wash away the road dust. Give you good afternoon, m'lord."

The viscount waved a careless hand and immediately began to speak of the arrival of the other Abbotts at Lansmere Park. The dowager had already made plans to see the baby again tomorrow. Knowing Eugenia Abbott's animosity toward her mother-in-law, I hoped we were not in for a dismal summer of arguments and hurt feelings.

Then I forgot them, forgot everyone and everything in fact, when I faintly heard someone whistling. My hand tightened on the stem of the glass I had just raised. We were sitting in the pergola at one end of the terrace, shaded from the late afternoon sun by quantities of royal purple clematis trailing gracefully over the columns and trellis. The brick wall that surrounded all the dower house property was far across the lawn behind me. And behind that wall, I knew, was Jaspar Hayes. It had to be he. Surely no one else here knew the old Cornish folk song he was whistling. Mentally I shook myself and the rest of the world returned. I saw the viscount was staring at me and I forced myself to sip the wine before I set my glass down. Carefully. Very carefully.

The dowager smiled. "Fleming had better not hear that man whistling," she said. "He is very like Napoleon you know, with the gardeners his troops."

"I see you have been working in the garden too, ma'am," I hurried to say. "Does Fleming approve of that?"

Successfully diverted, she explained the truce they had reached after a number of years. Then she picked up her basket and rose. "You remind me I have not quite finished that border I was working on. Do take m'lord down to the gazebo, Lucy. He has yet to see the pools and the water lilies."

The viscount was quick to express an interest. The dowager chuckled, but thankfully she had no further comment.

Left to myself, I would have been delighted to flee to my own rooms. This was all entirely too dangerous with Hayes nearby. Suppose he saw us, I thought as we strolled toward the path that wound through the woods. I concentrated on my steps for my knees were trembling.

Was he watching me even now, curious who the gentleman beside me was and what he was doing here? I wondered.

"Ah, it is cooler now, isn't it?" that man remarked as we entered the woods. There was nothing rustic about them for they were almost as well groomed as the formal gardens we had just left behind. The paths were well-raked and edged, and sunlight filtered through the leaves of the trees as we moved from light to shadow — shadow to light. The pools of flashing carp and the cool, fragrant lilies were duly admired before we reached the gazebo. Well beyond it through the woods, I could barely make out the boundary wall of the estate. There was no gate there. I was grateful for that and for the first time since I had heard Hayes's whistling, I was able to calm myself.

The gazebo had wide benches all around its eight sides. They were covered with colorful pillows. A wicker table placed in the middle held more wine and glasses, even a pitcher of lemonade. Had the dowager planned this? I wondered. Was she matchmaking again?

I was suddenly reminded the viscount had been silent for some time, and I looked at him askance.

"What have you been thinking?" he asked, more seriously than he had ever spoken to me before. As he turned me gently to face him, he added, "So many emotions have chased themselves across your face these last few moments. If I were a more conceited man, I might believe you were thinking of me — of our being alone here — of the kiss I might steal."

I pulled away and turned my back. This seemingly careless, irreverent man saw entirely too much. "My thoughts are mine alone, sir," I said as evenly as I could.

"You knew that tune the gardener was whistling, didn't you?" he asked next. "I could see it upset you. Why was that?"

For a moment I was tempted to deny it, but I knew enough now of Viscount Epstead even from our short acquaintance to realize he would not let me get away with that.

"Yes, I have known that particular air for a long time," I told him over my shoulder, proud my voice was so steady. "You're right. It does not bring back pleasant memories."

I was startled when I felt his hands on my shoulders. I had not thought him so close. Still, I did not resist when he turned me again so we were facing. He stared down into my eyes as if searching for something, something I knew I had no intention of letting any man ever find there.

He did not speak. Instead, he shook his head as if in resignation. Then he bent and kissed me. He didn't take me in his arms nor did he draw me closer to him. Only our lips met and I was aware I could pull away from the light grasp he had on my shoulders anytime I chose. For some perverse reason I did not do that. Instead, I let him kiss me. His mouth was gentle but firm, and it lingered, caressing my own. I did not respond. In a way I was reminded of two children, innocent of kissing and how it should be done, yet daring to experiment — both tentative, almost fearful of what they were discovering. I had been kissed that way once before when I was barely thirteen by a neighbor's son. Then it had brought a stirring deep inside me that had frightened me, and I had run away as soon as the boy let me go. Sadly, today I felt nothing at all.

It seemed a long time before Bradford Grey lifted his head just far enough to look into my eyes again. I searched his eyes as well, but like my own, they gave nothing away.

The shaft of sunlight we had been standing in had moved across the floor of the gazebo, and all around us the early dusk that had come to the woods began to invade the little outdoor room.

The viscount let me go, and stepping back he raised my hand and kissed it. A moment later he was gone and I was left alone in the shadows. I do not know why — I don't think I'll ever know why — but I sat down on one of the benches then and burying my face in my hands, I wept.

Chapter 6

When I left the woods I was relieved to discover the dowager had gone inside. I had tried to remove all traces of my tears but I was not at all sure I had been successful. The gardeners I had seen earlier were trundling heavy barrows to the gate in the wall. Only Fleming remained, hands akimbo as he surveyed the work that had been accomplished today.

I smiled as I neared him and he removed his cap and said, "M'lady? If I might have a word?"

I paused reluctantly.

"I've noticed a man about the place for some days now," he began bluntly, and the terror that the viscount's kiss had displaced, came back in a flood.

"He's not from around here, I know that, and he's not someone wandering the roads searching for work neither. No, he's a gentleman, he is, well-dressed and prosperous. And his horse is first-rate. But I don't want to worry Her Grace with this."

"But what can I do?" I asked. He looked at me as straight as Bradford Grey had done.

"I thought maybe ye knew him, or at least what he's up to, m'lady. Forgive me, but yer a bonny

80

lass. I wouldn't be a bit surprised if he was here because of ye. He hangs about, ye see, near the walls, and I suspect he's been in the gardens as well. I've found signs . . ."

I knew then that my rubbing out that boot mark had done no good at all. Fleming knew every inch of the gardens. Even if Hayes had left little trace of his presence, Fleming would know immediately that someone had invaded his kingdom.

"Late last night I thought I heard noises and I came out with a lantern," he continued. "I didn't find anything, but the gate was unlatched. I know I never left it that way. I always check it last thing."

"I see," I said slowly. "It does sound suspicious, doesn't it? But I can't help you, Fleming. I've no idea who the man might be, or what he might be after. Still," I went on, wondering at the accomplished liar I was becoming, "I quite agree with you we must not worry Her Grace. I do have an idea. Is the gate the only way into the gardens?"

When he nodded, I said, "I think an iron padlock might be a good thing to have, then. You could keep the key to it safe. And perhaps the drive gates could also be locked at night, if you think Her Grace would not notice."

"I'll see to that at once, m'lady," Fleming said. Then he added grimly, "And I'll do a bit more wandering about at night, lantern in hand. That might discourage the man."

81

He hesitated, turning his cap around and around in his hands. At last he said, "I think ye should take a groom with ye when ye go riding, aye, and be on yer guard. Yer too tempting a lass, indeed you are, and I'd not have ye in danger."

He turned scarlet under his deep tan when it dawned on him what he had said, but I thanked him seriously for his concern.

As I left him and went up the terrace steps, I wondered if, in spite of my earlier apprehension, this might not be a very good thing for me after all. Now at least I had an ally, no matter how unwitting an ally he might be, to help me avoid any more midnight surprises. Surely Hayes would have to stop coming to my room now. Surely there would be no more wild roses left there to torment me.

But as I reached my room and closed the door gratefully behind me to slump against it, I realized that no padlock or locked front gates, no middle-aged, stolid gardener, would be enough to keep Jaspar Hayes out. The walls were high, but not that high. They could be scaled. And surely there were plenty of places along their outer walls where the branches of trees hung tantalizingly close. As for Fleming, he could not patrol all night, every night. He had his daytime work to do. And by now Hayes probably knew every hiding place there was in the grounds. He was sly. I had always thought him sly.

I did not go down to dinner that evening. Instead, I sent word by Franklin that I was feeling tired and planned an early night. I had done this before in London several times; Faith Abbott would not question it or come to see how I did.

As soon as the maid had removed my barely touched tray, I dismissed her. Sure she had gone away, I got out of bed to wedge a heavy chair under the latch of the locked balcony doors. It was all I could think of to do. And if Hayes did come tonight, or tomorrow night and tried to get in, I would hear the door rattling and have time to get my pistol ready. It occurred to me then that if I shot him, now Fleming would come forward to tell what he knew of the interloper, and I would be exonerated. Grimly I wondered why that knowledge didn't make me feel better.

Back in bed I found I could not sleep in spite of my very real exhaustion. Instead my mind ranged over the past — the never-to-be lamented past — before it began to explore the present.

I was terrified and I admitted it. Even now, safe in the house with Fleming aware of the danger in his quarters near the stable, my ears were pricked for any sound near the doors. For a moment I toyed with the idea of asking the dowager if I might not move to another room. Perhaps I could claim the scent of the flowers made me sneeze. Then I could be in a room that overlooked the drive and the broad lawns that stretched to the front gates. There were no balconies there. I grimaced. I could not do that. It would be so singular it would be sure to be remarked. And the dowager would know it for the lie it was since I had spent so much time in the gardens with her and never sniffled once. No, I could not change rooms. I was forced to remain here and take my chances.

Was that a sound I heard? I sat up and fumbled for the pistol I had placed on my bedside table. Holding it in two shaking hands I peered through the darkness, hardly daring to breathe lest I miss the signal that Hayes was attempting to breech my defenses. Nothing happened until I heard the wind in the tree branches near the balcony, and the first drops of a sudden storm begin to strike the panes. I put the pistol down and clasped my hands to my rapidly beating heart. Cold sweat beaded my brow.

How was I to live this way? I wondered as I lay down again and tried to compose myself. How could anyone live this way?

I finally fell asleep glad to leave my torturous thoughts behind, but sleep held no refuge. Instead, I had nightmares, frightening, all-too-real dreams of Jaspar Hayes and what he wanted from me. I woke at dawn startled from sleep by an image of me running, always running but never getting away from Hayes close behind me, laughing as he reached for me.

Dear God, I thought, as I dragged myself from bed to set the chair straight and hide my pistol in the wardrobe again so Franklin would see nothing amiss — dear God, help me.

It rained all day. At nine I dressed, even used some discreet paint and powder to disguise my wan appearance before I made my way to the breakfast room. The dowager had already eaten. I could hear her discussing the day's orders with her butler and housekeeper in her morning room nearby. But Gareth Powell was there. He had pushed his plate away and poured himself another cup of coffee, and he was deep in the morning paper. Courteously, he rose to help me to my seat after I had selected my breakfast from an array of serving dishes set over spirit lamps on the sideboard.

"I hope I did not bring this steady downpour with me when I came, m'lady," he said as he took his seat again and folded the newspaper. I wished he had not. It would be so much easier for me to eat breakfast if he were hidden behind its pages.

"Rain is always welcome for the gardens," I said, proud of my composure. "Might I trouble you for the marmalade, Mr. Powell. Thank you."

"Something else has happened since I saw you in London," he remarked, leaning forward. "Something that has affected you deeply, ma'am."

"Are you a gypsy, sir?" I asked, trying for a smile. "And are you able not only to see the past and the present, but the future as well?"

"Hardly. But I know trouble when it stares me in the face. You are so beautiful yet so sad. So solemn. So frightened. Why is that, m'lady? What could possibly terrify such a woman as yourself?"

"I fear you are fanciful, sir," I said, ignoring

the hand he had stretched out to me by pretending to be intent on the scone I was breaking in two. "I did not have a good night. That is all that is wrong with me."

He did not take his gaze from my face. Even without looking up I was aware of it and it was all I could do to preserve any semblance of calm. Oh why, why had Gareth Powell had to come to the dower house? So all-seeing, all-knowing, and intelligent as he appeared to be?

"You are often troubled with disturbed nights, m'lady?" he persisted. "Surely that is not right. Perhaps you should seek the advice of a physician."

"Not you too!" I said, exasperated. "Her Grace is constantly after me to do so. And although I must thank you for your concern, it really is none of your business. As it happens however, I have seen a doctor. He says there is nothing wrong with me."

"Perhaps physically that is true. But there are other ways a person can be ill."

"Surely you are not suggesting I am going mad!" I said, professing shock. He grimaced and made a strange motion, as if he were washing his hands of me. He would never know how grateful I would be if he would do just that.

As I took a sip of coffee, he said, "I am afraid I am going to place myself further in your black books, m'lady. Still, I feel I must warn you about Viscount Epstead."

I lowered my cup to the saucer and looked at

him straightly. "Yes?" I said in my sweetest voice. "What about the viscount?"

"He is not a good man," Gareth Powell said, frowning heavily. "I cannot tell you why. Another is involved. But you may believe I am speaking the truth."

"But why should I believe you?" I asked. "I do not know you particularly well, and just because you are Faith Abbott's godson does not make you credible. To be frank, I find a man who maligns another something less than admirable."

I saw his face darken and held my breath, sure he was about to ring a peal over me that would put paid to any rapport we might ever had had. To my surprise he did not do so. Instead, as he picked up his paper again, he said, "Go your own way, then, m'lady. At least I tried."

It was very quiet in the breakfast room from then on, and I was able to eat in peace. In a way I was sorry it must be so, for I was left to my thoughts and they were hardly pleasant.

After breakfast I found the dowager writing letters. Not wishing to disturb her, I went to the library to find something to read. I had settled down in the window seat there with a novel when Mr. Powell came in. He bowed, but he did not speak to me as he went to search the shelves. Outside, the rain continued unabated. It turned out to be a lazy gray day that moved much too slowly. I read, wrote some letters myself to my London acquaintance, took a nap, and worked on my needlepoint. Fortunately the next day dawned fair.

I sent a message to Alicia Grey right after breakfast, asking her to ride with me that afternoon. I knew the dowager would be visiting her grandson, an event the rain had caused to be postponed. What Gareth Powell was doing I had no idea. And, I told myself as I went downstairs holding the train of my habit to one side, I didn't much care. Since that confrontation at breakfast, we had spoken to each other only when necessary. Fortunately Faith Abbott did not appear to notice.

I did not take a groom with me. I did not feel the need for one when I was with Alicia. I knew that Hayes would not try anything when there was another person present as witness. But I also knew he would not give up and go away. He had always been such a single-minded man, able to see only the course he had chosen and unable to deviate from it even slightly.

Whether it was the padlock, or the locked gates, he had not come again, but I was still not sleeping well. My mirror told me this lack of sleep would soon be remarked, for I was beginning to look wan and heavy-eyed.

Fortunately Alicia did not notice when we met at the crossroads she had suggested. I was not too surprised to see Viscount Epstead was there as well, mounted on a good-looking black mare with a white blaze and three white stockings.

"He insisted on coming. I could do nothing to discourage him," Alicia said, casting a dark look at her brother-in-law. "It is too bad. I had hoped we might enjoy our ride, just the two of us."

"Not at all the thing," the viscount said cheerfully. "Why, it does not bear thinking of, two such lovely ladies abroad with no man in attendance. Just think of all the dangers that might be awaiting you."

"What dangers?" Alicia asked. "What dangers could we possibly face here in the English countryside?"

I was reminded of Jaspar Hayes and found I could hardly smile at all this banter.

"Why, you might meet a band of gypsies intent on kidnapping, or worse." The viscount leered as we trotted off together. "Perhaps a mad dog or a runaway team might come pounding around that bend ahead. Or your horse might throw you if a snake slithered across the road under its hooves. Or perhaps —"

"Enough!" Alicia said, chuckling at his ridiculous list. "And, what, pray tell, could you do if anything like that did happen?"

"I haven't a clue," he answered promptly. "Especially about the snake. I hate 'em. Always have since I was a child. If we should see one, you will save me, won't you, dear sister?"

He turned to me then and smiled. Mounted, we were of a height and I could tell he was remembering the kiss he had given me and was daring me to remember it as well.

"Shall we canter?" Alicia asked crisply, and obediently, I dug in my heel. There was no more conversation until some time later when we reached the little village of Peasedale. The viscount suggested we dismount and investigate and Alicia and I were happy to leave our horses at the small inn the village boasted.

As the two Greys began to tease each other again, I looked around a little warily. It had suddenly occurred to me that perhaps Jaspar Hayes was staying here. It was only half an hour's ride from the dower house. I made myself forget him as we began our walk.

The village was busy this sunny summer afternoon. Women hung out their wash or leaned over their fences to gossip as their children played a noisy game on the common. Several men lounged about the blacksmith's shop and on the dusty road there was a donkey cart, two drays, and a dog and shepherd herding a small flock of sheep. To my relief, there was no sign of Hayes. We walked from one end of the village to the other, stopping once to watch some ducks on a pond near the mill race. At length we retired to the inn for some refreshment. I was looking forward to lemonade, if such a thing were to be found here. It was a warm day, and the exercise had made me thirsty. I was just thinking that at least tonight I would have no trouble falling asleep when the viscount stepped aside to allow Alicia and I to precede him, and I came face to face with Jaspar Hayes.

His eyes narrowed as he inspected me and my companions. Then he tipped his hat and stepped back so as not to impede our progress. Alicia smiled at him, but my heart was pounding so in my throat I could hardly make myself move forward and past him. He was so close to me! I cannot describe the horror of that moment.

I was glad to take my seat at a corner table and clasp my hands together under cover of that table. They were shaking badly.

Alicia said nothing until Bradford Grey went to order our drinks. Then she leaned forward and said, "Are you all right, Lucy? You look like you've seen a ghost."

I wished with all my heart Hayes was a ghost for I would not fear him then, but I only said, "No, I'm fine. I've been having trouble sleeping, and the ride has tired me. Please don't say anything about this, especially to the dowager. She tends to fuss over me, you know."

"I think you would do well to have someone fussing over you," Alicia said dryly, but she changed the subject when Lord Epstead returned with a servant bearing a tray.

He set himself to amuse us, telling of various inns he had stayed at over the years. Not to be outdone, Alicia gave her own account of inns abroad, especially in Russia. It was fascinating, and if I had not been so upset at encountering Hayes, I would have hung on her every word. Instead, all I could do was try to look attentive while I worried about seeing Hayes again when we left the inn.

The time for that came all too soon, but when we reached the yard and an ostler was sent running to fetch our mounts, Hayes was nowhere in sight. The viscount helped me to the saddle and I arranged the skirt of my habit and took up the reins, anxious now to be gone.

It was all I could do not to scream at the others to make haste, for it seemed an endless time before we started. A little way past the village there was a pretty cottage, set off by itself. Whoever lived there had planted a lovely flower garden and we stopped to admire it. It was then I smelled the wild roses again, stronger and sweeter than the other flowers on the afternoon breeze that had come up.

Alicia noticed the aroma too and she pointed to where the roses grew in profusion over a white trellis.

"Yes, they are the wild roses I was asking you about," I said, my throat constricted.

"They are lovely, and the scent is heavenly," she said. "I can understand why they are favorites of yours."

I was delighted to ride away. All the way home I thought of what had happened, and shuddered. But at least I knew now where Hayes was staying, and where he had found the roses, although I could not see that knowledge had given me any advantage. For after coming face to face with him, I knew I would never, ever seek him out, not for any reason.

When we reached the crossroads, the viscount insisted on seeing me the rest of the way home. I did not demur. For all I knew, Hayes could be waiting for me somewhere on the road ahead.

"Alas, to be a sister-in-law is not easy," Alicia complained as she prepared to ride on. "Pray I encounter no gypsies, mad dogs, or traveling snakes," she said, and chuckling rode away.

Bradford Grey did not seem in any hurry to reach the dower house. He kept his horse to a walk and I followed suit.

"Are you to remain here for the rest of the summer, m'lady?" he began.

"I believe so."

"And where do you live when you are not visiting the dowager?"

"Why, I have a house in London, in Portman Square. But I've asked my agent to sell it. Lord Blake's estate is in Cornwall. It is called Trecarag, but I have not been there since he died."

I looked at him, confused. "Do you know, I haven't even considered where I am to go next. Of course the dowager wants me to buy a place here, or possibly in Kent, but I am undecided."

"I have never visited Cornwall, although I have heard it's beautiful country, full of legends of valor and derring-do. They say the coastline is superb. Why don't you like it there?"

"I never said I didn't," I protested. "I just don't care to live there." Remembering what the dowager had said, I added, "It is too far from London, and the journey is long and hard."

I could see the walls of the dower house ahead. Bradford Grey must have seen them as well, for he reached out to take hold of my bridle and halt the horses.

"Don't worry about where you will live next, m'lady," he said, smiling at me. "I have that all planned. I think you will like my estate. Greys have lived there for over two hundred years, but I'll wager none of them ever had a bride as beautiful as the one I intend to install."

"Please," I said, looking straight at him and trying as hard as I knew how to show my sincerity, "I am not going to marry you or anyone. You waste your time supposing I am being coy. I disliked marriage. I want no more of it."

"You say so now, but you'll see," he said. Surely the man was the most maddening one I had ever encountered!

As he let go of my bridle and began to walk his horse again he said, "How are you faring with Gareth Powell? He can be a surly devil."

"For some reason he does not appear to like you either," I told him. "Why is that, I wonder?"

"I promise I'll tell you someday. What a comedy of errors it was that estranged us. Ah, we have reached the gates. I am so sorry. Tell me, will you ride with me again someday before Alicia's fete? Or go for a drive?"

I said I was sorry but I was going to be very busy with the dowager and could not be jauntering about on pleasure. He didn't look as if he believed a word I said. As I rode up the drive, aware he remained to watch me go, I wondered since he was so provoking, why he did not make me angrier. Why, in fact, he made me feel as if I were unique — someone special.

Chapter 7

As it turned out, I saw the viscount two days later. The dowager had returned from visiting her grandson with an invitation bidding her and her guests to dinner at the Park. She had accepted, but she assured me I need not go if I did not care for it. I smiled and said I would be glad, but later I wondered how much she had suspected about that Christmas house party this past winter. The duchess had been *enceinte,* of course, and much to my dismay, the duke had behaved rather foolishly, trying to get me alone, singling me out for attention, and generally making a cake of himself. I had been as cold to him as I dared, but I had been relieved when I had quit the Park and gone to stay with Faith Abbott. He had come often after that to the dower house, supposedly to see his mother, until at last I had had to be very straight with him. To his credit, he took my dismissal in good spirit and even apologized for distressing me. I could understand why he might yearn after another. Eugenia Abbott was not the most pleasant woman in the world, and since becoming a duchess had turned even more cold and distant.

When the three of us arrived at Lansmere Park

on the evening appointed, after walking the short distance from the dower house in the pleasant early evening, I discovered the Greys were also included in the party. The viscount came immediately to my side.

"How exquisite you look tonight in pale blue, m'lady," he began, still holding my hand in his.

I withdrew it gently. "Oh dear," I said, "you are not about to shower me with compliments, are you, m'lord? They become boring so quickly, don't they?"

"And here I thought women doted on compliments."

"Not I."

"That is only because you have heard so many of them, you have become jaded. Now if no one had said a kind word to you for six months, you'd be more amenable. Why is Powell glaring at us?"

"I told you he does not like you. And, I'm afraid, I am rather in his black books at the moment as well."

"I can't tell you how relieved I am to hear you say so, ma'am. Long may it continue. Why, just thinking of the two of you in such close proximity day after day makes me shiver. Powell has all the advantage, you see, living in the same house with you as he does. Be on your guard, ma'am. I am sure once he overcomes his pique with you, he'll discover he can conduct all his estate business from a distance after all. And I don't want him getting any ideas about the woman I have chosen to be my countess.

"Ah, Forrestal, my friend. How kind of you — and the duchess — to include me in the evening's festivities. I was sure I was unwelcome at the Park."

The duke grinned down at him. He was so tall he dwarfed most other men. "You are," he said bluntly. "Eunice was not aware you were visiting your brother and his wife, but of course, once apprised of it, she could hardly exclude you. Beg you'll behave yourself, Brad."

The viscount looked affronted. "Of course I will," he said. "I have superb manners which I sometimes even employ. You know Lady Blake, don't you? I'm going to marry her."

The duke looked at me, a question in his eyes. I shook my head.

"Pay no attention to her," Bradford Grey continued. "She says she does not agree, but she'll come around, you'll see."

The duchess arrived then to stand beside her husband. Her smile for me and the viscount was fleeting. "How delightful you could both join us," she said in her icy voice. "Forrestal, your mother is entirely too free this evening. She has just told the warmest story about the Prince Regent. Do go and have a quiet word with her, please."

Her husband looked around to see the rest of the party deep in conversation on the other side of the room. While he watched, the four enjoyed a hearty laugh and the duchess shuddered.

"She does not behave as a woman of her years

and station should," the duchess continued as the duke went away. I wondered if he were about to demand his mother repeat the story she had just told. I wouldn't have been a bit surprised if he had.

"How is the heir, Your Grace?" the viscount asked. He had all the signs of a man on his best behavior and doing the pretty no matter how distasteful he might find it. "In good health and sound of lung and limb, is he?"

"Reginald is doing famously," Her Grace said, sounding slightly more animated now. I braced myself for a detailed description of the firstborn son and future duke. The duchess did not disappoint me and I was relieved, as I assumed Bradford Grey was, when we were summoned to dinner.

Unfortunately, the viscount, by protocol, was seated beside his hostess. I was able to escape that fate, for I found myself next to the duke at the other end of the table with Gareth Powell to my right.

At first, conversation was general. The duke told us all the news of London. The Prince Regent had finally taken himself off to Brighton and many in society had flocked after him. There was some gossip about various members of that society to relate.

"I never would have thought Sir George Pennington would ever have the courage to bring a divorce proceeding against his wife," Faith Abbott marveled at last. "True, the woman has been deceiving him for years, but he always turned a blind eye to her affairs before this."

"I understand his hand was forced. He found them together in his own home," Gareth Powell contributed. "Sir George came back to town early from a race meet and surprised them. Still, he did not challenge Mr. Harvey."

"He is the most lily-livered creature!" the dowager said in dismissal.

"Has there been any news of Lord and Lady Canford? Lucy and I feel quite neglected by them, for we've not had a word since they left town."

Both gentlemen denied any knowledge of the newlyweds the dowager had so recently reconciled.

"Some more game pie, m'lady?" Mr. Powell asked me as a footman presented the dish. "Another roll, perhaps?"

"No, no thank you," I told him. I had rarely been so close to the man before this. I decided he was really not harsh looking, in fact his blue-gray eyes were very attractive under his dark brows. And his mouth was nicely shaped.

"Well, do I pass muster?" he asked, sounding amused.

I blushed a little. "Forgive me. I was rude to stare."

"You should have had more pie. It is excellent, as are the rolls. You've lost flesh lately, haven't you? You begin to look rather, er, pinched, ma'am."

I stared at him anew. How different he was from Viscount Grey with his fulsome compliments.

"There is something bothering you," he continued as he cut his meat. "I wish you would confide in me. I would be happy to be of service. And sometimes, just telling another makes a problem shrink in importance."

"You are kind, sir," I said, eyes on my plate. "But there is nothing to discuss, truly there isn't."

He snorted. "If whatever is bothering you is so delicate you feel you can't disclose it to a man, I wonder you do not take the dowager into your confidence," he said, ignoring my denial. "It is plain to see she loves you, and I know from my own experience she would move heaven and earth to come to your aid."

I was beginning to feel badgered and I took a deep breath lest I lash out at the man and destroy what little rapport was building between us. But before I could speak, he added, "It is entirely too bad for someone like you to be so frightened — terrified, even. I must believe someone is threatening you. I'll say no more now, but I beg you to reconsider letting me deal with the fellow. I assume it is a man, you see, and he has some hold over you. Such people are despicable, but they can be stopped, you know."

"My, you have a vivid imagination, sir," I said as evenly as I could. "I would not have supposed it to be the case. You appear typically masculine."

"And men are so imperceptive, ma'am? Careful now. You must not generalize. To do so is typical feminine behavior."

The duke asked me a question then and I was happy to leave Mr. Powell to Alicia Grey on his other side.

When next I looked down the table, I saw Bradford Grey considering me. He was not smiling, and I wondered at it.

He told me, of course, as soon as the men rejoined the ladies after their port, for he came immediately to my side.

"What were you and Gareth Powell discussing at such length during dinner, ma'am?" he demanded.

I must have looked affronted for he added with a grin, "If you please?"

"It was just polite conversation," I lied and I refused to say more than that.

The evening came to an end shortly thereafter when the duchess announced she still required an early bedtime. In the face of that bald statement, there was nothing for us all to do but give her our compliments and take our respective leave. I could see the dowager thought her daughter-in-law ungracious. The duke looked none too pleased either.

In the hall, Gareth Powell had the lantern lit that we had brought with us, for there was only a quarter moon and it was dark now.

"I would feel steadier if I had your arm, dear boy," Faith Abbott said. "And do take Lucy on your other arm. She can carry the lantern. It's not heavy."

We did as we were bade. It was a lovely night with a slight breeze that carried a host of fresh summer scents. The occasional rustling in the woods nearby told us nocturnal creatures were also abroad. Thinking of nocturnal creatures, I was reminded I had not seen a sign of Jaspar Hayes since encountering him at the inn in Peasedale. I knew Fleming was still locking the gates at night. He was probably waiting up for us to come home so he could do so tonight.

I tripped a little over a root and Gareth Powell's arm tightened in support. After assuring him I was all right, we fell silent again. It was as if none of us cared to interrupt the quiet peace.

When we reached the dower house, Faith Abbott suggested we sit on the terrace for a while. "It is such a lovely night, isn't it? It reminds me of evenings when I was young and my sisters and I, unwilling to concede the day was over, would linger in the gardens until late. My, how long ago that was, yet I can hear my mother's voice calling us in even now."

I smiled at the nostalgia I could hear in her voice, smiled for all her happy memories. She was lucky. She had been blessed with a wonderful family life as a child, then later married a husband she adored, had her son, her many friends . . . I made myself stop. Life was not fair. I'd known that for years.

I blinked as we stepped into the hall. With the candles blazing there, it seemed overly light. Gareth Powell looked at me, concern on his face, almost as if he knew what I had been thinking and sympathized with me. I told myself I was being ridiculous.

"Forgive me for not joining you, ma'am," I said. "I'm feeling tired. Best I have an early night."

Before she could question me, I went and kissed her, then bade Mr. Powell a civil good night.

Later, after I was undressed and had dismissed Franklin, I went out on the balcony. I was not concerned about Hayes. He would not dare try anything while the household was still stirring. Below me, on the opposite side of the terrace under the pergola, I could hear the murmur of voices. I wondered what Mr. Powell and the dowager were discussing. Were they talking about me? Was Powell telling her his theory that someone was terrorizing me? Filling her head with all kinds of surprisingly accurate surmises? Pray not!

The morning dawned misty and cooler. I had intended to help the dowager pick some bouquets for her friends that we were to deliver that afternoon. Perhaps the mist would burn off by then and we would not have to put it off.

When I came downstairs, the butler came forward with a letter. I had a sinking feeling as I eyed the black handwriting, all swirls and flourishes. I tried to appear at ease as I took the letter from his tray.

"I see this did not come in the post, Wells," I said casually as I examined it.

"No, m'lady. It was brought this morning by a young lad. Gave it to one of the gardeners, he did."

I thanked him and moved on to the breakfast room. Seeing both the dowager and Mr. Powell were there, I slipped the letter into my reticule. I told myself I would read it later even as I wished I never had to read it at all.

It seemed an age before Faith Abbott finished her breakfast and went off to confer with the housekeeper. Gareth Powell lingered over his coffee. He was not reading the papers this morning. Instead, he stared into the garden as if trying to see beyond the misty tendrils that had invaded the flower beds. They made even a common daisy mysterious. I finished my shirred eggs and buttered a muffin.

At last he rose. "Have you thought about what we discussed last evening, ma'am?" he asked.

I stifled my first reaction — a sharp retort — and said, "I have not, sir. Except to wonder why you insist on being so melodramatic."

Before I knew what he was about, he stooped and picked up my reticule where I had placed it against the leg of my chair. Holding it by its strings, he swung it gently back and forth.

"Nothing I have said is anywhere near as melodramatic as your feeling it necessary to always carry a pistol," he said. His voice was harsh, almost accusing, and I wondered wildly what on earth I was to say to him now.

As if aware of my predicament, he nodded grimly. "Think about what I have said, Lady Blake. Think hard. You are not the only one here who would be affected by whatever it is that threatens you. Do consider the dowager duchess. She is not young anymore, and she is getting frail. Wouldn't it be better for her to be prepared for any contingency? There is myself as well, although I hesitate to mention it lest you accuse me of cowardice. I am not a coward, but I dislike facing menace that I know nothing about and so can't prepare for."

He set the reticule down on the table while I stared at him, still speechless.

"You don't have to say anything now. But please, I beg you, reconsider your determination to go it alone. It is not only dangerous, it is unnecessary."

I sat staring blankly at the door he closed behind him. I had not even thought of Faith Abbott and I was ashamed. But surely Hayes would not attempt to hurt her. His quarrel was with me, and only me. Still, there was the possibility Powell was right and my dear friend was in danger.

It was a while before I remembered the letter and opened it. It was on cheap paper, the sealing wax a garish purple. Just holding it made my skin crawl.

It was not long and it was certainly to the point, once I got past the flattering opening compliments he must have been taught were the only way to begin, no matter how threatening and unsavory the rest of a letter turned out to be.

"I was glad to see you the other day and in London as well, *m'lady*," it began, "but I find chance meetings don't serve the purpose. I want more than that, just as I did four years ago, as *m'lady* is well aware. You tricked me out of my rightful place then, but I will have it yet. Yes, I intend to have *everything* that is coming to me.

"You can't buy my silence any longer. Gold is not enough. I've been wronged, and I want to be repaid for it in more than coin.

"You will meet me, alone. I've a plan for your future. No, it's more than a plan. It *will* happen. I'll see to that.

"Write to me care of the inn at Peasedale. If I don't hear from you by tomorrow, you'll be sorry. *Very* sorry, *m'lady*."

He signed the letter with the usual flourishes and only his initials. I read it again, more slowly this time, but it was no less horrifying and no more reassuring. He meant it then. He meant to expose me, tell the world what had happened the summer following my wedding. He meant to ruin me, unless I gave in to him. But I could not do that, I thought wildly, rising to pace the room. I couldn't! I'd die first!

It suddenly occurred to me that perhaps *he* might. Arrested, I stared down at my reticule where Gareth Powell had left it on the table. Just as he had done, I saw the shape of the pistol clearly through the soft fabric. I could not help the shiver that ran through me at the wickedness of my thoughts.

Dragging my eyes away, I went to the window. I did not see anything there, not because of the shrouding mist but because I was looking inward. I would have to write to Jaspar Hayes, I told myself, otherwise he would come here. Why, he might even ride right up to the front door and send in his card. I remember he had liked having calling cards and a handsome silver case to keep them in, even though he had nowhere to leave one. Lord Blake had given him the case, mocking as he did so. Hayes had not noticed, so intent had he been on admiring the heavy silver, the discreet initials.

I put my hands to my forehead and commanded myself to forget all these extraneous details.

Certainly I could not risk having Hayes come here. I must meet him. Bile rose in my throat and I forced it down. This was no time to be weak.

I returned to my pacing. More and more the thought of killing Hayes seemed inevitable — the only way out for me. But if I were to do it and escape punishment, I would have to make plans. Very careful plans, too. Somehow I would have to get him to come somewhere where I had the upper hand. Somewhere he would be uncomfortable, uneasy perhaps, feel out of place. And I would have to put him off his guard, get him to imagine I was about to agree to all his ghastly plans for my future. Dear God! A future with him did not bear thinking about.

So *don't* think about it, I told myself sternly.

Now, what to do first?

I needed time to think and think hard to perfect my plans even though I knew he was not prepared to wait. No, I must write today, explain I could not see him just yet, beg for more time. Try to make him think he had broken me, that he had the upper hand. Taking my reticule with me, I went back upstairs to my rooms.

An hour later I had my reply ready. I thought it would do the trick for I had pandered to all his vanities. In the letter I had claimed I was terrified of him. He would like that, bully that he was. I had said I could not possibly see him for several days at least, for I was much committed to the Dowager Duchess of Lansmere, and subject to her demands. He would like that as well. A *duchess*, no less. I begged him to be patient, claiming I did so on bended knee. He would like that, too, picturing me there at his feet, a humble supplicant. At the end I promised I would write again as soon as I could to arrange a meeting.

I folded the letter, sealed it, and rang for Franklin. Only when she had taken the letter away so a groom could deliver it to the inn at Peasedale was I able to relax my tight muscles, take a deep breath, and try to return to what consisted of normal for me now.

Still, I felt relief, sure I had protected Faith Abbott as well as myself. At least for a while.

And not once while making my plans or writing that letter had I even vaguely considered telling Gareth Powell — or anyone else — of the situation. I couldn't. It was as simple and damning as that.

Chapter 8

Mr. Powell did not press me again. True, in the next few days I often caught him observing me, but he said nothing more. I suspected this reprieve could not last; still, I was grateful for it.

Unfortunately he did not go to his new property as he had planned, and so on the day of Alicia Grey's fete, he climbed into the dowager's carriage with us, a look of determination on his face. I knew he would be an exemplary escort, but I sensed Bradford Grey had been right. Fetes were not high on Mr. Powell's list of pleasurable entertainments.

"I declare that hat is ravishing, Lucy," Faith Abbott said after we were settled and on our way. "Doesn't she look perfection herself in it, Gareth?"

"Lady Blake is always perfection, ma'am," he replied, adding after only a heartbeat's hesitation, "in her appearance."

I turned to the dowager and smiled my thanks, determined to ignore him. I was wearing a white muslin gown, deceptively simple but cunningly made. It had only a plain sky-blue sash that tied under my breasts. Franklin had assured me the white straw hat with its blue ribbons and forget-

110

me-nots and cloud of tulle was all the added decoration I needed. I remembered it was the hat I had bought in London the day I first saw Jaspar Hayes. This was the first time I had worn it.

I had not heard from Hayes since I had replied to his letter asking for more time. I was relieved, but in spite of hours spent pondering my dilemma, I was no closer to a solution than before. I had come to see the very idea of coldly planning a murder was inconceivable. I did not think I could kill him in cold blood. It would have to be in self-defense.

Beside me, Faith Abbott chatted away, all unconscious of my dark thoughts. I forced them from my mind when she asked me a question, and from then on made myself appear as gay and frivolous as any other young woman on her way to a garden party. The look in Gareth Powell's eyes told me he, at least, was not fooled. I even caught him looking at my reticule. Fortunately, I was not carrying my pistol today. In company, and at a private well-attended party I did not see the need.

It was true the Grey's gardens were nowhere near as lush and well groomed as the Dowager Duchess of Lansmere's were. Still, they were pleasant, and I admired Alicia's comfortable home. It had been built years before by an eccentric great-uncle, one who had devoted his life to fox hunting. His wife had devoted hers to chasing every new whim that came along. Thus what had begun as a simple country manor became the recipient of two new wings, a conservatory, French doors that opened directly on the gardens, a Moorish tower topped with a gilded onion dome, and deep in the woods, a deer park and a hermit's grotto. When Alicia had described the place to me earlier, she had wondered if Mr. Thaddeus Grey had ever repaired to the grotto to escape his acquisitive wife. Rumor had it, he had refused to pay a hermit to inhabit it. Childless, he had left the manor and all his wealth to Jack Grey.

When we arrived and greeted our host and hostess, I saw the manor was a delight, and not at all the weird collection of styles I had been led to expect. Of course it was a glorious summer day. Perhaps on a cold, sleety November afternoon I would feel differently.

We had not been there for more than a few minutes before Viscount Epstead sought me out. I could tell he was not pleased to see Mr. Powell, although he pretended to be gracious. To my surprise, he did not immediately try and detach me from the gentleman's arm. Instead, he took the dowager to see one of her old friends who had recently returned from a visit to Kent. Mr. Powell and I were left to investigate the grounds together.

"Her Grace will have a fine time here," Powell remarked as we stood by a graceful fountain and watched a marble cherub in the center pour an endless stream of water into the pool from an urn. He had such a mischievous expression, I

112

could not help but smile.

"You mean because it is not as perfect as her own?" I asked. "But not everyone loves gardening as Her Grace does."

"I know. But that won't stop her from offering all kinds of advice, and bullying Mrs. Grey into trying just a little border there, or a simple herb knot here, and perhaps a new set of waterways for variety. I suspect Mrs. Grey is more than a match for her though. She seems a woman of excellent judgment as well as diplomacy."

Feeling he was getting into dangerous territory — I hardly wanted him comparing my judgment to Alicia's — I asked him if we might explore as far as the hermit's grotto.

"I've never seen one," I said as we set off. "From what I have heard of them, they must be most uncomfortable."

"I quite agree. I've never wanted to live in a cave. Now, let me see. We've arrived at a choice of paths. Which, do you suppose, leads to the grotto?"

"This way seems wilder," I said looking ahead. "Surely you wouldn't set a hermit down among the rose beds."

We walked along for some minutes, greeting others who were on similar expeditions of exploration. At length we found ourselves alone, with no grotto anywhere in sight.

"How stupid of me," Gareth Powell said. "I should have inquired the way before we began."

"No matter," I told him. I could tell he was

vexed because now he did not appear omnipotent. It made me want to chuckle.

"Perhaps we should give up the search," he went on. "Everyone must be wondering where we are."

"I am certainly safe with you, sir," I said, my face carefully expressionless.

He looked at me sharply, then his mouth twisted. "Do you consider me so insipid, m'lady? So unlikely to treat you to wild passion now I have you alone? You must beware hasty conclusions. I am as hot-blooded as the next man."

"I'm sure you are," I agreed. "But since you took a dislike to me from the first, I hardly think I will have to fend you off now."

"Ah, but I did not take a dislike to you. Merely to your stubbornness and your misguided assumption that you know best."

"Because I refuse to be guided by a man, sir? Because, yes, I do feel I know what is best where I am concerned? Tell me, how would *you* like it if I suddenly began to advise you on your dress and your manners, your finances or your friends?"

"I should think it damned impertinent of you," he replied, stopping and turning to face me. "But I am not trying to advise you about any of those things, nor would I ever dare. How could I find fault with that glorious hat, for example, or your lovely manners? But about your ability to see beyond that pretty nose, why, yes, certainly I strive to correct you."

"I wish you would not."

"I am aware of your aversion to any interference; your single-minded decision to plunge into God knows what disaster. Yet still I find I must try and help you. I can't seem to stop myself, and believe me, I've tried."

I stared at him. He sounded so sincere, so deeply concerned for me, I could not help but be touched.

"Mr. Powell," I said, taking the hand he held out to me, "you are very kind, and I do appreciate your regard. I know I haven't always been gracious. I'm sorry. Tell me, do you think we could begin again? Try to be friends?"

"Friends?" he drawled, bending a little so he could search my face. "Only friends?"

"Only friends," I said as confidently as I could.

He put his other hand over mine. "I would give a good deal to know what there was specifically about the late Lord Blake that gave you such a disgust of men, and lovers," he said. I knew his language and his manner of speaking was unconventional but I did not pretend disgust or insist he apologize. I could not do that. We had gone too far in just a few minutes for such trivial matters as social niceties.

There was a discreet cough and we turned to see a servant bowing to us. "Begging your pardon, m'lady, sir," he said. "Mrs. Grey asks everyone to return to the manor now."

Obediently, we retraced our steps. In the distance, I could hear a string quartet playing, the laughter of the other guests, even the sound of the wind in the branches over our heads. The tall yew hedge beside us sheltered us from that wind. It was very warm and we did not hurry.

As we went up a flight of marble steps to the main gardens again, we found Viscount Epstead waiting for us. He looked very angry, and I felt a tremor of alarm. I hoped he was not going to do or say anything to ruin Alicia's party, but I misjudged him. He had perfect control of himself as he told Gareth Powell the dowager had been asking for him and that he himself would see to my care.

Powell bowed, his eyes conveying a secret message to me before he left us. Still, I felt uneasy as I took Bradford Grey's arm.

"Where have you been?" he demanded, speaking quickly and in an undertone. "You've been gone for quite some time. It has been remarked, and not only by me."

"We were trying to locate the grotto," I told him calmly. "Now stop this at once. I am not yours to command and I don't have to account to you."

He paused for a moment, engaged, I could tell, in a silent struggle. At last he said, "That is true, at least for now. But the future Countess of Epstead must be above reproach. I'd have no gossip attending you."

"I have told you and told you —"

"And I have not listened, nor shall I ever listen, so you might as well save your breath, my beautiful, desirable, darling Lucy. By the way, that hat

116

on you is enough to make every man here fall to his knees. Even Jack admired it."

Thankful for the change of subject and aware here and now was not the place to try and bring him to his senses where marriage was concerned, I said, "Yes, it was one of my best choices. Strange, that. I was abstracted when I chose it."

We had arrived at a large striped canopy that stretched from the house across the lawn. The other guests were taking their seats at tables set out there. At one end the string quartet continued to play sprightly country airs, while at the other, servants stood at a sumptuous buffet, ready to serve the guests.

The viscount installed me at a table already occupied by two other couples, and went to fetch our repast. I chatted lightly with the couples, agreed on the weather (beautiful) and the gardens (delightful), as well as the party (such a treat).

Later, replete with a variety of delicious entrées, compotes, aspics, salads, and some tempting cakes and confections, we rose to return to the gardens where we were to be treated to a puppet show written expressly for grown-ups.

I was surprised when the servant holding my chair gave me a note folded small. I slipped it inside my reticule and excusing myself from the viscount, I went into the house and found an empty room before I read it. My heart was pounding now, my breath came short. I did not need to see the handwriting to know it was from Jaspar Hayes. How had he managed it? I wondered, wishing I had not left my pistol at home. How had he gained admittance? Bribed the servants? How had he even found out I was going to be here?

"Come to the grotto at once," it read. "If you do not, I'll make a scene that will put paid to any chance you might have to be accepted by society ever again."

I asked a maid how to find the grotto and let myself out a side door. I knew Bradford Grey was waiting for me. He would be angry again, but I dared not risk Hayes appearing before this crowd and denouncing me. Eugenia Abbott was here as well as the duke, and several other of the haute ton to say nothing of Alicia Grey and Faith Abbott. Especially I could not face the revulsion that would be sure to come to their faces, their horrified gasps of disgust. No, I must see Hayes, and alone, too. I felt distinctly ill. I prayed I would not be sick.

Hayes grabbed me as I rounded the end of a hedge. I would have screamed in shock except he covered my mouth with his other hand so quickly, I did not have the chance. Still gagging me, he hustled me along a narrow side path to a small glade deep in the woods. No sun entered here. The leaves were thick overhead.

Hayes glared down at me. "Don't cry out! If you try, I'll throttle you, do you hear?"

His grip tightened cruelly and I nodded.

Slowly, he removed his hand, and when he saw I was not going to make any noise, stepped back and put his hands on his hips.

"Well, my fine lady, now I've got you at last," he said, his voice rich with satisfaction.

"What do you think you're doing?" I made myself say, thinking to take the initiative and the advantage from him. I knew cowering would only encourage him, so I must pretend a courage I had never had. "This is insane!" I continued. "I shall be missed, why, I daresay I've been missed already and there'll be a hue and cry before you know it. I told you I would write when a time to meet could be arranged. Why didn't you wait for my letter?"

He scowled at me and for a moment he looked perplexed. I had often thought in the past that Jaspar Hayes was not very intelligent. Sometimes it seemed to take him forever to grasp a simple point, and he was especially confused when bombarded by several different thoughts at once.

His face cleared then and he pointed his finger at me. "Wait? Not bloody likely, my fine lady! Not with them — *those* two gentlemen as hot on your trail as two dogs after a bitch in heat! I could see the way the wind was blowin', I could. You're not for them. You're mine, you are. You've always been mine, right from the start. And now yer goin' ter be mine again, d'y'hear me?"

I remembered Hayes, when excited, forgot the

119

careful diction he had acquired in his fruitless quest to be a gentleman. It was obvious he was beginning to forget it now. His voice had risen as well, something he generally managed to control.

"I hear you," I said coldly. "I daresay anyone within earshot can hear you."

Suddenly he came to me and I could not help flinching. That was a mistake, for he saw it and he growled in satisfaction.

"Are ye *afraid* o' me, yer ladyship?" he asked sarcastically. "Aye, well, an' ye should be, ye haughty wench. Ye think yer too good fer me, don't ye? Ye've always thought that. I could tell. Right from the beginnin' ye treated me like dirt under yer feet.

"Well, I'm as good as ye are — good as any fine lord. An' soon, ye'll see who's dirt!"

He grabbed me and shook me, his hands gripping my shoulders so hard, I knew I would have bruises there. Desperately I tried to think how I could escape him. He sounded almost mad.

"I'll teach ye, I will. When we get back to Trecarag ye'll feel my whip," he panted, then he let me go and pushed me away. I staggered back, but I managed to keep my balance. Breathing hard, I faced him, frightened of what would come next and trying hard not to show it. I could not keep my hands from trembling so I clasped them before my breast and prayed he would not notice.

Suddenly he rushed toward me and fell to his

120

knees. Grasping my legs, he buried his face in my muslin skirts. How strange we humans are! For a moment, in danger of heaven knows what atrocities, all I could think of was how crushed my gown was going to be, and how I was ever going to be able to rejoin the company looking so disheveled. Was anything more absurd?

Hayes began to cry then, deep wrenching sobs that rendered me even more untidy.

"Ah, lass, I didn't mean a word o' it. Ye know I didn't! I love ye — I love ye! It wasn't all the old man's doin', ye know. Fergive me, oh, please fergive me!"

"Lady Blake, where are you?" a familiar voice called. It came from a distance, but I knew rescue was almost at hand and it gave me courage. Hayes raised his head and stared up at me, his mouth loose. Ordinarily, he was not a bad-looking man. I mean, he wasn't ugly. But he was ugly then with his face distorted and running with tears, and his mouth agape like an idiot's.

Once more in command of myself, I said, "Let me go and get up at once. If you are found here, it won't matter if you denounce me, for who will believe you? You must run, run to safety!"

He got to his feet, clumsy in his haste. For a moment he hesitated, and I said urgently, "Go! If they find you, you'll be finished."

I was not sure even then I had convinced him, for comprehension was beginning to return to his face. Fortunately the voice came again, much closer this time, and another voice called as well, from a different direction. Hayes's eyes rolled up in his head for a moment. It was a horrible thing to see, for it made him seem more like a cornered animal than a man. Then he turned and without another word, raced off through the underbrush.

I waited until I could no longer hear him before I called. I had recognized the voices. One was Viscount Epstead's melodious baritone, the other, Gareth Powell's deep bass. I could hear them coming closer now, and I straightened my hat. I could do nothing about my damp, crushed skirt although I did try to shake it free of wrinkles. Looking down at it, I grimaced, wondering how I was to explain such disorder.

The two men arrived in the glade almost simultaneously. Their identically shocked expressions were ludicrous, but I was not tempted to smile.

"What happened to you?" Bradford Grey demanded as he reached me first and held out his hands to me. I took them gratefully and they tightened in support. Behind him, the taller Gareth Powell studied my face intently, but he did not speak.

"Oh, it was just dreadful," I said weakly. "I decided to go for a walk. To try and find that grotto, Mr. Powell. You remember. But I got lost. And then I heard an animal somewhere near in the wood and I ran away from it. Oh, I was so frightened."

I managed to shiver convincingly, and the viscount put his arm around me. "But why did you go off alone like that, Lucy?" he asked. "You knew I was waiting for you. I would have taken you to see the grotto. Who knows its location better than I, the brother of the owner?"

I thought frantically. "Yes, that's — that's true, but I wanted to find it for myself. It was foolish of me. I'm — I'm so sorry."

The tears that filled my eyes then were not at all a part of my playacting. I felt weak and spent, and all I wanted to do was escape these men as I had escaped Hayes, go home and climb into bed with the curtains closed and the door locked. And I wanted to sleep, sleep for days.

"That animal was probably a deer, more frightened of you than you were of it," Bradford Grey said soothingly. "Come now, don't cry, my dear. It's over now. You're safe."

I buried my face in his coat, as much to hide it as for support.

"I suggest we take Lady Blake back to the manor some way that will not call attention to her condition," Gareth Powell said, speaking for the first time. The viscount agreed. I could feel his heart beating strongly beneath my head. The smell of his clean linen and the soap he used was calming, it was so normal.

Slowly we began to return. I prayed we wouldn't meet anyone, but Bradford Grey saw to that, for he led us over the deserted paths the gardeners used that only an intimate of the estate would know.

When we were near the manor, Powell spoke again. "I'll go ahead and inform the duchess of what has happened; call for the carriage. I think it would be best to take her directly to the stable yard. There'll be fewer people to remark her appearance that way."

Although I was grateful to him for his quick thinking, I could not help but wonder why he had not said anything to me, asked me a direct question as the viscount had done. His silence seemed ominous somehow, and I shivered again. I did not see how I was to pretend nothing was wrong after this. It was obvious Gareth Powell had not believed my story about the wild animal. I even doubted I had convinced Bradford Grey of it.

Everything went smoothly. I do not think anyone saw me but a groom or two. I was handed gently into the carriage by the viscount. He promised to call on the morrow to see how I did. The dowager arrived, big with questions she did not voice. Instead, she produced a light throw which she wrapped around me. "For the shock, my dear," she said as she took her seat beside me and held my hand. Mr. Powell came at last, holding a small glass of brandy for me. I took it thankfully, for I needed its warmth and the false courage it gave me.

I closed my eyes then and leaned back against the squabs as we set off for home. I could hear my companions conversing softly, but I did not try to listen.

What was I to do? I wondered, and I was not thinking of my current predicament. I would have to hold to my story. Even if no one believed it, it could not be disproved. No, what was bedeviling me was what I was to do about Jaspar Hayes. His distorted face, wild with rage then wet with tears and agonized self-reproach filled my mind. I could not seem to banish it no matter how I tried. I knew now he could not be sane, therefore he was dangerous. Much more dangerous than I had imagined.

Back at the dower house, Gareth Powell would not let me walk upstairs to my room. Instead, he swept me up in his arms and carried me there, the dowager hurrying along behind. He put me down on my bed, his gaze keen as he inspected me. I confess I closed my eyes to avoid that gaze.

They left when Franklin arrived to undress me and put me to bed, and very soon I was huddled under a warm comforter with a hot brick at my cold feet. Tomorrow, I thought drowsily just before oblivion came. Tomorrow will be time enough to decide what to do about Hayes — about everything.

Chapter 9

I did not leave my room the following day; indeed, I barely left my bed. I had behaved this way many times in the past, but never had I had such a good reason for it. By now I knew it was an act of denial. If I did not get up — dress — join the others, I did not have to talk about my trouble or face it. If that made me the worst kind of coward I didn't care, I told myself as I cowered under the covers and my concerned maid brought me trays I barely touched.

I was reminded I must speak to Franklin soon. She was a sturdy, middle-aged woman who had been with me ever since I was widowed. She knew better than anyone that there was something wrong, although she had no idea what it was. Still, even as I dreaded it, I knew I must tell her something.

I had also come to realize I must tell the dowager and Mr. Powell something besides that tale of running away from a wild animal. It was just too lame to be creditable. Probably I must tell the Greys as well. Hopefully my confession could stop there. I did not want Eugenia Abbott to hear anything about it.

But what could I say? I agonized over this for

hours that day and at last I formulated a plan. It was not a very good one. There were all kinds of holes in it, but perhaps if I were convincing enough, it would pass muster. I would have to give a superior performance, pretending an openness that would be entirely false. By nightfall I was pacing my room, practicing that performance.

At last I threw myself down on the chaise. How terrible this was, I thought weakly as tears came to my eyes. How devious and despicable. But it was the only thing I could do to avoid complete disclosure.

The next morning even before I had breakfast in bed, I sent a note to Hayes at the inn as I had done before, telling him he must fly immediately. I told him someone had seen him at the fete and Viscount Epstead was insisting he be prosecuted for trespassing. To insure his cooperation, I asked him to let me know where he would be so I could get in touch with him when it was safe. Then I prayed he would do as he was told, for if he was found in Peasedale, I was ruined indeed.

After I was dressed, I sent Franklin to ask the dowager and Mr. Powell if I might have a few minutes of their time that morning. I paced my room again until she returned to say they were both waiting for me in the small drawing room.

I would have gone to them without a word except Franklin stopped me, pretending to adjust a ruffle on the bodice of my gown. She smiled at me then, a smile of encouragement and comfort.

It did comfort me, too, and when I went downstairs I was ready.

The small drawing room was situated on one side of the dower house, overlooking a sweep of lawn with woods beyond. It was a lovely room, done in peach and soft gray. Above the mantel, pastel drawings of some of the vistas around Lansmere lent a homey touch, and the sofas were heaped with silk cushions. It was a feminine room. Gareth Powell, so tall and masculine, seemed out of place there.

"I hope you are feeling better, Lucy," Faith Abbott said as I kissed her.

"Much better, thank you," I said as I took a chair nearby. Gareth Powell remained standing by the mantel. He did not speak.

"That is, I'm sure I'll feel better once I have told you what is on my mind," I continued. "You must forgive me for not saying anything about it before. I thought I could take care of it myself. Yesterday I saw that I had been mistaken, naive, even, not that Mr. Powell has not said the same many times."

"You have been badgering Lucy?" the dowager demanded of her godson. She sounded quite fierce.

"No, no, dear ma'am, not badgering me precisely," I hastened to say. "Merely pointing out I have been much at fault. And I have been. I know that now."

I drew a deep breath and stared down at the hands I had clasped in my lap. "It all began when

128

I was first married to Lord Blake," I said. Then I had to clear my throat. "We spent the first winter after our wedding in Portman Square," I went on. "I did not see Trecarag — his estate in Cornwall, you remember — until spring.

"Cornwall is a lovely place. I liked it from the beginning. But not long after our arrival, I began to feel very uneasy. There was a man in residence at Trecarag, a young man the viscount had befriended as a child, seeing to his education and his upbringing, for he was an orphan. I did not like this protégé of Lord Blake's and I told him so. But he had a fondness for the man and he ridiculed my concern."

I glanced around at both of them as I spoke, trying to gauge how my remarks were being received. Faith Abbott looked completely absorbed in the story, a little frown of empathy on her brow. Gareth Powell showed no emotion at all. I wondered what he was thinking.

"There was no way I could convince m'lord that this man should not live at Trecarag with us," I went on. "Believe me, I tried. As summer came, things became even more difficult. You see, the man began to think himself in love with me. It was most unpleasant, for I did not feel I could tell the viscount of his pet's infatuation, the trysts he proposed, the kisses he tried to steal. Lord Blake had been taken ill by then, and every day he grew weaker. I could not worry him at such a time."

I coughed a little and the dowager asked

Powell to pour me a glass of wine. While his back was turned as he did so, I hurried on. "You know of Lord Blake's death. Surprisingly, he had not left any provision for the man in his will. I was sure that had to have been an oversight, and I myself made arrangements to settle a generous sum of money on him."

Powell approached and held out the glass. I did not look up at him as I thanked him and took a sip.

"Did this man — good heavens, he must have a name! What is it, Lucy?"

"He is called Jaspar Hayes," I said, my voice shaking.

"Well then, I take it this Hayes was not properly grateful?" she asked.

I nodded. "He was distraught when he found he had been left out of the estate, and he accused me of forcing Lord Blake to have his will rewritten so he would get nothing. It was then I told him he was not welcome at Trecarag, that he must leave and never return. He — he threatened me. I had to threaten him in return with my pistol for I'm sure he would have harmed me if I had not."

"My gracious," Faith Abbott said. "You should have had the law on him! He had no claim."

"I didn't call in the law. I didn't think it necessary for he did go away and I didn't see him again until just before we left London.

"Do you remember the man you saw hanging

about Portman Square, ma'am? You mentioned him to me one day and wondered who he was."

"Yes, of course I remember. I was sure I knew him from somewhere, but I can't recall why, now."

"He was following me around town, everywhere I went. He even managed to get himself hired on at Severn's soiree as a servant. That was why I looked so white when you came over to me that evening, sir," I added, turning briefly to Powell where he stood again near the cold hearth. "I was so shocked he was there, of all places, you see.

"When we left town I hoped that would be the end of him. He was the main reason I told my agent to sell the London house. But as I am sure you have guessed, he followed me to Oxfordshire. He has been here in the gardens. Fleming noticed and took to locking the gates, not that either of us thought that would keep him out.

"I saw him yesterday at the fete. He confronted me when I was trying to find the grotto, and he begged me to be kind to him, marry him even, let him live at Trecarag. I do not think he is quite sane, at least where I am concerned."

I looked from one to the other of my intent audience. "I've been carrying a pistol here because I am afraid. Yet I don't see what I can do legally to stop the man. Yes, he has trespassed here, but no one has actually seen him. If you think of it, he has done nothing more than that. He hasn't committed a crime."

"Well, there must be something we can do!" the dowager exclaimed. "Gareth, dear boy, what do you think?"

"I think we have been treated to quite a fairy tale, ma'am," he said, pushing his shoulders away from the mantel and walking to the middle of the room. He did not look at me as he continued, "Some of it may even be true."

"Gareth!" Faith Abbott said. She sounded deeply shocked but she could not have been as shocked as I was.

"How can you say such a thing? Here is Lucy in the direst trouble and you accuse her of telling lies? I never would have thought you could be so insensitive!"

Powell turned to look at me. I couldn't seem to draw a breath deep enough, and my head was spinning. Just before I fainted, I heard the dowager call her godson the worst kind of blackguard and I quite agreed with her.

I have no idea how I got back to my bed. I assume Powell carried me there. When I regained consciousness, I was lying on top of the coverlet, Franklin holding a vinaigrette under my nose. I coughed and twisted away from its sharp bite.

"There now, m'lady," the maid said calmly. "I'll soon have you comfortable and all tucked up again."

I closed my eyes to hide sudden tears. I had done the best I could, but Gareth Powell had not believed me. Even in my distress I wondered

132

which part of my story had convinced him I was not telling the truth. I had deviated but little from that truth and still he had been able to catch me out. I wished he had never come to the dower house. I wished he were anywhere but here.

Viscount Epstead had called as promised the day before and this morning he had come again. Faith Abbott told me about it when she came to see how I did.

"He was most upset when he discovered you were still in bed, Lucy," she told me, her wrinkled old face full of concern. "I did not think you would mind if I told him of this Jaspar Hayes. I especially charged him to say nothing of him except to Alicia and his brother. He promised."

She looked away for a moment, a spot of color coming to her cheeks. "You may be sure I took Gareth to task most severely. I am still having the greatest difficulty believing I heard him speak as he did. Why, I was sure he was more than half in love with you."

I managed a weak laugh. "Hardly, dear ma'am," I said. "He doesn't even like me. He hasn't from first meeting."

"Then why can't he keep his eyes from you? And why has his new estate been relegated to a distant second on his list of priorities? He does not go there because he cannot bear to leave you."

I knew she was wrong but I did not feel up to contradicting her. After a moment, she went on,

133

"He has gone out riding. He told me he would keep an open mind, so he intends to visit every village in the immediate neighborhood, to see if Hayes has been staying nearby. I am sure he will discover he has.

"Now, if you feel up to it, please come down and have nuncheon with me on the terrace. You will not have to see Gareth."

She paused for a moment, then she added, "If you want me to send him away I shall do so, dear. I cannot have you upset — called a liar — even by my dear godson. Just tell me and he'll be on his way."

Her voice was soft now, sad, and I took her hand to hold it tight. "No, no, don't do that, dear ma'am. He is entitled to his own opinion, and truly, he does not bother me. Besides, I am sure we will both feel better with Jaspar Hayes roaming about heaven knows where, if Mr. Powell is in residence."

Her face brightened. "I never thought of that. Of course! I don't think I'll mention that to him, however. He is apt to be touchy where his dignity is concerned. His mother was one of my dearest friends. She died a few years ago. They were very close for his father was killed in the American revolution before he was even born. I know how he mourned his mother although he never showed it. I have never known a man so contained, so complete within himself. A rare talent, that, but not always the easiest thing for friends and loved ones to deal with.

"I will let you rest now, dear. Do try to come down at noon. It is a lovely day and the garden is flourishing."

She glanced wistfully toward the window and I squeezed her hand before I let it go and said, "Run along, as you have been longing to do. I'll not fail you, I promise."

I closed my eyes when she left. I could hear Franklin in the dressing room and I composed myself before I called for her. In essence, I told her much the same tale as I had told the others. She, like the dowager, believed me immediately.

"Yes, I understand now. I suspected there was a man. Those rose petals . . ."

"I thought I collected them all!"

"There were several caught in the covers on the bed, ma'am. I didn't mention them for I could tell you were upset."

I was relieved she took the whole thing so phlegmatically, although I had not really expected anything else. Franklin's competence and even temper, her steady head in any kind of crisis were only a few of the reasons I had kept her for my maid.

The afternoon passed pleasantly. I had a light meal on the terrace with the dowager. Nothing further was said about Jaspar Hayes, nor were there any more questions. How I loved this woman.

After our meal, she returned to her garden. Mr. Fleming had capitulated at last about the new rose beds, as everyone had been sure he would, and the dowager was there to supervise the men as they began to prepare for the expansion. I sat in the pergola with a book, a sketch pad, and my thoughts. It was amazing how calm I felt, how serene. I had not told all the truth about Hayes by any means, yet still I felt as if an enormous weight had been lifted away from me. The sun shone on me warmly, the story I was reading was both witty and wise, and the sketch I made of the dowager and Fleming leaped to life on the page. All my fears and apprehensions were gone. I knew this would only be a momentary release, but still I welcomed it.

Gareth Powell did not return from his foray around the countryside until quite late, and he only entered the drawing room where the dowager and I were sitting moments before dinner was announced.

Nothing of importance was discussed until the meal had concluded and the servants had been dismissed.

"Did you find anything, Gareth?" the dowager asked, all her anger at him gone.

"Yes, I did," he said. I tried not to stare but I could not help myself. He was looking at the dowager and from where I sat across from him, I was able to study his profile unobserved. It looked hard and firm, the curve of the mouth compressed. The one brow I could see was contracted, and there was a shadow under the eye. And even though he was correctly attired, he wore his clothes, this evening at least, carelessly.

"I found him," he said, and I forgot my musings to clench my napkin under cover of the table. Had Hayes ignored my warning? Or had he left his departure too late? If Powell had apprehended him, my life, as I had lived it up to now, was over.

"That is to say, I found where he *had* been staying at the inn at Peasedale," Powell continued, and I relaxed. "He's gone now, of course. He left early this morning, and no, no one seems to have any idea where he went."

Faith Abbott sent me a triumphant glance before she said, "Then he could still be somewhere about, couldn't he? Perhaps not at an inn, however. He might very well have made some acquaintances here who would put him up."

She turned to me then. "You never told us, Lucy. Does Hayes appear the gentleman?"

I could feel Gareth Powell's considering look on my face as I said, "Yes, I suppose you might think so. He can act the gentleman at any rate, till he forgets himself. And he has money to pay his way."

Faith Abbott frowned. "Do you think I should ask the duke for some men to guard the dower house, Gareth?" she asked. "I am sure Forrestal can provide them, and Lucy would feel safer."

"Oh, please, ma'am, don't do that!" I exclaimed before he could reply. "It would mean having to explain why we wanted them, and before you know it, my predicament would be all

137

around the county and in a few weeks, the country as well."

"Yes, but Lucy, dear girl, do consider —"

"I agree with Lady Blake, Your Grace," Powell interrupted. "I suspect Hayes may be a bit more circumspect now. If Lady Blake is careful never to go anywhere unattended, I am sure she will be quite safe."

The dowager still frowned, but eventually she agreed. I couldn't help but suspect she had been looking forward to setting up an armed camp here, complete with guards making their rounds. She was so intrepid I wouldn't have been surprised to discover she had taken to carrying a pistol herself.

We removed to the drawing room and I went to the piano, leaving Mr. Powell and the dowager to conversation and their books until the tea tray should be brought in.

The next morning, Viscount Epstead called again while we were still at breakfast. Wells brought his card to me and after scanning it, I handed it to the dowager with a questioning look.

She chuckled. "Ask the viscount to step in here, Wells," she said. "To be sure it is early for calls, even morning calls, but on the other hand, if he does not see for himself how you are, Lucy, there's no saying what the man will do."

I ignored Mr. Powell's snort.

Bradford Grey barely acknowledged the others as he entered and bowed. "I am delighted

138

to see you here, m'lady," he said as he pulled out the chair next to mine and sat down in it to capture both my hands. Faith Abbott raised her brows but said nothing.

"No, no coffee, nothing," Epstead said impatiently to the hovering footman. "You are feeling well now? Quite recovered?"

"Yes, thank you," I said, turning slightly so I would not have to see Gareth Powell's sardonic expression.

"What a relief to hear you say so! Alicia is so unhappy such a thing should have occurred at her fete. She has sent you a letter." Reaching inside his coat, he produced it and raced on, "At my request, Jack has set men to searching the countryside to try and locate this Hayes. When he is found, I'll take care of him, never fear."

I wished with all my heart he had not done that, and even as I thanked him I was silently praying that the cunning Hayes had in such abundance would stand him in good stead now. If he were found and questioned, everything I had done would be for nothing.

"Viscount Epstead," Faith Abbott said, her voice cool. As he turned reluctantly toward her, she added, "Yes. Good morning, sir. Please release Lucy now so she may finish her breakfast. And while she does so, you will have time to remember your manners, perhaps even exchange a few words with Gareth and me. Our presence seems to have escaped your notice."

The viscount dropped my hands and gave a

peal of laughter. "*Mea culpa,* Your Grace," he said. "Please forgive me. I know you will, for you are aware of my deep feelings for Lady Blake; my plans to share her future. Er, you said something, sir?"

He looked inquiringly to Mr. Powell, who after making a noise suspiciously like a growl of derision, had raised his napkin to wipe his lips.

"Nothing of import, sir," Powell said as he rose and dropped that napkin on the table. "Beg you excuse me, Your Grace, m'lady. Perhaps a morning ride will calm my stomach. I suddenly feel more than a little queasy."

Chapter 10

He left the room before the viscount could speak. The dowager lingered only a few minutes longer and Bradford Grey and I were left alone, which plainly suited him very well.

"Are you well enough to come for a drive, Lucy?" he asked, possessing my hands once again. "It is a glorious day."

"I'm afraid that won't be possible, sir," I said, freeing my hands. "I have several letters that must be written today, one most important one to my man of business."

"Ah, yes. Who do you employ? Is he satisfactory?"

"A Mr. Arthur Kittering, of Queen Street in London. He was in Lord Blake's employ. I have found him an excellent agent."

"I won't give up, you know," Epstead said as I rose and he was forced to do so as well. "Shall we drive tomorrow? Morning or afternoon? Or perhaps the following day? I warn you, I'll not leave until you set a date and time."

I agreed to an afternoon excursion the following day as we walked to the foyer. The viscount insisted on kissing my hand in such a lingering, ardent way, I was sure Wells and the

141

footman must be shocked.

In the library, I sat down to read Alicia's letter. I almost cried it was so dear, full of her concern and, more important, her encouragement. And although I looked carefully, there was not the slightest sign of revulsion for my getting embroiled with such an unsavory character. She told me she would always be my friend and if I needed her help, I had only to ask. I went to the desk then and there to answer her and thank her as best I could.

I spent another quiet day. I had no idea where Gareth Powell was. I didn't see him all day. That was a relief for I found it awkward talking to him now, knowing he considered me a liar.

Wasn't that strange? Of course I wasn't *precisely* a liar, since my sin was the sin of omission. Still, I could not really consider myself *honest*. Why then did I resent his assessment of me?

I worked in the garden side by side with Faith Abbott, overseen by a taciturn Fleming who came by every now and again to make sure we weren't uprooting some of his prize specimens. Later in the afternoon it turned positively sultry and we retreated to the shade of the gazebo with our needlework and one of those improbable romances from the Minerva Press.

There was a thunderstorm at dusk that unfortunately stayed far to our west. The gardens could have used the rain.

Gareth Powell seemed preoccupied at dinner. The dowager had to ask him several questions twice, and at last, with a shrug, she gave up and addressed her remarks to me alone. I wondered where Powell had been all day, but I knew I'd never find out. He was as contained and private a person as the dowager had claimed.

He did not join us after dinner either, excusing himself as we rose to leave him to his port. I could see Faith Abbott wanted to ask him why, but she must have seen something in his face that kept her from inquiring.

The two of us went out to sit in the pergola. It was still sultry; the thunderstorm had brought no relief and we resorted to our fans.

"It is always like this a few days every summer," the dowager said. "I try to pretend I am in India or the West Indies, but I've never managed to convince myself. All I can think of is how hot it is. Whew!"

I waved the fan gently before my face, stirring the humid air but gaining little relief. In the lights that streamed from the house, I could see a man walking in the gardens. I knew he was only there to serve as a guard for us. It embarrassed me suddenly, all the trouble I had put my dear friend to, her servants as well. Perhaps I should go away. Hayes would not know where I had gone if I were careful, and once he discovered my absence, he would leave himself, and peace would return.

"I declare you're as bad as Gareth, Lucy," the dowager said sharply. "Here I've asked you twice if you would care to drive out with me tomorrow to visit my old head groom, and I get no answer. It is too bad."

"I do beg your pardon, ma'am," I said quickly. "Ordinarily I would like that very much, but I am promised to Viscount Epstead tomorrow."

"I do hope you will be on your guard there, Lucy," she said seriously. "I've known Bradford Grey since he was a boy, and yes, he's a chameleon, almost a quicksilver creature. He's had his love affairs, but they never lasted. In fact, I've never seen him so obsessed as he is with you. I warn you, if you don't intend to have him, you had better dismiss him now, while you can."

"And how do you suggest I do that, dear ma'am? You know how he is. He will not take no for an answer. Every time I tell him I have no intention of marrying again, him or anyone, he simply ignores me."

"Oh, Lucy, Lucy," she said, reaching out to cover my hand with hers. "*Never*, my dear?"

"Never," I said firmly, staring straight ahead. The sounds of the night insects were a steady drone and down by the yew hedge fireflies hovered, blinking their little signals. Somewhere a chorus of frogs croaked out of tune and out of tempo. Still, I heard Faith Abbott's little sigh of regret clearly.

I mentioned my plan to leave the dower house then, but she would not hear of it. "I think that would be the worst thing you could do, dear," she said firmly. "Yes, of course you could escape the man for a while, but eventually he'd find you again. You are of society, and society's doings and whereabouts are well publicized. And I can't see you changing your name and moving to some horrid backwater to avoid him. No, better stay here — face him out. I'm sure Gareth will be invaluable to you. He likes tidy solutions. He'll see you have one, just you wait and see."

Not much later, the two of us went up to our rooms. It was then I discovered Mr. Powell had arranged for me to sleep in another room that night. Franklin said he had seen to it earlier, and so, after I was dressed for bed, she led me down the corridor almost to the stairs to a room on the front of the house. A room, I saw, that had no balcony. I must admit I fell asleep more easily than I had in weeks.

It was very late when I heard a faint commotion somewhere at the back of the house. Sitting up in bed, I clutched the thin sheet that covered me and strained to hear. Footsteps pounded up the stairs and down the corridor outside the room and I made myself get out of bed, throw on my robe, and lighting a candle, go and open the door cautiously. I saw the dowager's elderly footman near my former room. He held a branch of candles high in one hand. In the other, he brandished a poker. I gasped as Gareth Powell came out of my room. Even from this distance I could see his face was grim. There was a rustling behind me and the dowager, still pulling on her robe, ran by. She was waving an old dueling pistol, and concerned for the men ahead, I hurried after her, calling to her as I went.

Mr. Powell, who was still dressed except for his coat, came and calmly took the pistol from the dowager's hand.

"Here now, Gareth," she said hotly, "give that back! I can shoot as well as anyone else, I guess. All you do is aim and fire the thing."

"Not this pistol you won't," he told her. "It's so rusty it would have blown up in your face."

We could hear men calling then. They sounded as if they were in the garden.

Hayes, I thought, my heart sinking. It had to be Hayes.

Powell left us at a run, the footman behind him, laboring to keep up. Faith Abbott hesitated for only a moment, then she grabbed my hand and entered my old bedroom. We gasped in unison. It was obvious Jaspar Hayes had been there. Furious not to find me asleep, he had slashed the feather bed and pillows to shreds. Feathers were drifted everywhere, on the rug, the overturned furniture, the bedding he had tossed aside. Some even clung to the curtains. The air reeked of scent. He must have swept my perfume — everything from the dressing table — to the floor where it lay in a broken heap. Still holding my hand and picking her way through the chaos, the dowager went out on the balcony.

There were a lot of lights down in the garden, most of them clustered around the figure of Fleming's youngest apprentice. He lay on his back while Gareth Powell knelt beside him to ex-

146

amine him. The boy was not moving; I could not help but cry out.

Powell looked up at us then. "Go inside at once!" he ordered. "Are you determined to make yourselves targets?"

Suddenly realizing we could be seen easily not only by someone inside the garden walls, but outside as well, I pulled the dowager back through the disordered room to the hall.

"Let me go, Lucy," she said quite fiercely. I released her at once for never had she sounded so ducal. "That was young Macomber lying there. I must go to him," she said.

I went with her. I doubted I could be of any help, but to tell the truth, I was afraid to be alone. Perhaps Hayes had not left my room by the balcony. Perhaps after disposing of Macomber and destroying my room, he had hid himself somewhere on this floor. There were only three of us in residence; the dowager duchess, Powell, and myself. There were a lot of empty rooms.

We found the men, now joined by the dowager's elderly butler, in the morning room. They had laid Macomber on a sofa there. I felt tremendous relief when I heard him moan.

"How is he, Gareth?" Faith Abbott demanded, pushing her way past Fleming and the other gardeners.

"He's had a bad blow to the head, Your Grace, but outside of rendering him unconscious, I don't think it is serious. Still, he'll have a headache to remember tomorrow."

The dowager insisted on taking his place beside the boy to bathe his head with the cold water the butler brought her. "Tell me what happened, Fleming," she ordered as she began.

"I asked Macomber to walk about in the gardens tonight, Your Grace," he said gruffly. I could tell he was berating himself for putting the boy in danger. "I heard him cry out and I rushed to him, but when I got there he was lying unconscious. I roused the other men then, for I knew it had to be the work of that man who's been getting in here."

"How did you happen to go to Lucy's former room, Gareth?" she asked, wringing out the cloth again and putting it gently on Macomber's forehead. Was it my imagination or was there really a tinge of red on Mr. Powell's cheekbones?

"I suspected Hayes might have made for her room, ma'am," he said. "I hoped to catch him, but it appears he encountered Macomber after he had been in the house. He's long gone now."

The boy moaned again and stirred, and we were all relieved when he opened his eyes and looked around, confused.

Not many minutes later, the morning room was empty except for the dowager duchess, Mr. Powell, and me. The gardeners had taken Macomber to Flemings's quarters near the stable where Mrs. Fleming could care for him. Powell had sent the butler and footman back to bed.

Faith Abbott let him help her up from her knees and into a large comfortable wing chair.

He fetched brandy and three snifters while I put a footstool under her feet. As she settled back and inhaled the heady aroma in the glass her godson poured for her, she sighed. Holding my own glass, I took a seat nearby. Gareth Powell lounged against the mantel as was his custom.

"Well, what do we do now?" Faith Abbott asked. Her voice sounded old and worn. I looked at Powell in some concern.

"We leave here as early as possible tomorrow morning, ma'am," he said promptly.

"Leave?" she echoed.

"Oh, yes, it is more than time we were gone," he replied. "It is not safe here anymore, unless you want to hire an army to defend the place. And I would have no more destruction in your home. Hayes will not come here again, once he learns Lady Blake has left."

"But where can we go?" she asked fretfully, picking at a loose thread on her dressing gown.

"Why, ma'am, can it be you have forgotten my new estate near Chipping Norton?" he asked in a rallying tone. "How you promised to give me your advice about the grounds? There is that topiary garden. It is vastly overgrown, but I rely on you to tell me how it might be tamed again. And the flower beds are a disgrace."

Out of the corner of my eye, I saw Faith Abbott sit up straighter, and I wanted to cheer. Instead, I nodded to Powell although I do not think he saw me for all his attention was on his godmother.

He took a chair near her then. "We must leave early tomorrow morning, very early in fact, if we are to put Hayes off the scent. And no one here — *no one* — must know our destination." Anticipating her indignation, he added, "I know your servants are all trustworthy, ma'am, but it is so easy for a word — a phrase — to slip out, and then we would be undone. You can write to the duke later. His Grace won't worry when he learns you're with me."

"It sounds very exciting," Faith Abbott said. Her voice was livelier now, and when I looked, I saw her eyes were bright. "At dawn, do you think? May I bring my maid?"

"Yes, as close to dawn as we can make it," he agreed. "Of course both your maids may come. Tell them to pack only what is necessary for a few weeks, and remind them we go to a house in disarray. There will be no parties to dress for, no elaborate dinners. In fact," he added gloomily, "I only hope we don't have to eat all our meals off packing cases."

"Better and better," the dowager crowed. "It will be a permanent picnic."

"That reminds me. I must see to a basket of food. There is no way I can inform what staff I have, of our arrival. You will certainly have your picnic dinner tonight, ma'am.

"You are very quiet Lady Blake. Do you agree to my plan?"

He was looking at me intently, but I would not meet his eye. "Of course. You are very kind," I managed to say over the tightness in my throat. "I am so sorry this is necessary, indeed, I —"

"Nonsense!" he said brusquely. "It is not your fault."

We went our separate ways then. I rang for Franklin and she came promptly, already dressed after the commotion we had had. She nodded calmly when I told her the plan and immediately began to sort through my gowns. Fortunately Hayes had not invaded the dressing room, nor gone through the wardrobe. I helped as best I could, and we were able to snatch a few hours sleep before a knock on the door awakened me.

It was still dark, but there was only time to dress and drink a cup of coffee before Mr. Powell hurried us into the dowager's traveling coach. Our maids rode with us, facing back. Powell had elected to ride. The trunks were lashed to the roof and the boot filled with parcels of all kinds. Only one groom came with us. He sat up on the perch with the coachman. A large wicker basket of food shared the carriage with us. It was placed between the maids. I certainly had to admire Mr. Powell's ingenuity and organization. He had seen to everything.

Fortunately the drive to his estate near Chipping Norton only took a few hours, so the dowager was not cast down by it. We stopped once in a bustling market town where there were many carriages coming and going. It was a relief to get down and stretch, use the private parlor Powell arranged for us, eat a belated breakfast.

There was only one awkward moment. We were about to climb into the coach again, and Powell turned to me after helping the dowager. Then his eyes narrowed, and he reached out to remove a feather that had become caught under the white collar of the blue gown of Georgian cloth I was wearing. I wondered no one had noticed it before, for it was one of the feathers from my bed, or perhaps my pillows, that Hayes had slashed.

Powell's face darkened in an alarming way. I would have been frightened except the whole episode quickly became farcical. Have you ever tried to throw a clinging feather away? It refuses to cooperate, and no matter what Mr. Powell did, it stuck to his fingers or drifted back to my gown. At last, he marched up to an unsuspecting ostler holding a gentleman's horse nearby, and deposited the feather on the back of the fellow's homespun weskit. By this time I was having a difficult time not laughing aloud. From the set of Powell's jaw and his compressed lips, I could tell he was struggling as well.

I looked out the window near me with interest as the carriage slowed and turned in between massive wrought iron gates an hour or so later. The drive was gravel, but not well-cared for, and we were bounced and jounced unmercifully until we stopped at the front of the house. I knew Her Grace would have something to say to her godson about that.

The house itself was not pretentious. True, it had three stories and an imposing front with pillars and ornamental stonework, but it was made of mellow pink brick, and over to one side of it, I saw a child's swing dangling neglected from a sturdy branch of a large chestnut tree. The lower floors had wrought iron guards over the windows. Ivy had grown up and entwined them.

"But this is delightful, or at least it could be, Gareth," the dowager said as she stepped down holding the groom's arm and looked around. It was obvious she was eager to investigate the grounds. I knew she would have begun at once if she had not been so tired.

The housekeeper Mr. Powell had retained was flustered by the sudden guests, but she curtsied and bustled away to see to what had to be done to receive us. I learned later there were few servants. Powell had no butler, only a pair of footmen and a single upstairs maid. Franklin ended up doing much more than dressing me.

I sensed Gareth Powell was embarrassed, even wondering if suggesting we seek refuge here had been a good idea after all, and I hastened to say, "How grand it is to feel safe. I cannot tell you, sir, how grateful I am we are here. And please do not concern yourself with the accommodations. Her Grace and I are more than capable of doing without refinements, aren't we, ma'am?"

"Why, of course we are," she said, looking surprised anyone would even mention it. Powell's face cleared immediately. With a lady on each arm, he took us into his new domain.

There is no way to describe how disarranged and chaotic the interior was. Workmen were busy in the foyer, putting down a new marble floor. There were more in the drawing room, although we did not go in for the smell of wet paint was overpowering. Once we had to flatten ourselves against the wall as carpenters went by carrying long pieces of wood. At last we found a small sitting room near the back of the house which had yet to be torn apart, and we settled down there until our rooms should be ready. Clearly we could hear the housekeeper and someone I assumed was the cook having words somewhere nearby. Powell heard them too, for he excused himself to deal with the problem.

"Well, Lucy, what do you think?" the dowager asked as she removed her bonnet. I went to open the windows for it was still sultry and the room was stuffy from disuse.

"I think we will manage very well. Pray Mr. Powell does not fret overmuch about conditions here. There is this room, and surely there must be a few more where we may be comfortable. And there is always the garden to escape to, ma'am."

I had added that last remark slyly, in case she was also having second thoughts now that she had seen the confusion we had to deal with.

"How hot it is," she said, waving her bonnet before her face. "I do wish it would storm. A good storm often clears the air."

"I would enjoy some lemonade, wouldn't you, ma'am?" I asked. "However, unless lemons were packed in that basket we brought I don't think that will be possible."

"But they were packed," Powell's deep voice informed me, as he returned, trailing a nervous kitchen maid. He took the tray she carried from her before she could spill it, she was so in awe of serving a dowager duchess.

As he poured the lemonade, and over ice, too, I noticed gratefully, he said, "After you are rested, I'll take you down to the stream. It is cooler there, and much more peaceful."

As if to emphasize his remark, a loud banging began somewhere over our heads. Faith Abbott looked a little startled, but she was quick to say an afternoon by the stream sounded most enticing.

Suddenly I felt uneasy. Afternoon. *This* afternoon.

"Oh, no," I cried, putting a hand to my face. "Oh, how could I forget?"

Aware both the dowager and Mr. Powell were thoroughly confused, I explained, "I was pledged to Viscount Epstead this afternoon. He was going to take me for a drive. To think I forgot all about it! What shall I do?"

I saw a fleeting look of satisfaction cross Mr. Powell's face as the dowager said, "I am sure forgetting the drive was perfectly understandable under the circumstances, Lucy. Who could remember an engagement when that maniac had just attacked Macomber and destroyed your room? All your thoughts were on escape, and no one could take offense at that."

"I must write to him and apologize," I said as I set my lemonade down beside me.

"No, you won't," Gareth Powell said grimly. "That is just to take the chance Hayes will begin his tricks here, instead of at the dower house. Tomorrow I'll send a groom to the Greys with a carefully worded message of my own."

"Will you reveal where we are?" Faith Abbott asked.

"Yes, but I'll warn them to keep that information to themselves. They can tell everyone else we went on to — oh, London, I suppose. That will keep Hayes in the dark."

The dowager agreed it seemed the wiser way. I said nothing at all for I was still regretting treating the viscount in such an offhand way. Surely he must be offended, and I had not forgotten his gentle kiss; the way I had felt drawn to him, so quick and amusing as he was.

Chapter 11

By evening we were in much better order. Our rooms had been made up, the library and another sitting room as well which we would use for dining. The real dining room, I discovered, was in the process of getting new windows, a new ceiling, and a handsome blue and gold wall covering. We sat together in our impromptu substitute, after a dinner that was truly a picnic, and talked idly of the day.

"I must say cold meats and salads are all I cared for this evening, Gareth," Faith Abbott remarked, fanning herself in earnest. The weather had not broken. It was still very warm, even now at dusk.

She yawned and Gareth Powell and I exchanged knowing smiles. It was strange. Since the episode of the feather, we had been much easier together. That afternoon, lazy in long chairs by the wide stream, we had conversed about a number of things, although we had not mentioned Jaspar Hayes or Bradford Grey again. Perhaps that was why we shared this new rapport.

"You'll be early to bed this night, ma'am," I remarked. "I suspect we all will."

157

"It is not my age," the dowager said with dignity. "It is only I am not used to rising before dawn."

"I daresay none of us are," I hastened to agree. "I feel very sleepy myself."

But later, after I had been undressed and Franklin had gone to bed, I found I couldn't sleep. Even with the windows open, the room was oppressive. At last I gave up trying, and rose and put on my robe and slippers. I thought it might be cooler outside. There was a three-quarter moon. I would not have to bother with a candle.

Opening my bedroom door quietly, I crept down the hall to the stairs. This part of the mansion was not being renovated. I didn't have to worry about tripping over lumber or paint pots and ladders. On the ground floor I made my way to a side door. I was a little surprised to find it unbolted. Then I shrugged. There was no danger here. Probably no one ever bothered to lock up.

It was brighter outside and I could move more freely, but it was not much cooler. I decided to go down to the stream where I knew I would find relief. I had almost reached it when I heard a loud splash. Cautiously now, I went to the end of the hedge I was following and peered around it. A heap of clothing lay on the bank and I could see Gareth Powell swimming strongly upstream. I have to admit I envied him, knowing how refreshing that cool water must feel. I resented him as well for even being there. Was there anything more ridiculous? This was his estate, his grounds. It was his right to swim anytime he liked. I saw he was floating back downstream now, and I looked away. Perhaps he would leave soon? Perhaps I might even try the stream when he did?

It was a long time before Powell had had enough and began to wade ashore. He had played in the water, and how that had surprised me, a grown man frolicking there, diving deep and staying under until I grew concerned for him. Now I stared at him as he stepped up on the bank. He was naked and his body was beautiful. I know men are not supposed to be called beautiful, but he was. Long-limbed, narrow-hipped, broad-shouldered — he was not only powerful looking but put together so smoothly, every part of him flowed easily into the next. I found myself wanting to touch him, to explore that line of neck and shoulder, hip and thigh. Then I caught myself. What was I thinking of? He put up both hands to sweep his hair back and I retreated to the shadow of the hedge. When I dared to look again, I saw he wore his breeches and was buttoning his shirt.

Throwing the towel he had had the foresight to bring with him over his shoulder, he started toward the house. Then he turned and said, "If you decide to swim, m'lady, be careful. There is a strong current. Oh, and please bolt the side door when you come in."

He sounded matter-of-fact, as if we had been having a conversation. But how had he known I was there? I wondered. I am sure I was scarlet I was so embarrassed I had been caught admiring him nude. But he had not sounded perturbed. Perhaps he had not minded? Perhaps it was different for men?

I waited until I was sure he was long gone before I even ventured beyond the hedge. I had given up any thought of bathing, but somehow the slow-moving stream lured me on. Glancing around, I saw I was alone and I removed my robe, and more slowly, my night rail. Then, holding my hair to one side, I stepped into the stream. I could feel the tug of the current and since I was not a good swimmer, decided I must not go in too deep. A little way ahead of me was a flat-topped rock. I waded to it and sat down. Cupping my hands, I dipped up some water and dribbled it over my body. How good it felt, so cool and wet! I even shivered as it ran down between my breasts and over my stomach.

I stayed in the stream as long as Gareth Powell had, until I felt cool all over. Once safely ashore, I regretted I had not brought a towel. Next time I'll know better, I told myself as I used my night rail to dry myself before I put on my robe. Next time I'll bring a pitcher, too, and some soap.

As I walked back to the house I had the oddest feeling I was being watched. This feeling grew stronger with every step and I began to feel uneasy. Could it be Powell had not gone away as I had thought, but stayed to spy on me? Surely that was not the act of a gentleman, and never mind I had stared at him. I had not known he was there. The circumstances were entirely different.

Just then an owl hooted right over my head, and I jumped and looked up to see it regarding me out of its big dark eyes. For a moment, we stared at each other before the bird spread its wings and flew away, a dark shadow across the moon. So much for being watched, I told myself, chuckling a little at my foolishness.

Several uneventful days followed. We had a thunderstorm finally that ushered in cooler weather. It came one evening while we were eating dinner, and every time the thunder pealed closer and closer, louder and louder, Gareth Powell flinched a bit. He hid his nervousness very well, but I was watching him carefully and I knew. Somehow I found it endearing, this large, powerful man humbled by a storm.

He had said nothing to me of that night by the stream. I would have been surprised if he had, and although I had gone twice more on successive hot nights, I had not encountered him again.

The dowager spent every moment she could in the gardens. The head gardener was made of weaker stuff than her own Mr. Fleming, and he agreed to all her plans. She bullied Powell as well, insisting on a series of descending pools through the grounds, with fountains and waterfalls, and a much larger kitchen garden and herb knot near the servants' quarters.

"But of course," she exclaimed one morning as we sat at breakfast. "It's an aardvark!"

Bewildered, I could only stare at her.

"Of course it is," Gareth Powell said as he took another muffin. "Nothing else it could be. Knew that in a moment, for of all the many aardvarks I've seen, it is the most typical of the species.

"*What's* an aardvark, ma'am?"

She stared and then chuckled. "I'm sorry," she said, wiping her lips on her napkin, "I was thinking of the topiary garden and that one overgrown shrub I have not been able to label. You know the one, Gareth. It's near the stag but not as far as the dormouse. And it is definitely an aardvark."

"Doesn't that seem a bit, er, strange in an English garden, Your Grace?" I ventured to ask. I had no very good idea what the animal looked like — a long snout, wasn't it? — but surely they were not native.

"No, I don't think so," she said after a moment's thought. "A former owner might have seen one on his travels and developed a fondness for them."

"I wouldn't have said they were endearing, but then, I don't know anything of Viscount Clough's forebears," Powell said. "Er, don't they have scales? Aardvarks, I mean, not Clough's forebears?"

"Yes, I believe so," Faith Abbott said, frowning

now as she concentrated. "I know they eat ants."

"That settles it," Powell said sternly. "I'll have no ant-eating foreigner in my garden. We must find some other animal it resembles."

"Something with a long nose," I said, wanting badly to laugh. "Perhaps an elephant. A baby elephant," I amended.

We were all laughing when at last we rose from the table to begin the day. A baby elephant had been discarded, but so had Powell's suggestion we trim the shrub into a one-eared hare. The dowager remarked with dignity she thought we were both losing our minds, but she'd say no more about it.

As I went into the garden to pick a bouquet to decorate the sitting room, I wondered how long this blissful peace would last. We had been at Water House for almost a week. Surely Jaspar Hayes had discovered I was missing by now. Surely he would think of Gareth Powell soon, since he was missing as well, and then he would find out where he lived and come after me. I shivered. I had not forgotten how deranged he had looked in the woods at Alicia's fete, nor the fanatical fury he had shown destroying my bedroom. I doubted I would ever forget, not really. I shivered again.

"Are you chilly?" I heard Powell's deep voice ask and I looked up to see him leaning over the balustrade that separated the terrace from the grounds. Water House was built on a rise, the land sloping away from it to the wide stream that joined the Thames a few miles downstream.

I didn't answer immediately. Instead, I put down my basket and shears and went up the steps to join him. "I was just wondering how long it will be before Hayes figures out where I am," I told him. I went on and explained my reasoning, and by the time I had finished, he was frowning.

"We may have longer than you think," he said, looking down the slope to where the dowager was harrying the gardeners. "I've not owned this estate for long. Few people even know the deed has been transferred."

"Where did you live before?" I asked, curious.

"I had a small place in Kent. I have spent most of my life in London, except when I was traveling. My mother was fond of the metropolis."

"I'm sorry she died," I said, and I meant it, for even though I had cast off my family, I missed them still.

He didn't speak for a moment. Then he reached into his coat and produced a letter. "This came for you just now," he said. "It was forwarded with the rest of the post from Lansmere."

My heart had begun to beat faster, but only a glance at the handwriting told me Hayes had not sent this letter.

Gareth Powell nodded when I gave him a questioning glance, and I broke the seal. The letter was from Arthur Kittering and after a quick perusal, I knew all my peace and happiness were at an end. I looked up blankly to see Powell regarding me, his face serious.

I tried to smile at him. "Is there anything more vexatious than an officious agent who orders one to do this and that?" I asked in mock despair. "Here is my man Kittering telling me I must go to Cornwall without delay."

"Why?" he asked.

"He says he has a buyer for the property and begs me to inspect it once more before I make a final decision to sell it," I told him. "I suppose I must go. I owe Lord Blake that much, I guess."

Powell looked as if he had any number of comments to make, but to my relief, he only said, "Surely there is no need to tear off, is there, ma'am? Surely this buyer can wait till it is convenient for you?"

"I suppose you are right," I said slowly. Moments later I excused myself. I forgot the basket full of flowers and the shears I had left in the garden. The last thing on my mind just then was a bouquet.

Alone in my room and ignoring the racket the carpenters were making below me, I sat down to think. Why did it seem strange to me that a buyer had been found so quickly? True, Trecarag was a noble seat boasting more than five hundred acres. There were breathtaking views of the moors with the sea beyond. The mansion itself was handsome too, but it was isolated for there were no near neighbors and it was far from a town of any size. Indeed, it was necessary to travel many tedious miles across the moors to reach Fowey or Plymouth.

Who was this buyer? I wondered. And how had he learned Trecarag might be for sale?

Then I told myself I was seeing shadows where there were none. Trecarag had been vacant except for caretakers for four years. Any casual visitor to the area might have seen it in that time and admired it. More and more people every year were traveling about the country, stopping to see the sights and the country homes of the nobles. It was called "going on procession." Trecarag had surely been a destination for some of these people. That one had decided to purchase it now was only a coincidence.

I walked to the window then and looked out. Powell had put me in a large room facing the drive. More gardeners were working there below me, filling in the holes and raking the gravel smooth. We would have an easier time of it when we left than we had had on arrival. Suddenly I realized I did not want to leave. I felt safe here in Gareth Powell's new home. I refused to consider that might be so because he was here to protect me.

In my mind's eye I pictured him stepping out of the stream, pushing his wet hair back from his face. It was not the first time I had done so, either. Reminded I wanted nothing to do with a man, any man, I wondered why this vision persisted in disturbing me. I made myself think of my predicament instead.

Powell had said there was no need for me to tear off to Cornwall, and oh, how I wanted to believe him. But if there was a buyer for Trecarag, I did not want to lose him. I wanted to avoid owning the mansion for years as it got more and more decrepit as unlived in, unloved houses always did. And with the money from its sale, I could live anywhere in luxury and comfort.

If the problem with Jaspar Hayes was resolved, that is.

It occurred to me then that Cornwall would be the last place Hayes would think of looking for me. He knew how I had felt there; how quickly I had abandoned Trecarag. I nodded. Yes, I would go back, and once Hayes realized Trecarag had been sold to strangers, he might well give up his mad obsession with me. Of course, I told myself. I had never been as important in his scheme of things as Trecarag was.

Sadly I realized I could not ask Faith Abbott to accompany me, no, nor Gareth Powell either. The dowager was too old for such a long, tiresome journey, and I had no hold over Powell. He had his own life to live and this estate to set right. I recalled how he had begged me to give him my opinion of the library only yesterday. The paneled walls and the cases that fronted them were full of dry rot and must be destroyed. But when they were rebuilt, he had asked, did I favor a warm, pale wood like oak, or did I think a dark rich one would be better?

I had said surely that was his choice to make,

but he had persisted, as if my opinion was important. At last, to appease him, I had told him I thought mahogany would be handsome, with gold velvet draperies and green striped upholstery.

Suddenly all these meandering thoughts fled as a smart traveling carriage drawn by a team of grays came smartly up the drive. I wasn't at all frightened. I knew that even if Hayes had discovered I was here, he would not approach the house openly. That was not his way.

As I stared, Alicia Grey bent to take the groom's arm to step from the carriage. Her husband was right behind her, and smiling now, I hurried downstairs to welcome them.

I found Gareth Powell at the front door before me, and together we went out to greet the visitors.

"Do forgive us, sir, for coming without warning," Jack Grey said. "We only stopped to see how Lady Blake and the dowager were faring before we continue on our way."

"Surely you can spend the night," Powell said as he shook Grey's hand. "I warn you, we're all at sixes and sevens here, but we've a number of empty bedchambers, and Her Grace seems to be thriving amid the confusion."

"It does sound like fun," Alicia said wistfully.

The glance her husband gave her was brief. "Of course we would be delighted to stay, if you're sure," he said. "I must make London by tomorrow, however. We'll need an early start."

"How glad I am to see you, Lucy," Alicia whispered as the servants began to unload the coach. "I must say you look much better, rested — happy even."

We had no time to say anything more, for Powell was ushering us all before him, and enlivening the meeting by describing how we had found the place when we came. Alicia and Jack were still chuckling when we were seated in the sitting room we used. Powell ordered wine and tea, and sent a footman to tell Faith Abbott of the company.

One of the first things Alicia asked about was Jaspar Hayes. Had he returned to the dower house? Had he been seen here? What did we think he would do next, and what were we planning to do?

"I say, Alicia, you sound like a justice questioning suspects in some dire crime," Jack Grey said. I thought he looked weary from the travel, and I wondered if his leg was bothering him. Still, his face when he looked at his wife was full of love; hers, just as warm. I looked away immediately, embarrassed I had witnessed such an intimate moment.

"As far as we know, he hasn't returned to the dower house," Gareth Powell said grimly. "I'm sure he discovered Lady Blake was no longer there. He hasn't come here. It will take him some time to find this place, if he ever does."

"I'm glad," Alicia said, smiling at me. "It is frightening to think Lucy might be in danger from such a madman."

To change the subject, I asked for Viscount Epstead.

"Oh, Brad," Alicia said, shaking her head, "of course he was disappointed you could not keep your appointment with him to drive out, but he is so changeable. He was off the next day to London, claiming business there. Somehow I suspect your decamping had much to do with his own. Jack and I can never keep him in the country long, can we, my dear?"

I felt a pang of regret that the viscount, who had so often claimed I was to become his countess, had abandoned me so quickly, but I was not surprised by it. Bradford Grey was certainly the quicksilver Faith Abbott had named him.

I did not have a chance to see Alicia alone until much later. After some refreshment, Jack Grey excused himself to work on his papers, and Alicia was given a tour of the house and gardens by the rest of us. At last the dowager retired to take a nap and Gareth Powell was called away by one of the carpenters.

"How good it is to see you," I said as Alicia and I settled ourselves in the chairs set beside the stream. A tall oak provided welcome shade. "Forgive me for asking, but why are you and Mr. Grey traveling to London? I was sure you were spending the summer in Oxfordshire."

Alicia's face was serene yet I sensed something was wrong. "Jack has been called back by the

Foreign Office," she said. "The Secretary wants him to go to Russia sooner than we had anticipated. Indeed, his ship sails the end of this week."

I took her hands and held them tightly. "How you will miss him," I said, cursing the banality of my response.

She nodded, then smiled. "Yes, but sooner gone, sooner returned, you know. I had not hoped to see him till next summer. Now he may well be able to join me for the London Season."

Silently I admired her courage — wished I had some of it myself.

She asked me about my plans then, aware my stay at Gareth Powell's home could not last forever. It was then I told her about the opportunity I had to sell Trecarag, and how I intended to travel there soon.

"Alicia," I added eagerly, struck by a sudden thought, "I know I have no right . . . but it would be grand if you could . . . I mean, would it be possible —"

"For me to go to Cornwall with you, scatter-tongue?" she teased. "I don't see why not. It would be a grand adventure, and Cornwall is a part of England I've never seen. I'm sure Jack will agree for he knows I tend to brood in his absence if I am not busy."

"Oh, how famous!" I applauded. "I was dreading the trip by myself, for of course the dowager cannot do it, and certainly I cannot ask Mr. Powell."

In both instances I was wrong. Apprised at dinner of our plans, Faith Abbott was indignant to be excluded and to my great surprise, Gareth Powell insisted on coming.

"It is not at all fitting for ladies to go alone," he said seriously. "You need a man to see to everything for you and ease your travels, to say nothing of serving as protection. Forget this house. There is more than enough for the men to do until I will be needed to make decisions again."

"As for me, well, I am sure I will do famously," the dowager said, her voice determined.

"Especially if you travel by ship, Your Grace," Jack Grey remarked. "That will be much smoother and so much quicker than coach for everyone."

And so it was decided, to the delight of all. Looking around the table at them, I felt just as if a large burden had been lifted from my shoulders. Yes, I would go back to Trecarag even though I had promised myself I would never do so again, but I would have these good friends beside me when I did. How very fortunate I was.

Chapter 12

The excitement I felt must have remained with me, for I found myself awake very early the next morning. I could not go back to sleep nor was I content to lie quietly in bed making plans. Instead, I got up and after attending to my morning routine, went to the window to see what kind of day we might be going to have.

Below me, the Grey's coach was drawn up before the house, the grooms busy stowing Mr. Grey's portmaneau. It had been decided last night that Alicia remain with us, since her husband would be sailing so quickly.

As I watched, the Greys came in view as they walked slowly down the marble steps, Jack leaning heavily on his cane while he held Alicia close in his other arm.

He spoke to his men before he took his wife a little way down the drive behind the coach. They turned to face each other then and he spoke to her long and earnestly. Alicia smiled and nodded, before she said something in return. Then he took her in his arms and kissed her while the breeze set his cape to swirling around them as if to hide them from prying eyes. I could not look away even so.

He left her rather abruptly, I thought. One moment they were locked in a long embrace, the next he had entered the coach and given the signal to be off. Of course, I told myself, that was probably all for the best. But how brave Alicia was, standing there smiling and waving her handkerchief to him, even blowing him a kiss. I was shocked when the coach disappeared from sight and she turned back to the house, to see how she had changed. Ordinarily, Alicia was a handsome woman, but now her face was distorted with feeling and running tears, and she looked plain. I stepped back, praying she had not seen me witnessing the raw display of emotion that she had never intended anyone to observe.

Time seemed to move very quickly after that. Messages were sent in droves — to the Duke of Lansmere, my Mr. Kittering, and Mr. Powell's man of business. As well, Alicia had letters to send. In the evenings, we sat together in the small parlor when the house was blessedly quiet, and refined our plans. Powell's man had found a ship sailing from London westward in six days' time, and we were resolved to be aboard. With the exception of Alicia, we would not need to send for additional clothing since we would be attending no social occasions at Trecarag. Although I had said nothing of it to the others, I intended to be as quick as possible about this business. It would be horror enough for me just to be at Trecarag again where the very walls would remind me of my ordeal. No, I would not linger there. I would inspect the house, the grounds, the farms, and instigate any necessary repairs. Surely that would not take me more than a week. Then I would be gone, this time, forever. If the others protested such haste, we could linger in Cornwall, travel to Land's End, visit Tintagel where it is said King Arthur was born, even go "on procession" ourselves for the rest of the summer. Anywhere but at Trecarag.

When we finally arrived in London, we stayed at Lansmere House. I expressed doubts about this, but Faith Abbott would not hear them. "I am sure the duke will have no objection," she said sternly. "As for my daughter-in-law, she had better not say a word. This was *my* house for almost twenty years; best she remember it."

I caught Gareth Powell's eye as she turned away with Alicia, to climb the steps where the butler stood waiting to greet them. He was smiling at me and I smiled in return, wondering at how easy we were with each other now.

"You know, of course, Hayes is probably in London," he said.

I looked around, reminded suddenly it would be most unwise to let down my guard. Yes, Hayes could be here looking for me. No doubt he was furious at the lies I had told him. If he found me, I would not be able to lull him into thinking I was agreeable to his plans. Not this time, I wouldn't. I shuddered to think what he might not do to me to repay me for running away from him. "I suppose that's entirely possible," I said, resisting the urge to step closer.

"He may well be keeping Lansmere House under observation," Powell remarked. I wished he had not mentioned that as he went on, "Do not go out alone, or even in company with the dowager or Mrs. Grey. Instead, insist a footman escort you if I cannot do it. Better still, don't go out at all. We'll not be here long. Your man, and any others you may wish to see, can come here to you."

I nodded, looking forward to boarding the ship and sailing away. All the peace I had felt at Water House was gone and in its place, the terror and revulsion I had known before had returned.

Mr. Kittering came the next morning. I saw him in the duke's library. To my relief, he had seen to everything, sending word of our arrival ahead and arranging for extra servants and supplies for our comfort. Carriages would be waiting at the quay in Fowey when we disembarked, and riding horses had been hired and sent on to Trecarag for us. Kittering even supplied a large purse of money for my expenses. He told me the London House in Portman Square had been sold to a wealthy nabob, sniffing as he did so. I could tell he thought the very presence of trade defiled the house, but I was glad to be rid of it, and wished the new owner more joy there than I had ever had.

I did not leave Lansmere House, and the butler was instructed to admit no strangers, no matter how plausible they might sound. Alicia and the dowager were often with me, but Gareth Powell was out most of the time. I wondered what he was up to, although I knew it was none of my business.

I was surprised to learn all the Lansmere House servants thought we were planning a trip to Ireland. When I questioned Franklin about it, she said Mr. Powell had asked her and the others' maids to spread the rumor. It was clever of him for surely after we were gone, Hayes would be able to gain a confidant in one of the servants here. I did not count on him going as far as to travel to Ireland, but I would be delighted if he did. Only when Trecarag was sold would I truly feel free of him. Of course he might well decide to get revenge when he learned there was a new owner. I had already begun to think of traveling abroad after the sale was accomplished. Canada would be interesting but cold. Perhaps I might go to Bermuda instead. I understood it was a charming place fragrant with flowers almost all year long. And surely if I stayed away for a year, Hayes would forget me.

The day before we were to sail, the butler brought me a small package. I was alone at the time, reading one of the newspapers that came every morning. I did not open the package. Instead, I set it down carefully on a table beside me and stared at it. It was innocuous enough, about an inch thick, done up in brown paper and tied with string. My name had been printed in black letters, and there was no hint of whom the sender might be. Still, just looking at it made the hair stand up on the back of my neck. Few people knew I was here and none of those who did would be sending me anything. I told myself it was not at all cowardly to wait until Gareth Powell returned before I found out what the package contained.

He did not come back until mid-afternoon. I think I must have started to untie the string a hundred times by then, and the list of things I imagined might be enclosed, was almost as long. Because, you see, I knew the package came from Jaspar Hayes. I wished I might throw it away, but somehow I could not make myself do that.

Apprised of my dilemma, Mr. Powell took it upon himself to tear the paper off and open the lid of a cardboard box.

I did not try to see what was in the box. My gaze never left his face. I saw the disgust, the fleeting revulsion there, and I closed my eyes.

"There is no need for you to see this," I heard him say as he crumpled the paper the box had come in. I sensed him moving to the fireplace where even on an August afternoon there was a small blaze to take the dampness from the room. Still, I did not open my eyes.

"It's all right now," he said, and I forced myself to look at him. He stood with his back to the fire, effectively blocking my view. There was a faint, vaguely familiar odor I could not identify. Before I could do so, it was gone.

"That was from Hayes?" I managed to ask.

He nodded briefly. "There was no message. There wasn't any need for one. Who else would have done such a thing?" he asked. Then he came and sat down across from me. "So, Hayes knows you are here," he said. "How fortunate we are sailing tomorrow night."

I could not restrain a shiver. I was frightened. It seemed as if I had been living this nightmare for years rather than weeks. And Jaspar Hayes was so relentless.

"What are you thinking?" Powell asked.

"I was wondering if all our subterfuge will do any good in the end," I admitted. "Jaspar Hayes has no intention of letting me alone. He will continue to search for me until he finds me. I can't hide from him forever."

"I agree. He will find you, unless —"

"And there's nothing I can do to stop him!" I interrupted wildly. "I might just as well give myself up to him now."

"Granted you are distraught m'lady, but please don't dramatize yourself," Powell said coldly.

I'm sure I bristled, but before I could think of a suitably scathing reply, he went on, "What I was going to say was that he will find you unless we find *him* first."

"What good will that do?" I muttered, refusing to meet his eye.

"It will give us the advantage, of course, by having the meeting take place on our terms. I agree Hayes is persistent. If you are ever to have any peace, he must be disposed of — permanently."

I stared at him then. His face looked composed, hard even, and it was completely devoid of emotion. "Kill him, you mean?" I whispered.

"That would be one solution. There is another, simpler way. Hayes is insane. There would be no difficulty convincing the authorities he is a danger to society, now would there?"

I nodded, but of the two solutions, Hayes's death was preferable. He would not go quietly to Bedlam. No, he would shriek his ghastly revelations to one and all, and even though no one believed him, some taint must cling to me. Of course I did not tell Powell that, but I resolved to keep my pistol near me from this time on. I could afford no confrontation between Hayes and others and I certainly could not hope to reason with the man myself, plead for mercy, beg him to leave me alone. It had all gone too far for that. Much too far.

We left Lansmere House the following night at eleven. Our ship was due to sail at one in the morning when the tide was on the ebb.

I did not look around as I hurried to the carriage, Alicia beside me. Ahead of us, Mr. Powell escorted the dowager. She was all gay conversation about the adventure. I wished she would be quiet. I wished we could slip away like smoke, instead of betrayed by the servants' voices, the creaking of the carriages, the snorting of the teams and the jangling of their harness, even the noisy clatter of their hooves on the cobblestones when we were off at last. I huddled back in my seat, trying to make myself small. Hayes could be out there — on that corner — in that doorway.

When we arrived at the wharf, I was even more agitated. Surely a servant had told him the name of the ship we were taking. Surely he stood somewhere nearby in the shadows.

Unless he has booked passage as well, I thought, feeling cold sweat run down my spine. Without thinking, I reached out to grasp Powell's sleeve. When he turned and saw my face, he bent over me. I explained my fears in a quick whisper. He did not mock me. Instead, he covered my hand with his own large one and assured me we were the only passengers and there were no new members of the crew. I hoped the smile I gave him was not as woefully inadequate as it felt.

It was a calm night with little wind. It was fortunate we had the tide with us for the journey to the sea was long and slow. It seemed an age before we reached Greenwich, an aeon before the lights of Tilbury and Gravesend disappeared behind us. And the sun had risen before Margate came into sight and we were finally able to head south to the Dover Strait and the Channel beyond. I was not able to sleep. Instead, I paced the small cabin, envying Alicia. She had undressed, climbed into her bunk, and dropped off immediately.

At last I went up on deck. I knew I should be feeling relieved, now we were safely underway and Hayes could not threaten me. Still, my nerves were on edge and when I sensed someone nearby, I stiffened. I turned quickly then to find Gareth Powell regarding me. We stood frozen for a moment, like figures in a tableau, before he came and joined me at the rail.

"You couldn't sleep either, sir?" I asked, a little unnerved by his continued silence. Still I felt myself relaxing — growing calm — simply because he was close.

"I never do sleep, first night out," he said absently, staring straight ahead as if he could pierce the darkness. I wondered what he was hoping to see there.

It puzzled me that I should feel so comfortable. He was a man, wasn't he, and we were to all extents and purposes, alone. But it was as if we had known each other a long time, and good companions that we were, we did not find it necessary to make idle, pleasant conversation.

"What was in that package? Can you tell me?" I asked several long minutes later.

He did not try to parry the question and that pleased me. "It was a bird. A small, badly mutilated bird."

"You were right. He is not sane," I said softly, willing myself not to tremble. He was so close, he surely would have noticed.

Something else occurred to me then and I turned toward him. There were some lanterns lit

182

on deck, one at the bow, two at the stern. Far above us on the mast there was another one. I could just make out his profile. It seemed an intimate moment, and I dared to say, "Tell me, why didn't you believe me when I told Her Grace about Hayes, back at the dower house? Why did you call my explanation a fairy tale?"

He bent toward me then to search my face. "Because nothing you told us was so terrible, so revolting that it could not have been revealed long before. You said a man was in love with you. Of course he was. You said he was following you. Again, of course. You are a lovely, desirable woman. Why would his attraction have been something you could not mention? I'm sure many men have been drawn to you, confessed their love, annoyed you with their attentions. No, Lucy. There is something more about this Jaspar Hayes. Something much more serious, so serious you cannot bear to have it exposed, and mind, I do not mean his insanity where you are concerned. Since that is the case, your friends must accept your reticence, and I must try to help you even though I do not know what causes this terror of yours."

I bent my head, humbled. Easy tears filled my eyes. I blinked them away, glad the darkness hid my weakness. I was aware I owed Gareth Powell the truth. You will never know, as we stood there alone at the rail, how I longed to tell him — how I *ached* to unburden myself, but I could not. I simply could not.

The lines and the canvas that stretched so far above us rattled then. My skirts whipped around my legs as well. Behind us, someone gave an order, and I heard the slap of bare feet on the deck as the watch hurried to tighten sail. Aware Mr. Powell must be waiting for a response, I was only able to say, "I will never be able to thank you adequately for your help, sir. Please believe I do appreciate all you're doing for me, however, I, who am just a stranger. I — I can't imagine how I would have managed without you."

He put his hand over mine where it grasped the rail, loosening my fingers one by one so he could lift my hand and rub those fingers with his thumb. Back and forth. Back and forth, slowly and gently. I did not protest. It was so reassuring.

"But I wanted to help you," he said quietly, looking down at our clasped hands. "I think I will always want to help you, Lucy."

The ship heeled then in a sudden gust of wind and we staggered a little to keep our balance. The wind sent tendrils of my hair whipping across my face. Before I could smooth them back, Powell did it for me. I started when his warm, hard fingers touched my cheek, and deep inside, I felt a vague stirring, just the inception of sensation. I stepped away from him, confused.

"We seem to be moving faster now," I said, not knowing how to respond to his words, that gesture. If it had been another man, I would have suspected he was trying to seduce me. But surely that had not been Powell's intent.

"Yes, the wind's picking up. We'll make good time now," he said, interrupting my chaotic thoughts. "It is going to get unpleasant on deck. Go to bed, m'lady, try and sleep. I'm told it helps to pretend you're a baby being rocked in a cradle."

He reached out and took both my hands in his to press them between his own. When he released me, I did not feel the fragmented bundle of nerves I had before. Instead, I felt — serene.

I left him without a word; indeed, words were not necessary just then. A few minutes later when I was tucked up under a warm blanket in my narrow bunk, I found myself smiling, and not because the ship's motion reminded me of a cradle, either. No, it was because Gareth Powell had called me Lucy. And not just once, either. Twice.

Chapter 13

We had a good passage. The dowager especially was entranced with this new method of travel, and declared more than once that she intended to choose sail over coach in the future. And then she told her godson it was too bad he had so little respect for his elders that he would point out any inland journey made that very difficult. Fortunately, there were no storms to change her mind. I myself had worried about storms. I had never been on a ship before, but I had heard how sick some people became at sea. Alicia had reassured me, but still I found myself searching the sky and watching the height of the waves with trepidation. I never did have another tête à tête with Gareth Powell, something I chided myself for regretting.

We put into the port of Fowey early one morning, much to the crew's surprise, for the ship was indeed bound for Ireland. It heartened me they had not known our destination and therefore couldn't have told Hayes anything of it.

It felt strange being on land again. We all staggered a bit, trying to lose what Gareth Powell called our "sea legs."

Two carriages awaited us in Fowey, a saddle horse for Powell as well. We could have reached Trecarag Hall by late evening, but in deference to the dowager, it had been decided to break our journey at an inn on the moor. Naturally, we did not tell her that was our reason.

Once clear of Fowey, we headed northwest and the countryside grew increasingly wilder and more deserted. I saw Faith Abbott looking a bit perturbed at the vacant stretches of moor, the undulating ground that rolled away before us as far as the horizon with never a farm nor a village to break the solitude. I remembered how I had felt coming here as a bride of seventeen, glad in a sense to be away from the dreary London house, yet dreading what I might find ahead of me. Lord Blake had assured me things would be better in Cornwall. I remembered how I had pinned my hopes on that, and how disappointed I had been when nothing changed at all except to get worse.

We ate a picnic lunch somewhere on the moors. It was a lovely day, and blankets had been provided for us to sit on. Faith Abbott perched above us on the carriage steps, very queenly above her lowly servants. The warm summer scent of the grasses and the bracken was pleasant, the varied birdsong entrancing. Alicia seemed especially struck by the scenery.

"I see now why the Cornish are so clannish," she said as the maids packed up the remains of our meal and we went off by ourselves to a small copse of trees nearby. "They want to keep all this to themselves, of course."

"It is delightful," the dowager agreed, but I could tell she would have preferred a formal garden to all this untrammeled splendor. "Is all Cornwall so wild, Lucy?" she asked.

"No, the moors are unique. The one where we stay tonight is called Bodmin Moor. It is especially beautiful. Trecarag lies on its northwest border within sight of the Atlantic."

"I've heard moors can be treacherous places," Faith Abbott persisted. She sounded old and more than a little querulous, and Alicia and I exchanged glances.

"We will be perfectly safe," I told her, taking her hand and squeezing it gently. "The coachmen and grooms are Cornishmen. They would know the way blindfolded."

The dowager nodded, but the little crease on her forehead remained for the rest of the afternoon. The inn where we were to put up overnight was a bit primitive, but by the time we reached it, she was so glad to be set down, I do not think she would have demurred at a bed in a hedge. She went immediately to her room, so I knew the rough road and the hard carriage seat had taken their toll. Mr. Powell, Alicia, and I settled down near the fire in the fortunately deserted taproom. The inn sported no private parlors.

I was concerned my friends would scorn this simple hostelry, but both of them refused to listen when I tried to apologize. Alicia reminded me of her tales of Russian inns, and Powell confessed some of the taverns that had had his patronage in the Americas made this place look like a palace. Fortunately, the simple, hearty meal we were served was well-cooked, and the wine and brandy provided so excellent it was obvious it had never seen a customs officer.

Settling back replete in my chair, I admired the tawny color of the brandy before I said, "I've no idea how long a journey lies ahead of us tomorrow, for when I came before it was by land through Devon. For the dowager's sake, I hope it is not too tiresome."

"The coachmen tell me we should arrive by early afternoon if we do not dally in the morning," Powell said.

"I suspect that is Mr. Powell's subtle way of suggesting we make an early start, don't you, Lucy?" Alicia teased.

I saw his face light up, the flash of white teeth, and I wished he smiled more often, it changed his face so. Why, when he did, he looked almost handsome.

"Or the coachmen's," I agreed. "Best we get to bed, my dear. I suspect there will be a great deal of noise around dawn — ostlers calling, teams neighing, pots and pans being clattered in the kitchen, feet pounding up and down the stairs — the usual little hints, you know."

She laughed and rose. "Certainly an early start would be best. Her Grace will be happier when she is established at Trecarag. And if you have an overgrown garden, Lucy, she will be more than content."

That remark brought to mind my determination to finish the business at Trecarag as soon as possible, but still I said nothing of my intent. Time enough, I told myself as I followed Alicia up the steep stairs to our room under the eaves, to announce it when the rigors of travel had been forgotten. But still, I felt more than a tremor of unease as I lay down beside Alicia in the feather-bed we had been provided. Tomorrow, everything I had tried so hard for four years to repress would come back to me — everything I had suffered and cursed and fought with all my might. Tomorrow I would be at Trecarag Hall again.

We arrived at the Hall shortly after two the following afternoon. Gareth Powell was at the door of the carriage to assist us. I noticed he had to lift Faith Abbott down and when he set her on her feet, he kept an arm around her until he was sure she could stand alone. My heart went out to her, so little and frail, yet so *game*. For a moment, I was able to forget the building before me, postpone the inevitable tightening I would feel within when I looked at it square.

Do not misunderstand me. Trecarag Hall is a beautiful mansion. It was not built of local materials for its honey-colored stone had come, at great expense, from quarries near Bath. A goodly number of large windows paraded across its front. On one end, there was a hexagonal tower that contained six-sided rooms complete with bay windows on the front. A staircase against the inner walls connected the rooms. I turned my back and pointed out the remains of an old French chapel with its graceful spire some little distance away. I saw the dowager had revived somewhat at the gardens she could see that led up to it.

The grooms and coachmen were busy unloading the baggage, anxious, I am sure, to be on their way. The maids and Powell's valet supervised.

There was no help for it, and I knew it. Taking a deep breath I turned to the massive front door of black oak. I had barely set a foot on the first step that led up to it when it was flung open and Bradford Grey, Viscount Epstead, sauntered out to smile at us. I heard Alicia catch her breath, the dowager's little cry of surprise. For myself, I stood there, frozen.

"But how delightful to see you all," Epstead said as he strolled down the stairs to cup my elbow. Speaking so only I could hear, he said, "Now why did you feel you had to bring a party, my dear? It quite upsets my plans for us."

Then in a louder voice, he went on, "Whatever took you so long? I looked for you several days ago, for I told your Mr. Kittering I was anxious to conclude the purchase of the Hall."

"You!" I exclaimed. "You mean, you are the prospective buyer he told me about?"

He nodded, looking pleased with himself. I

191

was furious, and let me tell you, although I am not easily moved to anger, once provoked, I have a terrible temper. How dare he do such a thing, I fumed. How *dare* he trick me into coming here all for some precocious whim of his.

I wrenched my arm from his grasp and retreated to the drive where the others stood regarding him. He looked confused for a moment, then he said, "Come, come, m'lady. I can see you are angry with me — and may I tell you, you are magnificent, simply magnificent in that state — but surely you see that I had to see this estate you were thinking of selling. I hope I'll be able to dissuade you, for it is a handsome establishment and I am well pleased with it. But do come inside, all of you.

"Your Grace, you look as if you could do with a cup of tea, or perhaps something stronger? I shall have your rooms prepared at once. Rooms overlooking the gardens, ma'am?"

"Alicia, where is Jack? I did not expect to see you here, or Mr. Powell either. No matter, there is plenty of room and I brought an army of servants with me from London. We shall be very comfortable."

Seething, I followed the others into the house. The rage that I was experiencing had one benefit at least. It was so all-consuming, it allowed no room for revulsion.

"Lucy, I do apologize for Brad," Alicia whispered. She looked angry too, I noted, and perturbed any relative of hers should be so

192

overbearing and conceited. For it was conceit, I told myself as I handed my pelisse and hat to Franklin. Conceit to think what he wanted was acceptable to all. Conceit to imagine he had only to announce his plans for my future and I would agree to them at last. Well, the Viscount Epstead was in for quite a surprise.

"We'll speak of it later," I managed to say. "Not that it is at all your fault. How could you know the viscount would do such an unbelievable thing?"

I turned to see the man we were discussing standing at the door of the largest drawing room, waiting as host to usher us in, and my anger flamed even higher. No matter how I felt about it, this was still my property. He had not purchased it yet.

"I beg you all to excuse me," I said in an icy voice. "I have some things to see to."

"Of course, of course," Epstead said, never taking his eyes from my face. "I chose the best tower room for you, Lucy. It looked like it was designed for a viscountess."

I knew the room he meant. It had been mine when I was last here, and I was quick to say, "I do not care for the tower rooms. I shall choose another. No, sir," I added when I saw him beckon to a servant, "you must allow me to decide the accommodations. This is still *my* house, I believe?"

He had the grace to look a little abashed. Without another word, I signaled to Franklin and one of the footmen and began to climb the stairs. At the first landing, I turned and, looking down to all the uplifted faces, said, "I shall see your rooms are prepared immediately. Please enjoy your tea."

Before I turned away, I saw Gareth Powell push himself away from the wall he had been leaning against, and I was sure I did not imagine the approval I saw in his eyes, nor the little nod he gave me before he went with the others into the drawing room.

I chose rooms for Alicia and the dowager duchess that faced the gardens, and took the one between them for myself. There were no balconies at Trecarag. If Hayes ever came here, he would not be able to invade my room that way. Of course, since he had lived here once, no doubt he had any number of ways to get in. How glad I was there was no chance he would discover my whereabouts.

I sent Franklin to fetch a glass of wine for me before I investigated the other rooms on the floor. I saw Bradford Grey had appropriated the corner room nearest the tower for his own, and my lips curled when I remembered his "plans." I told the footman the room directly across from his was to be prepared for Mr. Powell, and content I had done all I could for the moment, retired to my room to rest.

I did not see the others again until dinnertime. I had dressed and gone down long before, determined to reign as hostess here no matter how it sickened me. Perhaps the little rage I still felt was a help. I know I surveyed the elaborately decorated drawing room without a single quiver. And Alicia joined me before I could begin to picture Lord Blake occupying his favorite chair by the fireplace, a large bumper of brandy at his elbow, and a determined glare on his red face as he told me what was expected of me. He is dead, I reminded myself. He can't give me orders ever again. And Jaspar Hayes would never again hover behind his chair, all but wringing his hands in his desire to please and ingratiate himself. That was over now. Done.

"I wonder you can bear to see me, Lucy," Alicia said as she came in and sat beside me. "I never dreamed Brad was so — so impulsive, so inconsiderate of others' feelings when he wanted something. Jack will be horrified when I tell him."

"Then don't," I said swiftly. "There is no need to upset him, and what can he do about it, after all? No, I'll handle the viscount, just see if I don't. And in a while we'll be able to leave here. I can't tell you how disappointed I am he wasn't really a buyer though. I am so anxious to rid myself of Trecarag."

I must have sounded desperate for she turned quickly to study me. "I don't understand," she said, frowning. "It is so lovely. And there is something invigorating in the air here. When I went up, I fell asleep almost at once, and I never nap."

"That's the salt air from the ocean. During a

gale, salt can be found on vegetation ten miles inland, the winds are so fierce. Yes, Trecarag is beautiful, especially on a glorious late summer day. But more often than not there are fogs — dense, penetrating fogs that last for days, storms as well. You wouldn't like it here then. I know I never did."

She looked doubtful, but there was no time for any more just then for Gareth Powell came in with the dowager duchess on his arm. I was surprised to see her. I had expected her to go early to bed after a tray in her room. But from the way she leaned forward when Viscount Epstead joined us a few minutes later, I suspected she could not bear to miss what she, at least, would be sure to call "the fun."

That fun began when one of the servants Mr. Kittering had engaged in London for me, and sent ahead, announced dinner. I could see Bradford Grey was surprised that his own choice of butler was not fulfilling that customary role. He was even more surprised when he discovered that instead of dining in the formal salon where he had arranged for us to sit opposite each other like man and wife, I had changed all his plans. Now, I led them to a smaller room, one much more intimate, and only one place was set at the end of the table — mine. I had placed Faith Abbott at my right, Mr. Powell beside her. I had been forced to seat Epstead to my left, in deference to his title. Alicia was beyond.

"Well, this is certainly more cozy than the

formal salon," Epstead remarked lightly as he pushed in the dowager's chair. The footman was assisting me so there was nothing he could do but take his own seat. I was careful not to look in Gareth Powell's direction as I signaled for the first course.

The meal that followed was one of the best I have ever eaten, due no doubt to the presence of two cooks in the kitchen, each intent on proving he or she was superior to the other. I wondered idly as I tasted a delicious dish of creamed shellfish with a hint of sherry, why no one else had ever considered such an arrangement. We concluded the meal with a rich chocolate cake and a luscious trifle.

Faith Abbott sighed in delight as she tasted that trifle. "I do not know how your Mr. Kittering managed it, Lucy, but I congratulate him," she said. "I hope we remain here for a considerable time. I have never had finer food."

"Perhaps it is the chef I brought with me who has made the difference, Your Grace," Bradford Grey said, signaling the footman to pour more wine before I could do so. Once again anger surged in my breast and I took a deep breath. Looking up, I saw Gareth Powell regarding me over his wineglass. As he set it down he smiled at me, and instantly I felt calmer. It was almost as if he had spoken to me, warned me not to lose my temper, assured me I was more than equal to the task of chastising the brazen viscount who had taken upon himself the role of host. I nodded to him only to find Bradford Grey staring at me before he turned to glare at Mr. Powell. To my relief, Alicia spoke up then, saying she could hardly wait to explore the grounds, ride out over the moor to the ocean tomorrow.

"For some reason, I have never seen the Atlantic," she confessed. "Is it as wild and glorious as I have been told?"

"It can be quite a sight from the cliffs," the viscount agreed. "I advise you not to ride alone, however. The grooms here are local. They know the moor and one of them will go with you. There is an abandoned tin mine on the property and it is dangerous. Some of the deeper shafts of it even go out under the ocean for a considerable distance."

Alicia shivered. "I've never liked caves, underground places," she admitted. "Thank you, Brad, for the warning."

"As for me, I intend to inspect the gardens," the dowager said. "From what I could see from my window, they have been much neglected, Lucy."

She sounded so disapproving, I would have apologized except Gareth Powell said, "But Lady Blake has not been here for four years, Your Grace. Of course the gardens show disorder. Gardens, like people, need love to thrive."

I was startled by his pronouncement. It seemed such an incongruous thing to say, especially for the severe, masculine Mr. Powell. Faith Abbott seemed to agree with me for she looked thoughtful when I gave the signal for the ladies to withdraw.

We were not permitted to do so, however. Instead, Bradford Grey rose with us, declaring he had spent quite enough time alone at the table while waiting for us to arrive. Gareth Powell joined us as well.

Alicia went to the piano while the men and the dowager enjoyed their drinks. I wandered over to the windows that faced the west. I felt the house closing in around me, imprisoning me, forcing me to remember the past.

That small slipper chair covered in rose velvet. Yes, I had often sat there in the evenings, pretending to read a book and wishing on one hand I might go to bed, while on the other I dreaded it.

The shadow of a stain on the carpet near the sofa. It had been made by Jaspar Hayes when he had carelessly dropped a glass of port. It had proved impossible to remove all of it. I remembered how Lord Blake had assured him it was of no importance, how he had clapped him on the shoulder and whispered to him while I supervised the servants who were mopping up the wine and picking up the broken pieces of his glass.

The portrait of the long-dead viscountess that had center place over the mantel. She still looked as disapproving of the events taking place at Trecarag Hall as she ever had. Lord Blake had said he intended to put my portrait there, but there had been no time for me to sit for it before he died. All the other family portraits, of his first two wives, his two sons, had been removed. If I squinted, I could just make out the faint rectangles on the walls where they had been hung.

In the reflection on the dark glass I saw Viscount Epstead rise and start toward me, and I made myself return to the others near the fire. He looked disappointed. I knew I would have to speak to him alone, and soon, but I did not feel up to it just then. When Faith Abbott excused herself minutes later, claiming fatigue from the journey, I went with her.

Still, it was a long time before I fell asleep, that first night back at Trecarag Hall.

Chapter 14

A misty beginning became the glorious summer day I had told Alicia that Cornwall had so seldom. I woke late to the sound of voices in the gardens, and steps outside my door. Ringing for Franklin, I stretched luxuriously. This room, at least, held no memories for me which was the primary reason I had chosen it. When I had been here before, this had been a guest room that had never been occupied during my tenure. I looked around it idly. It was a comfortable room with a large four-poster, a handsome mahogany dresser with an oval mirror above, some comfortable chairs by the window, and an escritoire against the far wall. The draperies had a charming floral pattern, the rug was thick and soft. I could almost pretend I was visiting in someone else's home.

But of course, all too soon I had eaten breakfast from the tray Franklin brought me, been dressed, and was ready to go downstairs. There had been a note on my tray from Bradford Grey, begging a private interview. I decided that would be my first order of business and asked a footman to tell him I was in the morning room.

This room was only too familiar to me, and although it was as innocuous as my bedchamber, I felt stifled once the door closed behind me. It was here Lord Blake and I had had some of our most memorable arguments, here where he had struck me for the first time, here where I had cried my defiance and threatened to betray him to the world. And it was here where I had sat innumerable mornings thereafter, trying — and failing — to stop my tears.

When the viscount joined me I was quick to suggest we go for a walk. He was most agreeable; indeed, I could see he was determined to win me over by charm and a cheerful acquiescence to anything I might suggest. For a moment, looking at his handsome face, that golden hair, those laughing eyes, I felt regret. I had not forgotten his kiss that afternoon at the gazebo, nor how it had affected me. But any tenderness I might have harbored for the man had disappeared in the face of his arrogant assumption that in spite of my constant denials, he fully intended to become my husband.

"I'm aware you were not only surprised to see me yesterday, but infuriated," he said as soon as we left the Hall. "I confess I had no idea you would react that way. You see, I did it hoping to please you — amuse you."

"You're right. I was not amused," I said.

"Well, suppose I promise, on my honor, I won't do it again?" he asked, laughing a little. "Will you forgive me then? Let bygones be bygones?"

I looked up into his smiling face. He was so sure of himself, this Bradford Grey, Viscount Epstead. Had he never felt uneasy? Had he never, even once as a child, felt inadequate? Out of place? Ignorant? Unsophisticated? Had he never wished he were anywhere but where he was? Never hated his looks, his voice, his body? Never wished he were someone — anyone! — else? Or were those particular self-doubts only reserved for more mortal men and women?

"You are forgiven, sir," I made myself say. "It was unconscionable of you to lead me to believe there was a buyer for Trecarag, make me travel all those miles to accommodate one. No, don't speak," I added when I saw he was anxious to press his case. "I've told you over and over I will not marry you. You refuse to believe me. Why is that? Surely you understand the word. Or has no one ever said it to you before? Well, sir, I do so now and I shall not change my mind. I won't marry you. I'll never marry you. I want you to stop badgering me."

He stopped walking then and turned me to put his hands on my shoulders, bending forward to stare into my eyes. "You mean it, don't you?" he said in the most humble voice I had ever heard him employ. "But *why*, Lucy? *Why* won't you marry me? I'll be faithful to you — I adore you! I'll even promise to curb my arrogance, and I'm wealthy beyond belief. What more could you want?"

I could hear the pain behind his confusion,

and I put a hand on one of his. "I don't want marriage," I said. "It is not personal. I don't dislike you. I just dislike marriage."

He brightened immediately. "But don't you see, darling, you shouldn't take old Blake as a model husband. For one thing he was piles too old for you and he had that dreadful laugh and the most boring conversation. I'm not like that, admit it. And although you'll probably think I'm being conceited again, I've been told enough times I'm a handsome fellow, unlike him with his paunch and bowed legs. And you have to admit there is no way our noses can be compared."

"I'll not dispute you are handsome and Lord Blake was not," I agreed. "It doesn't matter. I am indifferent to men. You may believe me when I say it will do you no good to press your suit. In fact, if you knew everything there is to know about me, you wouldn't want to."

"Why?" he asked. "Have you a secret, Lucy? Come now, confess."

I wondered he could change the subject so quickly, sound so eager. "Yes, I do," I said. "One no one will ever learn.

"Now, sir, shall we return? I must see the housekeeper, decide the menus. And that reminds me," I added as we set off for the Hall again, "I would appreciate it if you would remember you are a guest here. My guest, however unexpected. Do not give any further orders at Trecarag."

"Aha!" he said, shaking a finger at me. "Now I

have it. You're miffed because I usurped some of your authority. Now who would imagine the gentle little piece you are would rise up in wrath over such a petty thing? Well, I cannot tell you how that encourages me, to find out you are just like other women. You may be assured I shall not give a single, solitary order except possibly to my valet in the privacy of my room, but only if you have no objection to it, mind."

He chuckled and I decided to ignore him. I had done the best I could. Now I had only to show him by remaining cold that I had meant what I said.

Besides, I was not at all like "other women." How insulting!

I had another unexpected interview that same day. I had taken a book out beyond the gardens to a sheltered nook in the woods. It was only a small glade. There were no flowers there, no statues, no sweeping views to be admired. In fact, it had nothing to commend it. The only place to sit was on a fallen tree trunk, and little light filtered through the thick cover of leaves overhead. But this was my place where I had sought refuge during my marriage. I had spent many hours alone here, and now I was not pleased to look up and see Gareth Powell regarding me. For a moment, we only stared at each other.

"Do you want me to go away?" he asked, making no move to come closer. "I will, you know."

"No, oh, no," I said, closing my book and gesturing him forward, determined not to be rude. "It's just I was startled. I never expected anyone to discover this place."

"To be honest, I didn't just find it," he said as he sat beside me. The tree trunk suddenly seemed to have shrunk in length. "I followed you. I wanted to talk to you alone."

Not again, I thought. Another discussion like the one I had had that morning with Viscount Epstead would be too much. I should have known better. Mr. Powell had no amorous intentions.

"I'm concerned for my godmother," he said, scowling now. "Have you noticed the change in her, perhaps? She seems older to me suddenly, frailer. I wanted your opinion."

I thought for a moment. "Yes, I agree. She has been different lately. I had put it down to the rigors of travel, but perhaps it is more than that?"

"She hasn't even walked in the gardens today," he went on. "When I inquired for her, her maid told me she was resting. You know that is most unlike her."

I am sure I looked chagrined. To think I had been so involved in my own problems I had not even wondered how my dear friend was faring, never even asked for her or gone to see her. I was ashamed of myself.

"Do you think we should have the doctor? There is one in the area who attended Lord Blake in his final weeks."

"Yes, and I'll summon him myself so she won't

ring a peal over you," Powell said. Then he grimaced. "There's a very good chance she will refuse to see him once he is here. Faith Abbott can be the most maddening woman — stubborn, opinionated, blind to her own welfare . . ."

"Like me?" I asked innocently. "I seem to remember you saying much the same about me once."

He stared down into my face and I watched the light grow in his eyes, the barest quirk of a smile that appeared at the corner of his mouth, and I waited for his deep chuckle.

"Perhaps you are distantly related to the dowager duchess, Lady Blake?" he asked instead. His voice was even, controlled. It gave nothing of his amusement away.

I shook my head. "I wish I were," I said. "I'm sure she would have been a wonderful mother."

He must have heard something in my voice for he leaned closer and said, "Who are your people? Where did you grow up? I never hear you mention your background."

"I was a Tremont before my marriage. My father is Reginald Tremont. We lived near Stowmarket in Suffolk. But I don't speak of my family. I washed my hands of them after my parents forced me to marry Lord Blake."

"What happened to you was unfortunate. I was luckier, myself. Although my father died during the American Revolution, I still had my mother. She was a dear. I think I will always miss her."

I wanted to touch him, comfort him. His voice still held pain, remembering. He had not spoken of his mother before, not even when I had expressed my regrets about her death. That he would do so now, seemed significant.

"It could not have been easy for her, raising a son alone," I said at last.

"No, I'm sure it wasn't," he said, stretching his long legs out before him and picking up a twig nearby. "I was as much a devil as any young sprig. But she sent me away to school so I would have the company of other boys, and she made sure my uncles taught me to ride and shoot and hunt. She never hung on my sleeve, never begged me to remain by her side."

"She sounds remarkable," I said quietly. "I wish I had known her."

"She would have liked you," he said, surprising me. "She would have applauded your decision to solve your problems alone. After all, that is what she did."

"Are you sure she wouldn't regret your feeling you must assume responsibility for one who has no claim on you?"

He looked up from the twig he was stripping of its bark. It seemed a long time before he said, "There are claims, and then there are claims, as I trust you will discover, Lucy."

I could make nothing of that, and annoyed he was being cryptic, I rose and shook out my skirts.

As he rose as well, I said, "I think it past time we return to the house. There's that message to the doctor to see to, and I want to visit the dowager. I might be able to discover what's wrong with her."

Mr. Powell did not say aye or nay and I turned and left the glade. All the way back to the gardens on the narrow path through the woods, I was conscious of him following me, his eyes on my back. It made me clumsy.

When we reached the graveled paths, I stopped to wait for him to catch up. And as we walked through the gardens, I kept the conversation firmly on the dowager and the doctor. Powell seemed amused again. I ignored him.

I was disturbed when the dowager's maid answered my soft knocking and told me her mistress was sleeping. Beckoning her into the hall, I began to question her. Unfortunately she had nothing to report. In her opinion, Faith Abbott was only worn down by the travel, as she was sure everyone else was too, she added with a sigh.

I patted her arm. I knew it could not be easy for her. She had been with the dowager duchess since her marriage to Lansmere. They had grown old together. The dowager had told me she knew her Mathilda should be pensioned off, but she could not bear to do it. "I might just as well shoot her," she had said. "And she's as dear as any sister to me."

I told Mathilda of the doctor's call, and Mr. Powell's concern. She nodded and promised to do what she could to prepare Her Grace.

Unfortunately, Dr. Gates was not available until the following day. The message that came from his infirmary said he had been called to the site of a serious carriage accident where several people had been injured.

It was obvious Mathilda had told the dowager of the coming visit, for she appeared in the drawing room before dinner, looking militant. Mr. Powell and I exchanged glances.

She did not speak of the doctor during that dinner however, for which I was grateful. I watched her as unobtrusively as I could. She did not look or act sick. Indeed, only a militant haughtiness in her bearing was at all unusual.

Later, when we returned to the drawing room, she opened the engagement with no preliminary skirmishes.

"I understand from my dear Mathilda that you all consider me in need of medical attention," she said, glaring around the room indiscriminately. "I do assure you I have no intention of seeing a doctor. I am in perfect health."

"It is of course for you to say, Your Grace," Powell agreed easily. "But surely, just as a precaution . . ."

She snorted and he went on, "Or perhaps you would consider doing it as a kindness to me and your hostess? We are concerned for you, it is true, as are Mrs. Grey and Epstead. Why not do it to please us, ma'am?"

The dowager lifted her brandy snifter and swallowed the remains in it before she replied.

"You take too much upon yourself, Gareth," she scolded as she set the snifter down on the table beside her. "You have always had the most annoying habit of thinking you know best. Why, even as a child you were the same. I remind you no one is omnipotent."

"Including yourself, ma'am," he pointed out. "A Dr. Gates will call in the morning."

"And he shall be sent on his way," Faith Abbott said swiftly. I did not like her color. True, she had never had a rosy complexion, but now she looked almost gray. I tried to signal Gareth Powell to let things be, but I could not catch his eye.

"I'm tired of this," she said abruptly, gripping the chair arms hard to raise herself to her feet. "I'm going to bed and perhaps after you all come to accept how adamantly I feel about this doctor's visit, you'll . . ."

Suddenly she went down in a crumpled heap on the floor and Alicia and I cried out. As her godson knelt at her side and lifted her wrist to feel her pulse, I thought how tiny she looked huddled there. Not much bigger than a child, in fact.

Powell looked up, and speaking to me alone said, "Her pulse is very fast and thready. I'm going to carry her to her room. Can you ask Miss Franklin to help her, Lucy? I've noticed she's a strong, capable sort with her head firmly on her shoulders. Her Grace's collapse is sure to render her own maid of no use at all."

I nodded before I went to the door. Behind me, I heard Alicia ask what she could do to help. I shook my head as I hurried upstairs. There wasn't a single thing any one of us could do, and silently I cursed the situation that kept the doctor from Trecarag Hall tonight.

When I summoned her, Franklin went quickly to the dowager's room. Mathilda stood beside the bed weeping, her apron to her face. I was glad Franklin was there. Between us, we soon had the dowager undressed and tucked into bed, a hot brick to her feet. She regained consciousness moments later. I was not reassured when I saw her hand go to her heart. We did not dare give her anything to calm her, but that proved unnecessary. After only a few bewildered questions, she fell asleep.

Her maid insisted on sitting up with her even though Franklin said she would be there through the night. I decided I would take her place later. To that end, I did not return to the drawing room, but went to bed myself, after several fervent prayers for my dear friend's safe recovery.

I slept lightly and around four in the morning, I rose and put on a warm robe and some slippers. I found Franklin sitting by the window, her hands folded in her lap. On the other side of the room, the dowager's maid was fast asleep on a pallet. Franklin whispered the patient had not awakened and only barely moved, although her breathing seemed normal and her skin had ceased to feel cold and clammy.

Franklin would have stayed but I persuaded her to get some sleep, promising to call if I needed her.

Left alone with the two sleepers, I took the chair she had vacated. From where I sat I had a clear view of Faith Abbott's face. It looked as white to me as the pillow slip beneath her head. Her hands were folded outside the covers at her breast. Strange, I had never noticed how old they looked, the prominent veins blue, the knuckles slightly enlarged, and the skin wrinkled. I said another prayer.

Some time passed before I heard a soft knock and Gareth Powell came in. He nodded to me but all his attention was on the woman lying in the bed. As he bent over her he put his hand to her forehead. A moment later, he took her pulse. Coming to the window where I was seated, he hitched a chair closer so he did not have to raise his voice. "I see no change," he said. "I wish I knew more of medicine. I don't know whether that's good or bad."

"I've been praying it was good," I confessed. It did not make me self-conscious that we both wore only dressing gowns. In the light of the one candle, carefully shaded, beside the bed, I could see Mr. Powell had not shaved. Somehow the heavy dark stubble on his face made him seem villainous. I could easily picture him on a pirate's ship wearing an eye patch and waving a saber while the Jolly Roger flew overhead. That scene faded from my mind and a vision of him leaving

213

the stream at Water House nude that hot night of our arrival came instead.

"I wonder what you're thinking now, m'lady?" he said, interrupting my reverie. I am sure I blushed.

"If you'd like to go to bed, I'll stay with my godmother," he added. "I can't sleep anyway."

"I'd rather be here," I told him. "Like you, sleep has not come easy for me this night. I hope it won't be long till dawn. Everything always seems better when it's light, don't you think?"

He shrugged, his eyes going to the small figure in the bed again, and I fell silent. A long time later I remembered the animosity between him and Bradford Grey. It was in evidence every time they had to look at each other, or speak, and it was obvious they did everything they could to avoid each other's company.

"Tell me, what was it that estranged you and Viscount Epstead?" I asked as he returned to his chair after attending to the dying fire.

That certainly got his attention. His head came up quickly and he stared at me. "Can it be possible he has not given you his own, distorted version yet, ma'am?" he said. "I am surprised."

It was my turn to shrug. "He said he would, but he has not done so. What did happen? If you feel you can reveal it, that is."

"I suppose there's no harm in telling you. A few of the ton know." He paused for a moment as if to gather his thoughts before he continued, "Epstead and I are almost of an age. When I was

214

twenty-four to his twenty-two, a young cousin of mine was brought to London to make her come-out. Julie was only sixteen, a pretty little thing with red-blond hair and big brown eyes. Even the sprinkling of freckles across her nose could not detract from her looks and her charm. She was so lively and gay, and she had the most infectious laugh. Epstead made a dead set at her, and of course she fell in love with him."

He paused and stared at me. "Surely you have already divined the ending to this unhappy tale, haven't you?" he asked, his voice sardonic.

"She thought he was serious and wanted to marry her." I did not speak it as a question.

He nodded. "Exactly. When her father accused him of perfidy, he claimed he had made her no promises, that he had only been flirting with her. Unfortunately, my dear little cousin was not sophisticated enough to know the difference. Nor had she been clever enough to discern he was a man without honor who was incapable of feeling deeply about anyone or anything. Except himself, of course."

"But he was only twenty-two," I said in quick defense. "Surely he came to regret what had happened."

"I've no idea what he felt then, or what he feels now. My uncle refused to let me challenge him to a duel, saying the less said about the matter, the better. He took Julie back to Kent. She has never returned to society. Instead, a few years ago, she married a local squire. A poor match for her, although I believe her children give her some comfort.

"Were you thinking she went into a dark decline and died, as the more lurid novelists would have it? Julie was too strong for that."

"But you've never forgiven him, have you?" I whispered.

"No," came the bald reply. "I've no respect for men who think seducing innocent women is a sort of game. And do you know, although Julie smiles often, I have never heard that wonderful laugh of hers from that day to this. I'll not forgive him for that, either."

I nodded, but I said nothing. In my mind I could see Bradford Grey, his handsome good looks — his devilish smile — as he went his mercurial way, a golden god far above others who knew their shortcomings and agonized over their faults as they tried to live their lives in a way that would not hurt anyone else.

But perhaps I was not being fair to the viscount, I thought. I told myself I must hear his side of the story before I came to the conclusion he was nothing more than the flash of quicksilver Gareth Powell had painted him.

Chapter 15

The doctor arrived at nine. By that time, Faith Abbott was awake, and had even been able to drink a cup of tea and toy with a piece of toast. Her color was better, and she was lucid. I was afraid she would send the doctor away as she had promised, but to my relief, she agreed to see him. Only her own maid was allowed in the room during his visit. I was told I looked like a slattern and I should use the time to get dressed and have my hair done. I was smiling a little at this order as I shut her door and saw Gareth Powell waiting in the hall.

"She has agreed to see him?" he asked softly, leaning close.

I nodded. Mr. Powell had shaved and dressed in the casual clothes he affected in the country.

"She must be seriously ill," he said with a frown. "You remember how determined she was she would not see a doctor."

"I suspect her faint last evening frightened her. However, she is fast recovering her sangfroid. She just told me I looked like a slattern."

His face lit up in that so seldom seen yet welcome smile. "Did she now?" he murmured. "Now I'm concerned for her eyesight. As always, you look — delicious."

Beyond him I could see Bradford Grey watching us from where he stood a short distance away down the hall. His handsome face was cold. I knew he could not have heard what Powell had just said; still the two of us so close together while I was dressed in only a robe must have seemed an intimate moment. To appease him, I smiled and said, "Good news, sir. Her Grace is feeling better and she has not sent the doctor away — yet."

His face softened a little as he studied me. It was strange. Alone with Powell I had not felt at all uncomfortable. But the viscount's leisurely perusal made me want to clutch the neck of my robe together and hide my breasts behind crossed arms.

"You'll forgive me, I'm sure," I added when he did not speak. "I must dress before she needs me again."

"Surely her maid can care for her," he said. "I'd hoped we might ride to the shore this morning."

As I refused him, I wondered if Gareth Powell was still there listening, but when I turned, he had disappeared.

Later, in the morning room, Dr. Gates told us all the dowager would need bed rest for a considerable time, that her heart was not as young as it once was, and last night had been in the nature of a warning. He said he would send her a cordial and directed me to see she had no spirits or spicy food, and certainly no excitement. I felt guilty. Surely the dowager's illness must be laid to my door, mine and Hayes's, that is.

A week passed, and then another. It was September now, a golden September, its halcyon days strung out like pearls and disturbed only briefly now and then by mist or a shower of rain. The Cornish servants declared they had never seen weather like it, and predicted a storm to end all storms in the near future.

I spent those days conferring with my agent and riding out to inspect the farms and cottages, and the fishing fleet in the harbor with its village close by on the shore. From all these people came the rents that had sustained the Blakes for so many years.

I did not inspect the Hall. I left it to the housekeeper to tell me what was needed. I was not comfortable indoors. Too many memories clamored to be relived; indeed, there was hardly a room that did not remind me of something best forgotten.

When I rode out, I took a groom with me if Epstead or Powell was not available. Not from any fear of the tin mine, you understand, for I knew Trecarag land well. No, it was because as time passed and Faith Abbott slowly regained her health and her spirits, I found myself growing increasingly tense. I felt so strongly we had been here too long. Any day now it was possible Hayes would learn where I was, if he hadn't already. For even with all the clever deceptions we had employed, there were still those who could have learned where I had gone and would tell him, not even suspecting they were putting me in danger. If only we had been able to leave Trecarag quickly, as I had planned. If only the dowager duchess had not fallen ill and forced us to remain. Increasingly I began to see myself as bait, staked out here to lure a predator. It was beyond terrifying — I was numb with apprehension. I began to carry my pistol again, and I took to locking my bedroom door at night.

One glorious afternoon, Gareth Powell announced he did not think it would do any harm if he carried his godmother out to the garden. It was more like August than September, and because she had been growing impatient with her enforced exile, he thought a change would do her good. Accordingly I had the footmen place a chaise lounge in a shady spot near one of the fountains.

We were all there to applaud when Mr. Powell set her down in a nest of pillows and covered her with a silk throw. The dowager's cheeks were pink as she told us we were making much too much of a small thing. The viscount presented her with a posy of red roses — to my great relief, the wild pink ones had ceased to bloom — and we spent an enjoyable afternoon talking and reading aloud and listening to the dowager's plans for Trecarag's gardens. Watching her closely and seeing her animation, the stronger voice she had, I began to hope it wouldn't be much longer before we could all be gone. As yet I had made no firm plans to travel to Bermuda, but I knew I could not return to the dower house. I owed that much to my dear old friend, for if I were not there, Hayes would not be there either.

When the servants brought us a tray of cakes and lemonade, I watched the two men. I knew things had grown increasingly tense between them. Only a few days ago, Alicia had warned me I had better have a care, for if she were not mistaken they were almost at daggers drawn. Even today they had taken seats as distant from each other as could be managed, and not once had they spoken except to the ladies present. If I had had the slightest idea what to do to ease the situation, you may be sure I would have done it in a minute. But the viscount continued to believe I was on the brink of succumbing to his considerable charms, and as for Powell, I hadn't an inkling what he thought. Sometimes when I caught him regarding me, his eyes steady as if he were trying to fathom what kind of creature I might be, I was uncomfortable. Not only that, it annoyed me I couldn't discover what was going on in his mind. From things he had said, I knew he liked me. As for more, who could tell?

I had mentioned both men to Alicia one morning while we lingered alone at the breakfast table, confessed Powell especially puzzled me.

"It's no secret how Brad feels about you, of course," she said. "Talk about wearing your heart on your sleeve! And I must say I'm impressed he remains constant. He does not generally, you know. The number of ladies who have found to their sorrow Viscount Epstead is not interested in coyness or games, are legion."

"Perhaps it's because I am not being coy," I said gloomily. I stared down into my half-empty cup of coffee. It had grown cold as we spoke, and an unpleasant skim had formed on the surface. Grimacing, I pushed the cup away.

"I'm sorry for that. I would love to have been able to call you sister," she said, reaching out for my hand. "Are you sure you have no feelings for Brad? No desire to marry him?"

"No, nor anyone else," I said, turning to stare out the window. There was a heavy mist this morning. It might burn off by noontime, then again it might linger throughout the day. Until it did, we were all held captive in the Hall.

"Not even Gareth Powell?" Alicia asked, sounding surprised. "Somehow I suspected you were leaning toward him. Of course you know he is just as much in love with you as Brad is."

"How did you reach that conclusion?" I asked, my attention caught again. "I see no sign of the lover myself."

"Oh, my dear, he is waiting. Waiting for you to tell him he may tell you — dear me, how tangled that sentence is!" she said, chuckling and shaking her head. "I mean, you must give him a sign his declaration will be welcome before he troubles you with his feelings."

"No wonder he has never married. Most men would not be so nice."

She chuckled again, sounding genuinely amused. "I do assure you, dear Lucy, where you are concerned, Gareth Powell is not at all nice. He is the type of man who would surprise you with his kindness, overwhelm you with the extent of his love, and stun you with the passion he has for you. And before you can ask how I could possibly know such a thing about the very contained Mr. Powell, let me tell you my own dear Jack is just like him. If you loved him, you would be truly blessed."

That same afternoon, the viscount begged for a personal tour of the house. "Just those rooms I've not seen, of course," he said gaily. "It will give us something to do this gloomy day. And who knows what we might not discover in some dusty trunk in the attic? Perhaps a diamond brooch carelessly tucked in the toe of a lady's slipper, or a leather bag of gold coins."

Alicia and Mr. Powell were quick to say they would enjoy exploring, too. Relieved by the numbers, I said, "You're more apt to find discarded furniture, musty old clothes, and enough dust to make you sneeze for a week, but if you would care for it, of course we'll have a tour."

We began in the attics. They were surprisingly neat and clean, and nothing of any interest was found there. Beside them were the servants' rooms; we did not invade them. On the next floor were the nursery and the children's rooms. An elaborately carved old cradle rested near one window and some toy soldiers marched across the mantel. The schoolroom held a number of small desks and chairs. I was beginning to feel uneasy, and I was delighted to quit the rooms. I had only been there once before when Lord Blake had insisted on showing them to me shortly after our arrival at Trecarag.

Eventually we arrived at the tower rooms at the north end of the Hall. I would have given anything to avoid entering them, but to say so would be so singular it would cause all kinds of speculation. Speculation I had no intention of satisfying.

There were four rooms, stacked one on top of the other. They all had bow windows across the front; the top room that rose above the Hall itself had windows on all six sides. A staircase against the back walls connected the rooms. There were also doors that led into the main part of the house on each level but the last.

I hid my trembling hands in my skirts as I led the way, and prayed I would not betray myself in the next few minutes.

The ground floor room had been Lord Blake's private study. I could still smell the doggy odor there. He had owned a number of hounds, and here they had had full sway, wet or dry, sick or healthy. The furniture was worn and scarred. One old leather chair was particularly disreputable. It was where Lord Blake had liked to sit and smoke his pipe, the brandy decanter handy.

I was glad when Alicia raised her handkerchief to her nose and said "Whew!" for I could not have spoken then to save my soul and I was having the greatest trouble presenting a calm, unruffled front.

Lord Blake's bedroom occupied the first floor. It contained heavy oak furniture, dark with age now. The windows were covered in dark red velvet. Bradford Grey flung them open, releasing a cloud of dust. I was only able to stand there in the center of that room while the others explored and exclaimed, the viscount admiring the shaving stand, Alicia peering at family portraits. I wished they would hurry, lose interest.

"Why isn't this part of the mansion kept up, Lucy?" the viscount asked. "These are such unusual rooms, and they could be so pleasant."

"There is no need for them now," I managed to say, swallowing hard. Only two rooms to go, I told myself. Don't think about what happened here. Don't remember. This will be over soon.

"Shall we go on?" I asked, proud of my steady voice.

"Surely this must have been yours, Lucy," Alicia said as we reached the next room on the second floor. This room was in much better order since it was the one Epstead had had made ready for me. I tried to view it as a stranger might. The large bed was covered with a delicately embroidered silk coverlet and heaped with dainty pillows. Set in the bay were chairs and a table. There were bookcases along one wall, a large armoire and a small fireplace outlined in Dutch tiles on two others.

"It needs something," the viscount mused. "Flowers? Some figurines? It's almost cold-looking with all this silver and blue. But regal. Decidedly regal."

Warily, I watched Gareth Powell open the door that connected the room with the main part of the Hall. It was located under the last flight of stairs that led to the top of the tower. I realized then he had not said a single word since we had entered the tower, and I felt a shiver of apprehension.

To tell the truth, I had felt uncomfortable with Mr. Powell ever since Alicia had told me her theory about him that morning. I could not seem to put it from my mind. His kindness of course, I knew. But his love? Hardly! As for any passion he might have had for me, I could not believe it. Now I wondered what he was thinking, even what he was looking for as he walked the room, carefully inspecting everything. I must admit my heart beat strangely when he paused to stare at the large bed, then looked over at me, his gaze considering. Hurriedly, I suggested we go on.

When we reached the room at the top of the tower, the viscount said, "I've tried and tried to think what purpose this room served, but I've had no luck. Do tell us, Lucy."

"I've no idea. It was never used when I lived here, and even then appeared to have been empty for some time." I sensed they were waiting

226

for something more, and I added, "As you can see, there's no furniture. Perhaps it was used for lookouts. With windows all around, you can see a great distance in any direction."

I forced myself to smile, ignoring my clammy hands, the pounding in my temples. "Shall we go down? I'm thirsty, as I'm sure you are. Besides, I'm afraid this tour of Trecarag Hall was a great deal less exciting than you had hoped."

"We'll forgive you for not producing a treasure chest or any skeletons, my dear," Alicia said as she took my arm and strolled with me to the stairs. Bradford Grey was close behind us, although Mr. Powell lingered. I wondered why. It was only an empty room after all.

In the library again, the viscount challenged me to a game of chess. I thought him rude, for what were the others to do? Alicia however excused herself to go and read to the dowager and Mr. Powell settled down in a comfortable chair to peruse the journals, newly arrived from London.

I sat across from Epstead as he set up the board. I was still feeling unnerved by our tour of the house, yet proud of myself as well for the way I had acquitted myself. If only I had been able to play a better game. As it was, I was vanquished in short order, and the viscount took me to task for it as he poured us each a glass of wine.

"Your mind wasn't on chess, Lucy," he said, frowning. "What were you thinking about?"

I forgot Gareth Powell was there some little

distance away as I said, "I'm concerned by the length of our stay at Trecarag, and I'll not hide it from you. We've been here too long. I expect Jaspar Hayes will find me here shortly and then the whole nightmare will begin again. I'm frightened."

The viscount put our glasses down on the chess board so he could take both my hands in his. "He won't find you, darling Lucy," he said. "And even if he does, I'll protect you. You know, I wish he would dare come. I'd relish the chance to teach him a lesson for troubling you. Now, you're not to worry, do you hear? It puts a frown on your beautiful face and that will never do. Come now, smile for me."

I tried, but I knew it wasn't my best effort. He caught my chin in one hand and tilted my head up. I saw his gaze go over my face and linger on my lips, but when he bent closer, Gareth Powell coughed behind us. I jumped, although the viscount turned slowly and subjected the man he considered his rival to a long insolent stare.

He got as good as he gave. Powell put his newspaper down and rose slowly. He looked so threatening I felt my heart begin to pound.

"If you will excuse me, gentlemen," I said, curtsying to no one in particular before I hurried to the door. "I just remembered some letters I must write."

Calling myself every kind of coward I closed the library door behind me. I knew, if the butler had not been in the foyer, I would have put my ear to the keyhole, I was so curious about what would happen next in the library. Was there anyone so contrary?

Dinner that evening was not pleasant. Powell seemed lost in thought, Bradford Grey abstracted. Alicia and I exchanged glances. I missed the dowager. She would have had us all chatting and laughing, but she, alas, was still tied to her bed upstairs, and I did not have a tenth of her social skills, most especially with difficult, sullen gentlemen.

While I ate my dinner I decided to ride alone the next morning. Alone, that is, except for a groom. I might even venture as far as the village of Marghas. There was a stone church there I had admired before, and a few shops. It would be good to get away by myself, get away and not have to playact or pretend. I thought of Jaspar Hayes briefly and decided that even if he had arrived, he wouldn't try anything while I was with a groom. Besides, I would have my pistol with me.

But when I hurried down to the stables the next morning at first light, I discovered Gareth Powell before me. I was not only dismayed, I was angry when I discovered he had dismissed my groom and taken it upon himself to serve as my escort. And all without so much as a hint of an invitation, either.

As he helped me to the saddle and I arranged the skirt of my habit, I wondered why I had never acquired the art of dismissing someone without being offensive about it. Surely my mother had been most remiss, forgetting such an important part of my education.

I was silent, silent and stiff as we set out following the road that went to the shore. He had not even asked me where I would like to go and I brooded about that as well.

"Are we to proceed in silence, ma'am? For our entire ride?" he asked, controlling his mount easily when the horse would have shied at a rabbit running alongside on the verge.

"I did not expect to see anyone this morning," I forced myself to say. "I wanted to escape the Hall and everyone in it. That's why I'm out so early."

There, I thought. Make of that statement what you will, sir.

"I see you are touchy in the morning. My mother was much the same," he remarked, his deep voice understanding. I longed to hit him. "She was the sweetest thing after she had an hour or so to collect herself. I learned early never to bring her a problem until then. I shall keep my own counsel, ma'am. Do let me know when you have come out of the sullens."

Once again, he had left me with nothing to do but seethe, and seethe I did as we rode over the fragrant moor. There were no flowers now, although I recalled carpets of them in spring and early summer. Still, the moor was attractive even so. Outcroppings of granite gleamed in the sunlight amid low bushes and grasses, and I could smell the wild thyme and bracken on the soft breeze that blew in from the ocean.

By the time we had nearly reached the mine, I felt ridiculous. True to his promise, Gareth Powell hadn't said a word, nor so much as looked at me. He made me feel I was sulking, much as a spoiled child would, and I halted my mare. He was quick to pull up as well.

On horseback the difference in our height was much less noticeable and we were almost eye to eye.

"I do apologize, sir," I said. "I've been ungracious, and that's a poor trait for a hostess. I ask you to forgive me."

"Surely we've progressed beyond hostess and guest, and therefore there's nothing to forgive," he said easily.

He pointed his crop at the falling-down buildings ahead that comprised all that was left of the mine. "When was the place closed?" he asked.

"Shortly after the death of Lord Blake's first wife in 1790. He named the mine for her. It was called Wheal Angela. But although it had brought great profits at first, eventually the veins of tin petered out."

"I find it strange it was just left there. Surely it's dangerous to have all those shafts open to the sky."

"As it turned out, it was fatal. Seventeen years later, Lord Blake's two young sons by his second wife came to grief here. They were having a horse race to the shore and both of them tumbled down the same shaft. They died in the fall;

the horses had to be shot. But nothing was done after that. I believe Lord Blake was devastated by their deaths; perhaps he was incapable of acting decisively."

"Did you have a particular destination in mind today, m'lady?" Powell asked, looking around.

I didn't hesitate. "I thought to ride as far as Marghas. It's a pleasant little village and a complete change from Trecarag."

"By all means let's go there then, and make a day of it," he said promptly. "I'm sure we could both use a complete change.

"Shall we ride on, ma'am?"

Chapter 16

As we set off, I didn't trust myself to reply to his last remark. Mr. Powell seemed different today — more open, easier somehow. I glanced sideways at him as we cantered along. Yes, I had not been mistaken. He looked as if he were about to smile, and as I knew, his smiles were hard-won. I would have smiled in response until I remembered he was probably only gloating, for by capturing me alone, he had put one over on the viscount.

By unspoken consent, we reined in at the cliffs. The beach stretched out below us, at low tide a long gray-brown stretch of sand. Overhead, gulls floated effortlessly on their white wings. Far out, I could see part of Trecarag's fishing fleet hard at work. I drew a deep breath of the cool, briny air.

It took an hour to reach Marghas, and we saw few people on the way, certainly none who resembled Jaspar Hayes. There was no inn in the village, but I knew of a woman there who would be glad to let us stable our horses in her shed, even prepare a meal for us if we wanted one. I led the way to her cottage.

"Why is the place called Marghas?" Powell

asked as we took the horses to the shed. "A strange name, that."

"It's Cornish for market. None speak the old tongue anymore, but place names remain. In the early days this was probably a meeting place for farmers and fishermen to trade their crops and catch. There's more than the harbor you saw, there's an estuary, as well as a busy cross-roads."

"Do you know many Cornish words?" he asked as he lifted the saddle from my horse.

I shook my head, wondering how long Mr. Powell intended to remain here. "Only a few. A ryn is a hillside, porth a bay. And of course Trecarag means homestead on a rock."

"Forget Trecarag," he said almost harshly. I must have looked startled for he added, "At least while we're here. In fact, let's pretend it does not exist, shall we?"

I was only too glad to agree, and I nodded as I took his arm and we set off down the Front to see the sights. We stopped to inspect shop windows and to admire the slate-roofed cottages, each with their neat square of yard filled with flowers, the vegetable gardens and sheds behind.

When we reached the church of St. Mary's we went inside to admire it as well. Like many old churches, it had a distinctive smell of cold stone, burnt incense, and the ever-present damp. Dust motes floated in the light from the stained glass windows, all brilliant blue and gold and red. Powell seemed intrigued by the richly carved ends of the pews with their strange depictions of fabulous birds, animals, and people. The altar held the church's pride and glory, an ancient Flemish triptych of the Annunciation.

To my surprise, Gareth Powell bowed and entered a front pew where he bent his head over his clasped hands in prayer for a moment. I wanted to join him, but the only thing I could think of to pray for was to be spared Jaspar Hayes, and to even think his name in this holy place was a desecration.

There was no one in the church but ourselves, and we took our time inspecting every apse and nave, every old brass burial plaque.

Outside at last, Powell led me toward the graveyard on one side of the church. Many of the older stones had fallen over, and some were so covered with moss and lichen it was hard to make out the faint inscriptions. Still, Powell bent to study one, gently scraping the vegetation away with a small stone. When he was finished, he said quietly, "Look here, Lucy."

Obediently I bent closer. Under a woman's name and the dates 1585–1634, there was an inscription.

"Sleep here awhile, Thou dearest part of me," I read aloud softly. "In little time I'll come and sleep with thee."

We did not speak. My throat was tight with the unshed tears those tender words invoked. Surely a husband had composed them for a beloved wife and I marveled at such love. His gravestone stood beside hers. He had died only a year later, in 1635.

The verse — the church itself — had made me pensive and I said nothing more until we reached the banks of the estuary. There was a stone wall there and we sat down to study the scene before us. Nearby on the muddy banks two little boys were busy digging a channel to the river's edge. They were almost completely covered with mud. I hoped their mothers would not be too harsh with them. Out in the stream, three sailboats drifted with the tide, the skippers exchanging greetings. On the other side, a man sat as if made of stone, a fishing pole motionless in his hands. Over this scene the black and white oyster catchers dipped and darted, sounding their quick, seeping cry. It was so peaceful, I felt my eyes grow heavy, and afraid I might fall into a doze and end up with my head on Powell's shoulder, I said, "Are you hungry, sir? Mrs. Barrows would be glad to provide a meal."

He smiled down at me. I was startled by the intimacy of that smile. "But that's not necessary," he said lightly. "I've come prepared. I saw a pleasant place on our ride here. Shall we go there and eat?"

I nodded, although I wondered when he had accomplished everything. Last evening after dinner when I had sent a message to the stables?

While Powell saddled the horses, I chatted with our hostess and paid her as I had done in the past.

236

At last we were mounted and headed for home. No, not home, I reminded myself as we cantered north along the shore road. I felt bleak when I realized I had no home anymore, hadn't had one for some time in fact.

The place Gareth Powell had chosen was on a stretch of beach easily reached on horseback. We tied the horses to a branch of a stunted tree, and Powell put his saddlebags over one arm. As we walked over the towans, that bit of wasteland between the sea and the earth with its mixture of sand and sea rush, he said, "I've no blanket for you to sit on, Lucy. I hope you don't mind."

I smiled as I settled down on the warm sand. "I don't need one, sir. But what do you have in those saddlebags? I admit I'm ravenous."

Proudly he spread out his feast. There was a stone bottle of lemonade, still cold, and some fruit and cake, as well as two fat pasties. At least I assumed they were pasties, for they were much the worse for wear. Powell's face darkened when he saw they had been crushed, and now the meat and gravy were oozing from the crust.

I laughed as I took one from his hand. "Don't fuss! It looks fine, and this is a picnic, remember? Mmmm. Try yours. It's good."

He joined me then on the sand and we made short work of the food. Satiated, I sighed and stretch out full length. "Do we have to leave now, Gareth?" I asked, my eyes closed against the glare of the afternoon sun. "I'm so sleepy."

I wondered his voice should sound so constricted as he replied, "No, there's time. Sleep if you wish."

I needed no further urging. Lulled by the sound of the waves breaking on the shore, the harsh cry of distant gulls and the warmth of the sand at my back and the sun on my face, I began to doze. Just before I slept, I realized how safe I felt in this man's company. Hayes could not touch me while I was with him.

I have no idea what woke me later, but suddenly I opened my eyes to see him leaning over me, studying my face. I could only stare in return. "Lucy," he said, his voice a caress. I remembered Alicia saying he only waited for my encouragement before he showed me his love and something I had no control over wanted to believe she was right. I held out my hand to him — smiled.

Somehow I wasn't surprised when Powell did not take me in his arms and kiss me. I hadn't believed Alicia any more than I had the dowager duchess that he was mad for me. But I was surprised when he reached through the slit of my habit skirt and removed the pistol I carried in one of my pockets.

As he inspected it he said, "I suppose you can fire this? And hit something when you do? Er, something you were aiming at?" I sat up, disconcerted and flustered at the liberty he had taken.

"Of course I can," I said indignantly as I smoothed my skirt. "I wouldn't carry it, else."

"At least it's been cleaned and well oiled, and

it's loaded," he went on, almost to himself.

I took the pistol from his hand. Holding it to one side, I scrambled to my feet. "Choose a target, sir," I said. "I'll be happy to show you my skill."

He looked around. "Do you see that pile of stones over there? The darker one near the top? Hit it, if you can."

I took my time. It had been a while since I had done any shooting, and although I knew my pistol well, I was on my mettle here. At last I squeezed the trigger as I had been taught. There was the usual loud retort. Behind me, I could hear our horses neigh in fright.

We had to walk up to the stones to see how I had done. To my disgust, I hadn't hit the darker stone, but the one next to it. When I shook my head, Powell chuckled. "Don't be too hard on yourself, my girl," he said. "A man is bigger than a stone. You would have hit him all right."

I felt a little happier then until he said as we walked back to pick up the remains of our picnic, "It only remains to be seen whether you can fire if the man should become a reality. Shooting at a human being is different from target practice."

I was not even tempted to make a quick retort. Instead, as I knelt beside him I thought carefully. It was all very well to tell myself I would be able to shoot Jaspar Hayes. Heaven knew his death would remove a terrible burden — free me to begin some sort of life again. But could I shoot him? Actually pull the trigger deliberately to accomplish that end?

239

"I don't know," I said as I took the hand offered. On my feet I gave Gareth the paper our pasties had been wrapped in and said, "I would like to think I could, but I'm not at all sure. To be truthful, I hope it wouldn't come to that."

"Would you be able to fire if he were threatening someone you loved — the dowager, or Mrs. Grey, for example?"

I didn't have to think about that. "Yes," I said firmly. "In a moment."

"Good girl," he said. For some reason my spirits rose although I knew how bad it was to feel elated, complimented on such a regrettable act.

Walking back to the horses, I said, "Does your questioning me about all this mean you believe Hayes might be coming here, even as I do?"

He looked away from me for a moment to study the sky. The sun had disappeared behind a bank of high, thin clouds and suddenly the air had a bite to it that foretold autumn. "Like you, I feel we've tarried here too long," he said at last and I swallowed. "It's entirely possible Hayes has discovered your whereabouts by now. All we can do is hope we have some time left. The doctor thinks the duchess will be able to travel in another week. I've a man looking into ships bound for London from either Fowey or Plymouth."

"I'm glad," I said, not a bit perturbed he had taken such arrangements into his own hands.

As he tossed me into the saddle, he said, "Where will you go from here?"

I mentioned my tentative plan to visit Bermuda. As I did so, I wondered why the ease I had felt only moments before had disappeared.

He looked up at me, his gaze considering. I found it strange, looking down into his stern face with those dark brows and serious eyes.

"Lucy," he said.

I waited, but when he did not continue, I bent toward him a little. "Yes?" I said, my voice a question.

He shrugged. "Nothing," he said. "Just 'Lucy.'"

I stared at him as he untied the horses, mounted, and led the way back to the road as if anxious now to be gone. I wondered about it all the way back to Trecarag.

As we drew abreast of the old mine, I began to worry about Viscount Epstead's reaction to my being absent most of the day, and in Gareth Powell's company, too. With some trepidation I stared ahead to where Trecarag Hall waited for me, standing solid against the sky, the high tower an exclamation point at one end. Behind it, the lonely moor ran unchecked in undulating waves to the horizon. I was sorry my day of freedom was over, sorrier I had to return. As for Bradford Grey, even though he had no control over me, that would not stop him from assuming he did. I just knew he was going to be unpleasant.

I was right. He came from the library as I walked into the house, intent on pulling my leather gloves from my hands. As I caught sight of his face, I was glad Gareth had taken the horses on to the stables alone.

"There you are at last, m'lady," Epstead said. "Dare I hope you might spare me a few moments?"

"Of course, m'lord," I said, ignoring his sarcasm. "The dowager is well? There are no problems?"

He waved a careless hand as he closed the library door firmly behind us. "The dowager is fine," he said, his voice barely concealing his rage. "Where have you been?" he demanded. "Where did you go all day, and with Powell, too?"

"For a long ride," I admitted before I remembered I did not have to answer to him. "I see I must remind you once again, where I go and with whom is not your concern. No," I added, raising my hand, "let me finish. It will never be your concern."

I saw him clench his fists, saw his handsome face grow cold, and I was sorry. But whether I was sorry I had spoken so sharply or sorry he refused to understand me, I could not have said.

"So, he's asked you to marry him, has he? What did you say?" he demanded, grasping my shoulders.

I was shocked. "No such thing," I said quickly. I shrugged away his hands and walked past him to the windows. There was no sign of Gareth coming up from the stables, and for that I was grateful. Taking a deep breath, I turned to face

Epstead again. "I am not going to marry anyone, and I'm getting very tired of telling you so. Can't you just leave it, sir?"

He came to me then, and my heart sank when I saw he was smiling. "No, I can't let it go, Lucy. Not ever. You see I want you, and surely by now you've discovered I always get what I want."

"You won't this time," I said wearily as I removed my riding hat and tossed it on a sofa. Sitting down beside it, I wished I might go to my room — call for a bath — rest.

Epstead poured me a glass of sherry and I was forced to accept it. As he sat down across from me, I remembered something. Not at all loath to change the subject, I said, "Do you know, you've never told me why you and Mr. Powell don't like each other and you promised you would some-day."

"So I did," he agreed. I was listening carefully, but I could detect nothing in his tone but boredom with the subject I had chosen. "Some years ago, a young relative of Powell's came to London for the Season. She misinterpreted some little attentions of mine, made a fuss about them in fact. Powell took exception, but he must have known it was all in the chit's imagination, for he went abroad soon afterwards. He broods about the slight to his family name still. Silly of him, isn't it?"

"What happened to her, do you know?" I asked.

He shrugged. "I've no idea. I imagine she married eventually. She was a pretty little piece. But not, you understand, outstanding enough to become the viscountess she had hoped."

I put my glass down and gathered up my belongings. Epstead rose leisurely as I did. "You'll excuse me, I'm sure, m'lord," I said evenly. "I must bathe and change before going to the dowager."

He smiled — a lazy, knowing smile. "And I shall greatly enjoy picturing you doing so," he said as he took my hand and squeezed it. "Bathing, you know. Not seeing the dowager."

I did not smile as I freed myself and left him.

The foyer was empty as I crossed it, indeed, I couldn't hear a sound from any part of the Hall. It was almost as if everyone had disappeared and left me alone with Viscount Epstead. I was berating myself for such a silly thought when the housekeeper came through the baize covered door at the back of the foyer and asked if she might speak to me.

I did not know this Mrs. Langley well of course, for Mr. Kittering had hired her. However, our dealings since my arrival had been conducted to my complete satisfaction. The woman knew her job. The household and the servants were in good order so I smiled as I indicated a sitting room nearby.

"There's no need, m'lady. What I have to say won't take long," she said, standing very stiffly with her shoulders back. She had always reminded me of a fierce sergeant major. She did so now.

"Yes?" I said to encourage her when she seemed lost for words. It was then I noticed her hands were twisted in her apron, and I felt a shiver of apprehension.

"At first I thought everyone must be mistaken, but I don't think that anymore," she began, her eyes never leaving mine. "Someone's been in the Hall, ma'am. Yes, and more than once, too."

So, Hayes was here, I thought bleakly. He had found me and I was not to be granted another week to make good my escape. "How do you know?" I asked, stalling in order to compose myself.

"Telltale things really. The cooks have mentioned a quantity of food missing, and the maids speak of things that have been disarranged. For example, Agnes — she's one of the downstairs maids — says that every morning when she goes to do the drawing room she finds things out of place. An ornament moved from a table to the mantel, chairs shifted. This morning there was an old shawl draped over the big wing chair by the fireplace. I never saw that shawl before. None of the servants have.

"I don't believe in ghosts, m'lady. Certainly not ghosts that steal food. But that means someone real is getting in somehow and doing all these things."

I put both hands to my forehead and closed my eyes. It had to be Lord Blake's shawl. He had often spread it over his legs in the evenings when he began to feel a chill. I wondered where Hayes was hiding. We had inspected the Hall thoroughly only yesterday and I had seen no sign of him. A little cough reminded me the housekeeper was waiting and I thought quickly.

"I shall investigate, Mrs. Langley. I believe you are a Londoner?"

As she nodded, I went on, "It well might be one of the former Cornish servants. The Cornish are noted for holding a grudge, and I know there was bad feeling when they were dismissed four years ago. This is only a childish trick; still, trespassing cannot be allowed. I'm sure we'll soon get to the bottom of it."

Mrs. Langley looked slightly more cheerful as she curtsied. As I went upstairs, I felt in my pocket for my pistol. Before I called Franklin for my bath, and questioned her about the intruder, I intended to clean and reload it. And sometime tonight I must warn Gareth — the viscount and Alicia as well — that Hayes was here. I only hoped it would be possible to keep the news from reaching the dowager's ears.

In my room at last, it did not make me feel a bit better to discover a dusty book of sermons from the library had been laid on my bed. It had been opened to one titled, "A Treatise on Wifely Obedience." When I looked up and caught a glimpse of myself in the pier glass, I saw my face was ashen.

Chapter 17

As I bathed, I told Franklin what I had learned. Although she had seen no sign of Hayes herself, she had learned of him today from Mrs. Langley. I did not mention the book of sermons. How could I without going into detailed explanations?

"We'll have to be sure the dowager doesn't learn he's come here," I said as I poured a copper can of clean water over me to wash off the soap.

"You're right, m'lady. It's too bad that maid of hers has a tongue that wags on both ends. She'll never be able to keep it from Her Grace — never."

"What do you suggest, Franklin?" I asked as I stepped from the tub and took the heated towel she held out.

"Maybe we could persuade her she's as sick as her mistress," Franklin said promptly. "Mathilda fancies herself quite the invalid, and believes she has what Her Grace suffers. She's been talking about her poor heart for days now."

"Of course. We'll convince her she must keep to her bed, tell her one of the other maids will take care of the dowager."

"That had better be me, m'lady. She won't do

it, else. Trusts me she does, because she knows me better."

"I hate to ask it of you," I said as I dried myself.

"It's nothing, m'lady. There's little enough for me to do, here in the country," Franklin said calmly as she took the towel and handed me my shift.

When Mathilda came in in answer to my summons, I begged her to sit down. I told her I was worried about her health, but she would not consent to take to her bed until I mentioned how much Faith Abbott depended on her.

"Yes, and she has told me you're as dear as any sister to her," I said to the simpering, elderly maid, hoping I wasn't overdoing the flattery. "I'm sure it would be fatal if anything happened to you. Franklin can maid Her Grace while you have a few, well-earned days in bed. Now, which maid would you prefer wait on you?"

It was the mention of this last luxury that toppled Mathilda's defenses. In half an hour she was tucked up in a spare bedroom at the end of the hall, the upstairs maid at her beck and call.

When I went to see the dowager, I explained Mathilda's absence with all my best lies.

"I knew she was feeling pulled, but I did not suspect she was in such bad twig," Faith Abbott said with a frown. She was sitting near the window reading, a silk throw over her knees. "You're sure she will be all right?"

"The doctor will check on her tomorrow,

ma'am. She's asleep now. My Franklin will see to everything you need."

The dowager admitted she preferred Franklin's ministrations, but felt so guilty when she did so, she could not enjoy the experience. We both laughed.

Content I had solved one problem at least, I went down to dinner. I knew I would have to wait until later to speak to the others. I don't think I have ever been so impatient. It seemed an age before I was able to rise from the table and invite the gentlemen to have their port in the drawing room as was now the custom.

It only took me a few minutes to apprise Alicia and the men of Hayes's arrival, and what I had done so far.

"So, he's traced you here, has he?" Epstead said, rising to pace the room with quick, nervous steps. "Determined chap, ain't he? I wonder how he got in?"

"I've no idea, but since he used to live here, he must know every nook and cranny. He probably even has a key," I added glumly. "Besides, there are times — why, this afternoon after I left you, sir, there was no one at all in the foyer. Anyone could have walked right in the front door unnoticed, for all the servants were either at their supper or busy elsewhere."

"Don't you suppose he must still be in the Hall?" Alicia asked, looking around the drawing room as if she expected Hayes to pop out from behind one of the sofas. "We are so isolated here."

"He could be in the stables or one of the other outbuildings," I said.

"Or perhaps in that ruined French chapel," the viscount contributed. "Since he's been stealing food, we can assume no one nearby is harboring him."

"Perhaps he's down a mine shaft," Gareth Powell said, speaking for the first time. He sounded sarcastic and I wondered at it.

"Before we allow our fancies full-flight here, let's remember we are only dealing with a man. One man, and there are four of us," Powell went on. "Hayes must reveal himself sooner or later. It's Lucy he wants. He'll come for her. We'll have him then."

I shuddered. "How reassuring," I murmured.

"Perhaps if one of us was with you at all times, he wouldn't dare try anything," Alicia suggested.

Both men frowned. "Yes, but that will only delay the inevitable," Epstead said. "Lucy must face the man sometime. Why not get it over as quickly as possible?"

They began to argue the situation, and I let my mind wander. Yes, Hayes was here. How was I to keep him from revealing everything I had kept secret for so long? It occurred to me it was to his advantage to keep that secret, too, for if he divulged it, he would have no further hold over me. That made me feel better. No, I told myself, he would not dare speak out. To do so would be to admit his own background and dastardly behavior and he would be scorned. I knew he would do anything to avoid scorn.

As the level of the port in the decanter sank lower, Bradford Grey invented wilder and wilder schemes to dispatch Hayes. I wished he would not drink so heavily. He would be of no use against a man as sober and determined as Hayes.

"May I suggest we lock our doors when we go to bed?" I said. "My maid stays with the dowager tonight, and she intends to lock them both in."

"You don't care for my scheme to set the grooms and gardeners to patrolling the halls?" the viscount asked. He sounded disappointed.

"The less the servants know the better," I replied.

I found myself avoiding looking at Gareth Powell. I sensed he was studying my face. He had done so at intervals throughout the evening, and I found it unsettling. What was he thinking now? I wondered.

We lingered in the drawing room long after the tea tray made an appearance. I knew I remained because I did not want to have to face my room alone, for even locked in, I wouldn't feel safe there.

I had not mentioned the book of sermons, so the others were not aware Hayes knew the location of my room. How could I possibly explain it, or the reason it had been left there?

Hayes was showing his usual cunning. He was toying with me, slyly planning every move he could to disconcert me and punish me for banishing him as I had banished the servants here four years ago. Yes, he wanted me as he wanted Trecarag, but not as desperately as he wanted to make me pay for every iniquity, every slight, every little bit of pain he had suffered from birth. That such a thing was unreasonable did not matter to him. He was not sane, not where his rights and Trecarag were concerned.

Alicia and I finally went up to bed together. I went to wish the dowager good night, and as I left her I whispered to Franklin to lock the door after me. With my candle held high, I went down the hall to see how Mathilda did. I knew only a great deal of attention would keep her playing the invalid, and indeed, she was already fretting because she was not with Faith Abbott. It took me a long time to reassure her that Franklin had things well in hand, and of course I would go back immediately and instruct her on the way Her Grace preferred to have her hair braided for the night.

I felt weary when I locked the door to my room and put my pistol in the drawer of the table beside the bed. The long ride and the fresh air, to say nothing of the fright I had had since had exhausted me. I undressed quickly, clumsy with the fastenings of my gown by myself. The last thing I did after washing and cleaning my teeth was to check the door to the hall to make sure it was locked.

To my horror, the door opened easily when I tried it. Gasping, I whirled and pressed my back against it, my eyes darting from one shadowy corner of the room to another. Hayes had to be here somewhere. Where was he? Did I have time to get my pistol? I tried to still my fast-beating heart long enough to listen for another's breathing, but that was impossible. It thundered in my chest.

"All right," I said, my voice shaking. "I know you're here. Come out."

"Not if you're holding your pistol," a deep voice said from the direction of the bed. "I'd rather not be shot."

"Gareth?" I squeaked, feeling weak with relief. "What on earth do you think you're doing?"

He rolled out from under the bed and got up to brush himself off. He had only removed his evening coat, I noted.

"I'm here to watch over you, of course. I'd hoped you wouldn't notice the door was unlocked. I begged the key from the housekeeper earlier," he added when he saw the question in my eyes. "If Hayes is coming anywhere, he's coming here. I thought unlocking the door would make it easier for him."

Stunned, I watched him sit down in a chair by the window. The one candle that still burned cast strange wavering shadows on the walls, and only lit parts of his face. It made him look dark, threatening. Slowly, I pushed myself away from the door and moved to the center of the room.

"You can't stay here," I whispered. "What will everyone think?"

"Everyone won't know," he added, speaking as softly as I had. "Your maid is locked in with the dowager, the others have gone to bed. Epstead might, in a self-serving moment, consider coming to guard you, but I rather think the amount of port he consumed this evening will forestall that. I'll leave around dawn. No one will see me, Lucy. Your reputation will be quite safe. Oh, except for Mrs. Langley, but she's thought I was your lover ever since we arrived. You see, I asked for the key then. Fortunately she's a Londoner. You're a young widow. She doesn't think a lover a bit out of the ordinary, so don't fret.

"Why don't you get in bed? You must be tired."

Stunned, I stared at him. It was only when I remembered how revealing my lawn night rail was that I hurried to get under the covers. I saw Gareth was watching me and I remembered that hot night by the stream at Water House and how I had felt someone's eyes on me. The image was fleeting. Other, more pressing problems intruded.

"What are you going to do?" I asked, the coverlet clutched to my breast. "You can't sit up in a chair all night."

"Yes, I can," he said, stretching out his long legs before him as if to show me how comfortable he would be. "Don't worry about me. I have my pistol.

"May I suggest you don't attempt to use yours, no matter what happens? One man looks much like another in the dark and you're too good a shot."

"All right," I said. I felt a quiver of nerves as he rose and came to stand beside the bed, looking down at me.

"Come now, time for bed, Lucy," he said. It never occurred to me to disobey him. He took the coverlet from my hands and tucked it under my chin. I stared at him until his fingers closed my eyelids and trailed down my cheeks.

"Hayes won't hurt you," he said. "I won't let him."

Before he moved away he bent and kissed me — my eyes, my cheek, and finally my lips. I know I didn't imagine those fleeting whispers of sensation.

After he left me, I lay still for a long time, trying to breathe deeply, trying to stifle my fears of a confrontation with Hayes.

"Go to sleep, Lucy." Gareth's voice came from the depths of the chair he had gone back to. Only then did I sigh, turn on my side, and fall at once into a deep, dreamless slumber.

Hayes did not come that night. When I woke to the sound of birdsong at first light, the chair by the window was empty. Only the indented chair cushion showed where Gareth had been. I climbed out of bed and padded to the door. He had locked it behind him, and I smiled as I went back to bed again, hoping he was sleeping now, too.

When I went down to breakfast later, I discovered both the Greys waiting for me. I thought Alicia seemed uncomfortable while the viscount had an unusually determined air about him this morning. As I filled my plate with shirred eggs, a slice of ham, and a small piece of apple tart, I pretended nothing was wrong. But as I took my seat and poured some cream into my coffee, I said, "Come now, what is it? I'd have to be blind not to see something's afoot. Why, you've even dismissed the servants. Alicia?"

A flush stained her cheekbones, but she didn't look away. "Very well, Lucy. Brad and I have talked and we've decided that we've all been held hostage for far too long by this Jaspar Hayes. As have you, my dear. We can't for the life of us think why. Who is this man that he can threaten you with such impunity? Why have you run from him when you should have had the Bow Street Runners after him months ago? I'm your friend. Surely you can tell me, can't you?"

Throughout her speech, I had sat numbly, and I did not attempt to deny anything she said. Her brother-in-law began to speak to me then, putting forth his arguments as to why Hayes must be dealt with, and dealt with now. In the midst of his lecture, Gareth came in. He looked at all of us, but to my great disappointment he did not intervene, not even after I sent him the most pleading look, too.

"Well, Lucy?" Epstead said firmly. "What have you to tell us? Come, you must see we cannot help you if you are not more open with us."

I put my napkin down carefully beside my untouched plate and rose. My knees were trembling and I had to grasp the edge of the table for support. "I'm sure you have only my best interests at heart," I began. Alicia's face cleared a little. "I appreciate it. Indeed, I have appreciated all your help. But I've a very good reason for my reticence and I cannot reveal it. Perhaps it would be better for you to return to London and leave me to deal with the situation. Yes, I think that would be the best thing —"

"Don't be an idiot!" Epstead snapped. "Leave you to deal with a maniac alone? You must think us loose screws!"

"I didn't ask you to come here," I said lashing out at him, as I lost my temper at last. "I wish you would go away!"

"Lucy, dear, please don't say things you will later regret," Alicia reminded me. "You're upset. We're all upset but we're in this together."

"Sit down, Lucy," Gareth Powell said in his deep voice. "Eat your breakfast. You should have told the Greys how you hate confrontations first thing in the morning."

His calm reasonableness was the last straw. Pushing back my chair I ran to the door. I didn't mean to slam it, honestly, I didn't. It just slipped from my hand.

Once in my room, I changed quickly to my habit. Making sure I had my pistol as well as my crop and gloves, I hurried to the stables. It seemed to take a very long time before the groom had saddled a horse for me and I was able to trot through the archway that led to the drive.

For a while I rode aimlessly. Strange, I gave no thought to Jaspar Hayes. It never even occurred to me he might find me out here alone. I was in such mental turmoil I did not think of the danger. Part of me knew my friends were right. Hayes must be dealt with. But part of me hated them for forcing me into a corner and demanding I tell them the truth. Surely it was my life and my secret, wasn't it? I asked myself childishly. My secret, to keep if I wished?

At last, when the mare I was riding stumbled, I slowed to a trot, and then a walk to rest her. Wheal Angela lay behind me. I had not even been aware of it in my fury and confusion. For a moment it occurred to me that if I'd fallen down one of the shafts, my problems would be over. Then I scolded myself for being so stupidly dramatic. I did not want to die. I had no intention of dying.

I could not judge what time it was when I turned back. It was a gray day. The wind had come up, too, blowing from the ocean and bringing with it the familiar damp, briny mist that was such a part of life in Cornwall.

I felt exhausted, beyond feeling, and I had no idea what I was to do next. All around me lay Trecarag, the symbol of everything that was evil in my life. If it had not been for Trecarag, or the Blakes, or Hayes . . . but there was no sense in crying over spilt milk, as my nanny used to tell me when I was a little girl.

As I watched the mist creeping toward the Hall, I saw three ravens circling the roof and the tower, calling to each other as they flew. I remembered another old saying then, this one Cornish, that ravens crying over a house meant bad luck for someone in it. Very bad luck.

Chapter 18

There was a note waiting for me in my room. Franklin was there as well. She did not question me about my unexpected absence, she merely spoke casually about the dowager's health and state of mind. Excellent Franklin! Truly I had been blessed when I acquired her for my maid. When she curtsied and left me to return to the dowager, I opened the note.

I knew it was from Hayes. I had recognized the handwriting. Strangely I felt no terror now, only a numb resignation to whatever was going to happen. The message was brief and to the point. It summoned me to Lord Blake's bedroom in the tower at one that same afternoon. I looked at the clock on the mantel. It was almost one now. I was glad of that. The less time I had to think about this, the better. I checked my pistol even though I knew it was loaded, and slipped it in my reticule before I let myself softly out the door. I was not tempted to call on Faith Abbott as I passed her room. I hoped I wouldn't meet anyone, in fact I positively scurried by Epstead's bedroom door and Gareth Powell's opposite. This was my time alone, to do what I had to do — handle the situation myself. I would plead with Hayes if need be, promise him half Trecarag's wealth, give him anything he wanted that was in my power to give. If that wasn't enough, well, I would have to see. The pistol in the reticule that dangled from my wrist was a constant reminder I had another way.

The tower was quiet when I entered the room that had once been mine and closed the hall door behind me. For a moment I listened carefully, but there wasn't a sound. Picking up my skirts, I started down the stairs to Lord Blake's room, as I had been instructed. Halfway down the flight, I stopped in surprise. Alicia was there seated by the window, Epstead as well, standing behind her chair. Gareth Powell leaned against the mantel over by the hearth. My hand went to my throat.

"What are you all doing here?" I demanded. "Who told you of this meeting?"

"I did, m'lady," Hayes said behind me. I had not heard him coming down the stairs. His right arm imprisoned my waist to hold me close to him. He held one of Lord Blake's dueling pistols in his other hand. I remembered he was left-handed.

"Once I thought it best no one know who I am, but now I see it doesn't matter," he said in a chatty easy way as he forced me down the stairs before him. "M'lord, if you'd be so good as to put that pistol you carry on the center table? And you, sir," he added, gesturing to Gareth, "I'll have yours as well."

When neither man moved, his arm tightened cruelly and I gasped in spite of myself.

"I'd remind you, fine sirs, Lady Blake is at my mercy. If you care for her — and I know you do, both of you — you'll do as I say. Otherwise I'll hurt her."

Gareth did not hesitate. "Put the gun on the table, Brad," Alicia ordered her brother-in-law when he did not move as quickly.

"Now that's more like it," Hayes said, his tone of voice an obscenity. He made me walk before him to the table, and pushed me into a chair there before he pocketed both guns.

As he did so, I was able to see him for the first time. He had obviously dressed very carefully for this confrontation. He wore a coat of the best blue superfine, spotless linen, and tight-fitting pantaloons. But his lapels and the brass buttons on his coat were too large, his cravat too elaborate, and his waistcoat far too florid — they all proclaimed him a failure as the gentleman of taste and discernment he longed to be.

You are wondering how I felt? Only numb. Yes, I was aware the moment when everything I had worked so hard to conceal was about to be laid open for the world's perusal, but strangely it didn't matter. I was so tired of subterfuge. So tired of running and being afraid. Now I felt as if I did not even inhabit my body anymore but rather floated in a disinterested way above the others, high among the dusty rafters.

"No questions?" Hayes sneered as he looked

from one to the other of my friends. He ignored me. He was not playing to me, after all, but to this new audience he had acquired. That didn't matter either.

"Well, I'll tell you, since you're too nice to inquire. I'm your Lady Blake's lover. Now, what do you think of that?"

He paused for a moment and looked around triumphantly. I did not even bother to look at the others although I heard Epstead mutter something and move impulsively.

Hayes leveled his pistol at him. "Nay, my fine lord," he said, hurrying over his words, he was so anxious to tell them everything. "Stay where you are, sir. Lucy don't need you to protect her good name. Besides, I spoke the truth.

"Didn't I, Lucy? Didn't I?"

I sat there, staring down at my clasped hands. There was a dent in the table right by my little finger, and a white circular stain as if someone had spilled wine there. By rights, the table should have been refinished long before, but Lord Blake didn't care about things like —

Hayes grabbed my chin and forced it up and I had to look into his gloating eyes. "Tell them, m'lady. Admit I've been your lover right there in Lord Blake's own bed. Do it, if you know what's good fer ye!"

He released me and I drew a careful, shallow breath. "Yes," I said, surprised my voice was so even. "Yes, it's true what he said."

Alicia gasped and the viscount stifled an oath.

Only Gareth Powell made no sound at all. I looked up then and inspected them one after the other. Alicia was pale and her eyes were full of tears, but she did not look as if she hated me. I had expected her to hate me. Gareth Powell still leaned against the mantel, his eyes steady on my face. As always, I could read nothing from his expression. Hayes might have been discussing the weather for all he appeared affected. But Bradford Grey more than made up for their forbearance. He had tried to school his features, but he could not hide the revulsion he felt. It was there in the twist of his mouth, the drooping eyelids that could not conceal the scorn in his eyes. I studied him well. It was to prevent this kind of reaction I had pretended all this time. And now? Well, now I found it didn't matter what he or anyone thought of me. How very strange.

"I've come back, I have, to get Lucy and claim Trecarag," Hayes continued, forcing me to concentrate. "I'm not some nobody, y'know. I'm Lord Blake's son. And ever since his other two sons had that accident and fell down the mine shaft, I'm his only living heir."

"Of course!" a new voice exclaimed and we all turned to see Faith Abbott entering the room from the hall of the main building. She was dressed and leaning on a cane, which she raised now and pointed at Jaspar Hayes. "I was sure I knew you from somewhere when I saw you watching Lucy's town house in Portman Square. It's the nose of course. It's just like Harrison

264

Blake's, 'pon my soul it is."

Hayes beamed at her. "I'm left-handed too, like he was," he confided.

The dowager pointed to his legs and said, "Be thankful you didn't inherit his bow legs as well. And may we hope you've been spared that truly awful bray he called a laugh?"

Hayes looked confused, and I remembered again how hard he found it to handle more than one simple thought at a time. Still, he recovered quickly enough.

"Please sit down, Your Grace," he said, bowing deeply. "I'm sure I'm sorry I didn't invite you to the party. I thought you were too ill."

"I am very well," Faith Abbott said as she took the chair he indicated. "And I certainly wasn't so sick I didn't know something unusual was going on. But do continue, er, *Hayes,* I believe you are called?"

In spite of my detachment, I cannot tell you how much I admired the Dowager Duchess of Lansmere then. The breeding of centuries was in her voice, her manner. And that one simple query of hers had the power to put Jaspar Hayes firmly in his place.

"Yes, well, it's true I'm not legal-like. I admit it," he blustered, his face growing red and his hands nervous on the pistol he seemed to have forgotten he held.

"I've never tried ter hide it," he lied. "But it don't matter. There ain't — *aren't* — no other heirs. I'm the only issue left. That's what *he* called me, he did, an issue. Trecarag should be mine an' I intend ter have it!"

"This grand estate go to a *bastard?*" Epstead said, speaking for the first time. "One moreover whose father did not even name him in his will as I am sure he named his butler and his valet? And may I remind you, Hayes, gentlemen may take their pleasure with the lower classes but they don't marry them, and their bye-blows can't inherit. The very idea, and you the son of a barmaid, no doubt."

"No, I wasn't a barmaid," my maid said calmly as she came forward from the doorway. Her hands were clasped over a spotless apron, her head was held high, and she was as neat as a pin.

She curtsied to the dowager. "You shouldn't be here, Your Grace," she said. "It will be too upsetting for you."

Faith Abbott only stared at her as hard as the rest of us were doing.

"Franklin?" I asked weakly. "You are Jaspar Hayes's mother?"

"I'm not Franklin, m'lady," she said. "That was my mother's maiden name. I am Sarah Hayes. Miss Sarah Hayes, as you so correctly divined, m'lord."

"Tell 'em, Mother!" Hayes urged. "Go on, tell 'em wot happened ter ye!"

She gave him the same considering look she had given the rest of us. "You mustn't get excited, Jaspar," she said. "You know it is bad for you when you get excited."

Turning back to me, she said, "I came to Trecarag with the second Lady Blake's sister. They were close and she was here to keep her sister company the first year of her marriage. Lord Blake seemed to prefer me to his new wife, especially after he got her with child. As you might expect, no one consulted me about the arrangement and I could hardly refuse him for I would have lost my place. But when Lord Blake discovered me in the same condition as his wife, I threatened him. He was frightened his wife might miscarry if she learned what he had been up to — his first wife had died childless. To keep me quiet, he was forced to buy me a cottage outside Marghas, and provide me with an income adequate for me and the child. I raised Jaspar there and saw he had the proper schooling. I never let him forget who his father was. I saw no reason he couldn't be a gentleman. You see, I was the only child of a poor clergyman who had some nobility on his family tree. Not that that did me a bit of good. When he died, I was forced to become a lady's maid to survive. But with my blood and m'lord Blake's, why shouldn't my son better himself?"

We all looked at Hayes. He was leaning forward, his mouth ajar as if he were hearing this tale for the first time. I wondered at the woman's ambition. Was it possible a mother's love had blinded her to the fact her son was deranged?

"He was not always this way," she said, as if she could hear my misgivings. "As a boy, he was quite normal."

267

"Here now, wot's all this?" Hayes demanded. "Are ye sayin' I'm not's good as any other gentleman, Mother?"

"Of course you are, Jaspar," she said, but she didn't smile at him. "Now go and sit down over there and be quiet for a bit. You're getting yourself worked up and all to no purpose. Besides, I want to finish my story. I always let you finish your stories, don't I?"

He nodded as he sat down on the edge of a chair. I noticed he chose one that gave him a clear view of everyone in the room. He might not have all his wits, but he was still canny. One leg jiggled incessantly as his mother spoke. I tried not to look at it.

"When Lord Blake died, my income stopped," the woman I would always think of as Franklin continued. "And, I admit, I was angry Lord Blake hadn't named Jaspar in his will. You were right, m'lord," she said, turning to Epstead, "he did remember his butler, his valet — all the servants. But his *son* — the son he had thought to use for his own purposes, no, he got nothing. Nothing."

Her voice had risen and I tried not to cringe back in my chair. Over to the side I could hear Hayes mutter, "Am not nothin'. Am not. Good as anyone, I am. Better, even."

"It was when Jaspar came and told me you had promised him money to leave you alone and never reveal what had been going on in the house, Lady Blake, that I decided to take a hand.

I learned of your plans to abandon Trecarag and go to London, and I knew when you let all the Trecarag servants go. So I leased my cottage and went to London myself. And although it took some doing, I managed to get you to engage me as your maid."

"However did you manage that?" Alicia asked. She sounded fascinated by the story. I could hardly blame her.

"Her former maid told me the name of the agency Lady Blake had used before. I went there and waited until she came."

"But you had references. Up-to-date references," I protested. "I wrote and asked your former employers about you."

She actually smiled as she said, "I wrote those references myself, ma'am. Remember, I was a clergyman's daughter and educated. I also replied to your queries. It wasn't difficult. I simply intercepted them when you gave them to me to post, waited the necessary time, and then replied in glowing terms. I knew you'd find me satisfactory. You did, didn't you?"

I did not answer. Instead, I said, "But why did you want to be my maid?"

"I was afraid the time would come when you would forget to send Jaspar the money, and we would both be destitute. And when I'm gone, who will look after him if he has no income? Under the circumstances, I saw no reason you shouldn't live at Trecarag with him. He's half a Blake, and you could leave the estate and income

269

to any children you might have together. A tidy solution."

"That's right," Hayes said eagerly. "That's what I want, too. I was her lover. What ter be again. Want Trecarag. Babies get money, right!"

"When did you decide all this was not feasible, Miss Hayes?" Gareth Powell's deep voice asked. For a moment, I was startled. Intent on the story, I had forgotten others were in the room.

For the first time she looked down, to avoid his eyes. "When I saw the things Jaspar was doing at the dower house at Lansmere, and later too, of course. I knew then it would be better if there were no children. He has changed these past four years. Changed considerably."

"What do ye mean?" Hayes demanded, rising to his feet so quickly his chair tumbled over. "Changed? I've not changed, Mother. I still want Lucy an' Trecarag, an' everythin'! Are ye sayin' I'm not com . . . comp . . ."

"Competent?" Bradford Grey asked as he walked forward. He put his hands on his hips and subjected Hayes to a slow, searing examination from head to toe.

I held my breath. Surely it was madness for Epstead to taunt the man when it was obvious he was not only deranged but armed as well.

"I don't think you're competent to muck out a stall," Epstead drawled. "As for being a gentleman, a monkey would make a better job of it."

I almost expected Hayes to cringe as he had so

270

often in the past when faced with criticism and forced to admit his station, but he did not do so. Instead, he raised the pistol he held and pointed it straight at the viscount. He had to use his other hand to steady it, he was shaking so.

"Don't ye call me no names," he panted. "I'm heir to Trecarag! Good as ye any day, I am!"

Before he could fire, Epstead coolly shot him with a small pistol he had concealed in the palm of his hand.

Hayes was right next to me. I swear I heard the dull thud the bullet made striking him. Horrified, I watched his face change to a look of surprise before he dropped the pistol he held. His right hand came up to cover the wound in his chest just before he crashed to the floor.

No one had tried to interfere. No one had cried a warning or even moved, not even Franklin. But now she went to her son and knelt beside him. She did not weep or cry out. She only took his hand in both of hers and held it with her head bowed. I looked at Epstead. He was pale but he was composed.

"Oh, Brad," Alicia said softly, "why did you do that? You teased him about the one thing he wanted most — to be a gentleman. And you knew he was deranged."

"Yes, I knew. I baited him deliberately because it was the best thing I could do," he answered quickly. "The man was a maniac, a danger to everyone he came in contact with. He would have been put away, and I've heard even death is preferable to Bedlam where the criminally insane are kept.

"Besides, there was that dastardly lie he told and forced Lucy to agree to. It was a lie, wasn't it, Lucy?"

I stared at him. He was offering me a chance to escape. All I had to do was say I had never slept with Jaspar Hayes. That his accusations were the rantings of a madman. No one would call me a liar for I was the only one alive who knew the truth. And the only people who had heard Hayes say he was my lover were here in this room. And Franklin was the only one of them all likely to try and make trouble. But I did not believe she would do so. She was fond of me. I knew that over the years we had been together, she had come to care for me. Now I knew she had worried about me when she saw her son's sanity slipping away from him as his obsession with Trecarag and with me gained control of his mind.

"It was a lie wasn't it, Lucy?" Epstead prompted. I could tell he was proud he had provided a way out of my difficulties for me. Not that he wanted to marry me anymore, for he didn't. Not now. I was as sure of that as I was of my own name. But he was a gentleman and I, no matter what horrid sins I had committed, was a lady. He would help me if he could. I wished I could have felt more gratitude.

"Lucy?" he repeated.

I shook my head, knowing I couldn't take the

easy road and turn my back on the truth. Not even to save myself and my reputation. Not when a man lay dead at my feet. "No," I managed to say. "No, all he said was true."

Bradford Grey stared at me, his face showing the disbelief he felt anew. I was sure he was not aware that he had stepped back slightly, as if I had suddenly become unclean somehow.

A hand gripped my shoulder. I knew it was Gareth without even turning my head to see. He at least did not condemn me for what had happened here four years ago.

There was no time for any more. The butler and two footmen arrived, concerned about the shot they had heard. Gareth took charge. He ordered a groom sent to fetch the nearest justice and told the butler no one was to enter this room until the justice had seen it before he ushered us all out and closed the door firmly behind us. I saw he was especially gentle with Sarah Hayes as he gave her into Alicia's care. The rest of us went down to the drawing room where the usual small fire was burning. I went to look out the window. The mist had thickened. It obliterated the landmarks and clung close to Trecarag's walls, as if to shield us all from the prying eyes and eager speculation that was sure to come.

Chapter 19

As Bradford Grey seated the dowager in a comfortable chair by the fire, I watched her carefully. She appeared to be holding up well. Still, she raised the snifter of brandy and water Gareth gave her with both hands and she took a healthy swallow. In contrast, I didn't feel I could summon the strength to lift the glass he handed me.

"We have considerable time before the justice will be here," Gareth remarked, taking his usual place before the hearth. "The fog's so thick he may not be able to come until tomorrow. That's in our favor. We'll have time to agree on our stories."

"Why should any story be necessary?" Faith Abbott asked sternly. "The man was insane. He was also a housebreaker and he was threatening us. Fortunately, the viscount was carrying his pistol and he shot him. Period."

"But what of the pistols Hayes took from us?" Gareth asked calmly. "He not only had his own, but two others. Why would he carry so many? And if we admit to ownership, how are we to explain why we felt it necessary to go armed at a private house party?"

The dowager shrugged. "Obviously you don't admit it," she said, sounding testy. "I suggest we continue to maintain the man was mad. No one can contradict us, not even his mother. And who knows why such people behave as they do?"

"But why would Hayes attempt to rob the house in the daylight when it was full of people coming and going? And why were we all in the old tower?" Gareth persisted.

"Surely none of this matters," Epstead said. He had been standing all this time. Now he threw himself down in a chair opposite Faith Abbott. I realized I had taken a chair a bit removed from this cozy circle of friends. By design? I wondered.

"The local justice will be no match for Her Grace, or for either of us, Powell," the viscount continued. "He's sure to be a simple country squire. He'll believe what we tell him. As for why we were in the tower, we were advising Lady Blake on decorating plans, since she wished to refurbish the rooms. A perfectly logical explanation considering their condition."

"You are forgetting the one aspect of this that we cannot control," Gareth persisted. "Hayes's mother. Surely she will not agree to any story that maligns her son. I doubt she will even admit he was mad. Remember, she saw you shoot him. She is sure to consider that murder."

The viscount stared at him, his eyes narrowing. I was reminded these two men did not like each other and had been at odds for years.

Faith Abbott must have remembered it as well, for she was quick to say, "We must buy her silence. I do not think it will be that difficult. Do you remember how she said she was angry that Lord Blake did not name Hayes in his will? How she sought revenge?"

"Of course!" Epstead said. "We'll see to it she has another cottage somewhere other than Cornwall, and an annuity. Nothing could be simpler. And I beg you to recall how she took her son's death. She did not weep or cry out. She was more than stoic; she was stony. It made me shiver, her indifference."

"I doubt the woman will take anything from your hands though, Brad," Alicia said as she came in to join us. She patted my shoulder in passing as she went to another chair. "I've given her a dose of laudanum. She's asleep now. Before she dropped off, she told me to tell Lucy she was not to worry, that her secret was safe. I don't believe she'll be vindictive, although I suggest you play least-in-sight, Brad. You taunted Hayes and you shot him deliberately, for all he aimed at you first."

"Must we keep harping on it?" the viscount demanded, running his hands through his blond hair. "At least *I* had the courage to act in a way that saved Lady Blake."

"Stop it," the dowager said firmly. "We'll have no cock-crowing here. A man is dead. Have the goodness to remember it, sir."

I could only look from one to the other, completely passive. I wondered why I didn't feel relieved. Why, inside, I wasn't dancing with joy, if it came to that. Oh, I knew I was in shock that a man had been killed right next to me, and disturbed by the blood that had pulsed from the wound to stain the rug and the floor beneath him. I could still see it, as vividly as if it had just happened. But even taking my shock into account, I should have thought that deep inside, I might be celebrating my new freedom. That just knowing I would never have to worry again about someone discovering the scandalous truth would make me feel elated. But I didn't feel elated. I didn't feel anything. It was then I realized I would never have any peace until the rest of the story had been told, at least to these few who had traveled the road with me. For after all, they did not know everything. I wondered how I was to begin.

"I suggest we discover how Lucy wishes to proceed in the matter," Gareth said. "She has said nothing so far."

All eyes turned to me and I thought for a moment before I said, "I agree there is no need for the rest of the world to know what happened here this afternoon. That means we must stick to our tale of a madman invading the house in search of valuables. The justice for this part of Cornwall is a Lord Benning. He is an elderly man, but he is sharp — not at all the country bumpkin you envisioned, m'lord," I added, for Epstead's benefit.

"He was a friend of Lord Blake's. He was very kind to me at the time of his death. I foresee no problems there. It won't even matter if Lord Benning recognizes the Hayes nose. A bastard who was forgotten in my lord's will makes our explanation even stronger."

Bradford Grey looked more cheerful. Even though what he had done had been at great risk to himself, it was still murder. I told myself I must not be a hypocrite. I must remember all the times I had contemplated killing Hayes to get rid of him. Still, I could not picture myself thanking the viscount for doing it for me.

"Well, I'm glad that's settled," the dowager said as she set down her empty glass and looked at it longingly. Neither gentleman obliged, and she sighed.

"Do you think we'll have to remain here much longer, Lucy?" she asked next. "I find I've a great desire to go home to Lansmere."

"I'm sure you'll be able to travel in a short time, ma'am," I reassured her. "All of you. You've been very good to me, giving so freely of your concern and your care, to say nothing of your time. I would not ask more.

"However, before you go, I'd like to tell you what did happen to me when I married Lord Blake. I feel I owe you that much after all the trouble I've put you to."

Bradford Grey raised his hand. "Certainly not, m'lady," he said sternly. "There is no need to distress yourself. I'm sure I speak for all of us when

I say we've no desire to hear more."

The slight revulsion in his voice made me cringe. Obviously he thought I wanted to try and excuse my adultery. I could see from Faith Abbott's face she at least was eager to hear me out, and although Alicia did not betray the same interest, neither did she side with her brother-in-law.

"You're wrong, Epstead," Gareth Powell said. "Oh, not that there is any need for Lady Blake to explain anything to us. I didn't mean that. *She* needs to do so, for her own sake. We are all adults here, and between us I'm sure we've heard all there is know of vice. I suggest we listen."

I tried to smile at him gratefully. It must have been a poor effort, for he did not return it.

I took a sip of my neglected brandy and water and tried to summon every ounce of courage I possessed. This was the hardest thing I had ever had to do in my entire life.

"I am sure you are all aware my parents arranged my marriage to Lord Blake," I began. "It was the *on dit* of that year's Season, the twice widowed lord marrying a girl more than forty years his junior.

"You know the customs as well as I do. I was not consulted. Naturally I did not want to marry the man, but my parents' wishes prevailed. Lord Blake took me to London after a quiet wedding at my home. It was January then. I had just had my seventeenth birthday.

"London was thin of company. I was glad of

279

that. I hoped by springtime I would be able to appear content with my lot. Oh, do not misunderstand me. Lord Blake was not unkind to me. He bought me lovely clothes and furs, gave me jewels and trinkets, promised me a dozen things I didn't want."

I left my chair then to pace the room. This part of the story was difficult for me, and no matter we were all adults as Gareth Powell had claimed. Still, I could not falter. My friends must know what had happened if they were ever to stop forgiving me for the lapse of good manners I had suffered when I took Hayes into my bed. Taking a deep breath, I turned to face them again.

"Lord Blake was not a successful lover," I said baldly. Faith Abbott looked thoughtful, Epstead frowned. Gareth and Bradford merely looked attentive.

"He tried, over and over, but he could not consummate the marriage," I went on, so intent on keeping my voice steady, I did not have time to worry about the indelicate things I was saying.

"At last, in desperation, he announced we would go home to Cornwall. And there, he assured me, things would be better, for we would be away from town with its many distractions, the endless late nights he spent with his cronies eating and drinking intemperately. Here, at Trecarag, we would live a simpler life with good fresh air and a wholesome routine of exercise and careful diet, and things would improve. Or so he claimed.

"They did not."

I stopped to take another sip of brandy water. My mouth was dry, but I felt I was past the worst part of the story.

"M'lord became annoyed with me," I went on. "He blamed me that we were not truly married, and there was no child coming. And he told me that was why he had married me. His two sons from his second marriage had died tragically in an accident at a mine shaft, and there were no more Blakes in existence. Not a cousin, not a nephew — not a soul —"

"I remember now," Faith Abbott interrupted in her impetuous way. "Of course. The news of his marriage to you was a terrible scandal, and not only because you were so young, Lucy. No, everyone was shocked he remarried less than four months after his sons' deaths. But the talk died down when you went to Trecarag. Hah! You wouldn't have had to worry about schooling your features during the Season. If Blake had stayed in town, he would have been royally snubbed, and you along with him."

She sniffed. "The old goat," she said. "To blame you after the life he led. Oh, yes, he was famous for his mistresses, the prostitutes he had. It's said his first wife died of a disease he passed on to her from one of them. As for his drinking — he was always in his cups. Yes, there are stories I could tell you about m'lord Blake that would shock you, but I shall say no more."

She sat back in her chair to my great relief. I

wanted nothing more than to finish this story and have done with it.

"I can believe that, Your Grace," I said. "He began to drink heavily again here, and he took to secluding himself for hours in his study with his dogs, to brood about his misfortunes."

I paused again to compose myself. There was no need for anyone to know how unpleasant those days had been for me. No need for them to learn how he cursed me and screamed at me, even how he had struck me when I would not do the things he suggested that he said would excite him.

"At last he summoned Hayes." I made myself go on. "He had been hovering about the property for some time trying to ingratiate himself with m'lord. M'lord had pointed him out to me when we first arrived at Trecarag, even bragged about this bastard he claimed was only one of many he had produced with different mothers.

"Hayes was installed in the house and treated like an honored guest. I didn't know why, but I was to learn in short order. Lord Blake told me I was to admit Hayes to my bed so he might get me with child. He would be a surrogate husband and father, he said. And since he was half Blake himself, what could be better? At least the child would have some of his blood."

"Oh, no," Alicia cried softly, her hand to her lips. Beyond her, the dowager sat with her fists clenched in her lap. She looked as if she wished she had Harrison Blake here so she might tell

282

him exactly what she thought of him. Bradford Grey lounged in his chair, one hand shading his eyes. I could not see enough of his face to discover what he thought of my story. When I looked at last at Gareth Powell I almost gasped. His dark eyes were blazing with the contempt he felt for my late husband. I swallowed and turned away.

"I refused to have anything to do with Hayes," I went on after another sip of my drink. "I told m'lord I didn't care if the practice was often employed in like cases the length and breadth of England. I wouldn't do it, and that was that. I disliked Hayes. He was a servile creature, always bowing and being obsequious when his father was about. Even then I suspected there was something that wasn't all right about him.

"The threats and pleas and punishments went on for some time. At last, after I was released from the room at the top of the tower where I'd been imprisoned for a week without any human contact and little to eat but bread and water, Lord Blake said he would try no further to persuade me to his way. He even apologized for what he had done to me. Hayes, however, was going to stay, he said. He had grown fond of him. I was wary hearing that, but I was so anxious to believe him, I relaxed. That evening after dinner, I felt unwell. Just before I fainted, I wondered if Lord Blake had poisoned me in hopes of marrying a more pliant, agreeable girl."

I paused again, to collect myself. The room

was quiet except for the crackling of the fire. Everyone but Epstead was staring at me; still, no one interrupted now.

"When I recovered consciousness much later that night, I found myself undressed and in Lord Blake's bed. It didn't take me long to discover Hayes had been with me there. Lord Blake told me so himself the following morning at breakfast while Hayes strutted about preening until I became ill. So ill, in fact, the doctor had to be summoned. I was put to bed and Lord Blake was told I was to be kept very quiet with no visitors and only invalid food. It didn't matter. I couldn't keep anything down, and whenever Lord Blake or Hayes came into the room, I pretended to have hysterics, and swoon. Afraid I might die, m'lord left me alone then. By the time I recovered, he had become ill himself."

I shrugged. "I confess I was glad he was ill, for concerned with his own well-being, m'lord lost interest in an heir. Hayes tried to come to me but I threatened to stab him if he even touched me. That, added to my scorn, convinced him not to bother me again.

"Eventually, after a long, painful time, Blake died. It was late August then. We had been at Trecarag for only four months, and I had been married for only twice that time. I buried him with all the pomp a lord of the realm deserved and with a great deal of hidden satisfaction as well. I make no apologies for that. He ruined my life. I hated him. I still do."

"I knew you did," Gareth said, speaking when I sipped my drink again.

"How did you guess?" I asked, curious. I'd been so sure I had managed to hide my true feelings for Blake.

His one-sided smile held little of amusement. "Because you have never, not once in all the time I've known you, ever called him by name. You never even said 'my husband' or 'my late husband.' No, it was always 'm'lord,' or 'Lord Blake.' "

I thought for a moment before I nodded. I hadn't been aware of it but I could see how it might have been so.

"I've told you almost everything," I said. "I let all the Trecarag servants go for I couldn't bear to have anyone near me who might have guessed what was afoot. Not that there was much danger of it. Lord Blake was anxious to claim the child as his own. Hayes was only an instrument he used to gain that end."

I shook my head. "Poor man," I said. "He was so sure his fortune was made and his future safe. So very sure Lord Blake not only valued but loved him. And then as soon as the funeral was over, I sent him away from Trecarag and closed the place before I escaped to London. No wonder he went mad. He was as much a victim as I was."

"To think I never guessed," Faith Abbott mourned. "To think I was so insensitive I did not realize what was making you sad and depressed, my dear girl. I wish you had told me all this sooner."

"But you see why I couldn't tell you, or anyone, don't you, ma'am?" I asked.

"Of course. Such a vulgar, gross thing for you to have to discuss, and you so young. Still, I wonder I didn't think of it long ago. I've known of another case like this, more than one, in fact. There's never any proof, of course, although there may be speculation about why the heir doesn't resemble his father in any way. But with Hayes, Lord Blake wouldn't have had to worry about that. You'd be astounded at the grooms and footmen who've been pressed into service, and then sent on their way a great deal richer."

I stared at Faith Abbott, speechless. This had happened to other women? My situation was not unique? How truly awful men were!

"I've heard that sometimes a husband merely leaves a wife to her own devices — gives tacit approval to a discreet affair," Alicia contributed. I stared at her as well. She sounded as if she were only discussing some unusual local custom. "Turns a blind eye to her amorous adventures, and then when she finds herself with child, claims it as his own. And who shall say different if the husband won't admit he's been cuckolded?" she concluded.

"Why didn't I ever hear tell of such things?" I asked, almost indignantly. "I thought I was the only one . . . that Lord Blake was a monster —"

"Oh, he was a monster, all right," Gareth

agreed. I tried not to look at him too long, but I cannot tell you how much I hoped he had believed my story, and understood why I had been acting as I had. Somehow that was very important to me.

"Yes, this has been very interesting, but surely it has been painful for Lucy to relive," Epstead said brusquely as he rose. "If you'll all excuse me, I think I'd prefer to have some time alone before the justice comes. Your Grace? M'lady? Alicia?"

"I think we had all better go and compose ourselves," the dowager agreed, rising and beckoning to Alicia. To my disappointment, Gareth pushed his shoulders away from the mantel where he had been leaning and followed them all to the door. There, however, he paused and turned, made me a deep sweeping bow. I confess I blushed crimson when he put his hand over his heart and paid me that homage, just as if I had been a queen.

As the door closed behind him, I sank back into my chair, a little smile on my face. He did understand, he did.

Chapter 20

Justice Benning arrived at Trecarag an hour later. He was as portly as I remembered, with the same snapping hazel eyes and surprisingly delicate hands and feet. After I had received him and his men, I took them to the tower room where Hayes's body lay. Lord Benning patted my hand at the door and told me to run along for there was no need for me to revisit the scene and distress myself.

Some time later, we were all summoned to the drawing room to be questioned. The dowager duchess was haughty and indignant such a thing had happened when she was a guest, Gareth Powell was matter-of-fact, and Alicia properly shocked. Viscount Epstead claimed he always carried a small pistol and had since he had attended a ball in London a few years ago that had been invaded by a number of jewel thieves. The Gladdings ball. Perhaps the justice had heard of it? It had been a brilliant occasion.

As for Hayes's arsenal, none of us had the slightest idea why he felt three pistols were necessary, nor did we have any explanation for why the man had attempted such a daring feat in the daylight.

"Perhaps he thought the fog would aid his escape," the justice suggested, as his clerk scratched diligently away, recording the proceedings. "I met Hayes once when Harrison — m'lord Blake, y'know — was alive. I thought him a singular young man. Strange, too. He insisted I take his card although I am not generally accustomed to doing so right after being introduced and while on horseback."

He coughed behind his hand, looking at both Gareth Powell and Viscount Epstead. "Wasn't difficult to see where he sprang from though, was it?" he said in an aside to them I barely caught.

A short time later he took his leave, bowing to both ladies and giving me a kiss on the cheek. I was told I was not to worry about a thing. He would rule death by misadventure, and if I liked, see to the removal of the body himself.

I hesitated. Franklin had not been called. The justice did not know she was Hayes's mother since we had not thought it necessary to mention it. Still, I felt she must be consulted about her son's funeral.

"It is kind of you, sir, but then, you've always been kind to me," I told him. "I think no matter what the man did, I should see to his burial myself."

Lord Benning harummphed and blew his nose, somewhat at a loss for words since I had as good as told him I knew of Hayes's connection to my late husband. Finally he said it was just like me to be so thoughtful, and by the time the drawing room door shut behind him and his men, I was quite undone by his overblown compliments.

"I must say I was astounded to hear you volunteer to bury the man Lucy," Epstead drawled. "Surely there's no need for it."

I was tired and I longed to rest. I supposed I would have to dress for dinner. Life did go on. But just then I was out of patience with Bradford Grey and heartily wished to see the back of him.

"But there is since he was Lord Blake's son. His burial here is only a small thing, but it might comfort his mother."

"Your maid?" Epstead asked, astounded.

"My maid has feelings, too," I told him.

"But to return to a more important subject. May I suggest it might be wise to plan your departure, sir, now the justice has accepted our explanation for Hayes's death? He might think of further questions and call again."

He stared at me for a moment before he said, "I shall certainly do so, ma'am. But I don't like to leave Alicia and the dowager duchess here, and no woman I know can pack and leave a place with less than three days' notice. And even then they are apt to forget some prized possession."

"Prepare to be astounded, sir," Alicia said. "You forget I'm a seasoned veteran of foreign travel. On occasion your brother has given me only an hour. As for the duchess, she always travels light, don't you, ma'am?"

She turned to me then. "Are you sure it's all

290

right if we go, Lucy? Wouldn't you feel better if we kept you company until you are able to put all this behind you and leave as well?"

I went and kissed her. "No, for I'm fine, now," I said and smiled to prove it. "Hayes's death, and telling you all my secrets has lifted the enormous burden I've been carrying. I assure you, I feel quite rejuvenated."

"I should think this place would have such horrid memories you would want to quit it as soon as possible," Faith Abbott remarked.

"Since I'm never coming back to Trecarag, there are things I must do before I leave. Please, you must not worry about me. Oh, would you be so kind as to carry a letter to my man Kittering in London? I want him to find me a house there. And when I am settled, I expect you and Alicia to be my first guests."

Diverted, the dowager began to discuss the merits of various London squares and the more fashionable streets. I let her talk, only smiling and nodding now and then. I was very conscious of a silent Powell seated to my right. I wondered what he was thinking, not that I had a chance of discovering it, of course. It was maddening he was so undemonstrative.

When I went to my room at last, I found Franklin there laying out my evening clothes. As I paused in surprise, she curtsied.

I went to hug her tight. She did not cry, but I heard her uneven breathing, and felt how unsteady her hands were as she put me away from her.

"There now, ma'am, I'm all right," she said as she turned away.

"You shouldn't be here, Franklin — I mean, Miss Hayes. You should be lying down, resting."

"I tried to do that. It gave me too much time to think," she confessed as she took a pair of sandals from the armoire.

"Tell me," I said slowly as I sat down at the dressing table to remove the pins from my hair, "would you like your son to be buried at Trecarag?"

I was watching her reflection in the mirror before me, and I saw how she started and turned to me.

"You'd do that?" she almost whispered. "You'd allow Jaspar to be buried here?"

"I don't see why he shouldn't be. He is half Blake and the last of the line, if it comes to that. And none of what happened was his fault. If his father hadn't manipulated him — made promises he had no intention of keeping — given him hopes there was no way of satisfying, I don't think Jaspar would have begun to follow me. He might not even have gone mad.

"I'll see the vicar first thing tomorrow; arrange for a suitable coffin. We'll bury Jaspar in the Blake graveyard with his ancestors. Then we must attend to your affairs. Whatever you decide to do, you'll have ample funds."

I paused, for Sarah Hayes had covered her face with her hands. She was weeping at last.

Jaspar Hayes was buried two days later. Everyone was still with me, but only Gareth Powell and his valet and groom followed the coffin to the graveyard. They were somberly dressed, the servants wearing black gloves and armbands.

Of course Bradford Grey was nowhere in sight, and as was the custom, no women attended. I was glad of that for surely it would have been difficult if Franklin acknowledged she was the thief's mother. As it was she sat with me in the room at the top of the tower where we could watch the proceedings and read our prayer books.

I admit my eyes seldom left Powell's tall, upright figure. I had not asked him to serve as mourner; indeed, I had not expected it of him or anyone. But he had seen the need, to comfort Hayes's mother and make his death seem less scandalous. Still, I was sure all the terrible doings at Trecarag would be discussed over many a fireside for miles around, not only now but through the winter months. Gossip is hard to come by in Cornwall then.

After the service was over and Franklin had left me, I wandered down the stairs to the tower room that had once been mine. It was here Bradford Grey found me. I could see he had a lot on his mind, and when he asked to speak to me, gestured to the chairs in the bay window.

"I gather from your suggestion the other day that you would prefer I quit Trecarag," he began, leaning toward me earnestly. A sunbeam turned his hair golden; limned his handsome face.

"I've also had to accept the fact you'll never

marry me," he went on. "You know I'm sorry for that."

He paused and I told myself I must not rush into speech. There was no way on earth Epstead could have been cajoled into marriage with me. Not now. Not after what he had learned. In his eyes I was soiled beyond redemption, no fit mate for the Viscount of Epstead. I knew this. I even sympathized and forgave him. To be truthful, I didn't really care although I knew remembering the impetuous suitor he had been would always make me smile.

"Oh, do give over, sir," I said lightly. As his brows rose, I went on, "You don't want to marry me now and we both know it."

He sat back then, all the subtle signs of tension gone from his body. "And you don't want to marry me. That's quite understandable after your first experience.

"Do you know, like Her Grace I feel so stupid! While such situations as yours are not common practice, neither are they that rare. But I never once considered it."

He sounded annoyed he had not been more perceptive and I hid a smile. I knew I should not ask he keep this delicious bit of scandal to himself. He would be insulted if I did. And truly, as mercurial and careless as Bradford Grey was, I knew he wasn't evil. Even the way he had treated Gareth's pretty cousin had to have been more a young man's carelessness than intentional arrogance.

"Her Grace and Alicia are packing. I hope you will not linger here for long after we go. London will be desolate without you."

He rose as I did. "Tell me, m'lord, is it possible for you to converse with a woman without flirting with her?" I asked.

He appeared to think, but only for a moment. "But of course it is," he said haughtily. "When you consider how few lovely, alluring women there are. Why, I've been known to go for weeks without voicing a single gallantry."

As we reached the door, he kissed my hand. "Please allow me to say one more thing, darling Lucy. Do not, I beg you, jump too quickly into yet another matrimonial stew. You're young yet. You can take your time. Be sure."

"You've never listened to me when I told you I've no desire for marriage, now have you?" I asked. "It is so vexing!"

He chuckled and hugged me tight for a moment. "I'd be willing to wager anything you like, m'lady, you'll have to eat those words by this time next year," he said.

I pushed him on his way, glad my complexion betrayed nothing of my feelings. His prophecy would not come to pass and I knew that full well. I wondered why I hadn't seen Gareth Powell. Both the dowager and Alicia had sought me out for a private farewell. Faith Abbott had been full of advice about my future. I knew she intended to do more than find me a new house in London. I was sure she was going over her list of eligibles even now, discarding them one by one if they were too old, too boring, or too impoverished, but putting a little tick next to a pleasant earl's name, or that of a wealthy and fashionable widower.

As I went down the stairs to see if the afternoon post had arrived, I wondered which list her godson's name was on.

We had a pleasant dinner together that evening, the five of us. Bradford Grey especially was full of high spirits, carrying us all before him with his outrageous stories and quick-witted ripostes. Faith Abbott laughed so hard she had to wipe her eyes on her napkin, and even Alicia laughed heartily. Gareth Powell was quieter, but he seemed to throw off his abstraction and dislike for the viscount to enter into the occasion. It occurred to me he must be glad this adventure was over, glad he could return to Water House and his own affairs. Perhaps that was why he was so cheerful. I realized he had given me a tremendous amount of his time — well, so had they all, this band of friends. I told myself I would be forever grateful, and had to wipe my own eyes on my napkin. Fortunately, Brad had just told a very amusing jest, and no one remarked my sudden flood of tears.

I rose early the next morning, determined to see my friends off. I was glad it was such a lovely day. Faith Abbott had begged to make the trip in one day, rather than stay on the moor overnight, and so it had been decided. The ladies embraced me; Bradford Grey as well. I turned at last to Gareth Powell. He was checking the cinch on his horse a short distance away, and I went to join him. Behind me I could hear the viscount giving orders about the disposal of the baggage, and the dowager demanding her salts since she was sure to need them almost immediately.

"You weren't planning to ride away without saying good-bye, sir, now were you?" I asked, holding out my hand to him.

"No, I wasn't going to do that," he told me as he pressed my hand gently.

"I would thank you again for all your help, but I'm sure you've heard me do that too many times already."

"Indeed I have. Please spare me."

"Then there is nothing to say but good-bye, is there?"

"Not good-bye. Adieu."

"Aren't you going to kiss me?" I asked, wondering at my boldness. "Everyone else has."

"So I noticed. But I've no intention of kissing you before the grooms and footmen, to say nothing of my godmother's sharp eyes and both the Greys' heroic attempts to pretend indifference."

"I did not think you such a coward, sir," I scolded, trying not to show how wounded I was.

One side of his mouth lifted in a smile for a moment. "Ah, Lucy, if you only knew," he said.

"Knew what?"

He shook his head. "You'll not trap me that

way, my girl," he said as he reached out and turned me away from him. "Run along before I forget myself. You are in great danger. Run!"

He gave me a little push and there had been something in his voice — in his eyes — that made me hurry to obey him. Still, after the servants had returned to their duties, and the carriages had pulled away, the two men on horseback leading the way, I stood for a long time on the steps alone and wondered what Gareth Powell had meant by the things he had said.

Or perhaps, more important, by the things he hadn't.

Four days later, I was still settling household and estate matters. The servants the viscount had brought with him had gone on their way, happy, no doubt, to return to London. The servants Kittering had hired for me would stay on until I left myself. Mrs. Langley had consented to remain at Trecarag with a small staff to oversee the household and be available to show it to any prospective buyers. I was relieved she had agreed to do so. She was a competent woman and she got along well with Cornish folk. There would be no need to worry with Mrs. Langley in command.

Now, after a morning spent in the stillroom and the linen room with her, I excused myself and escaped to the garden. It was a cool day. When I had looked from my window that morning, the sea had been a deeper blue than I had ever seen in Cornwall. Now I could feel a nip in the air whenever I moved from a patch of sunlight into the shade. The garden looked attractive. There were still flowers blooming and I picked a late rosebud. It had a lovely fragrance. Beyond the garden near the Blake burial ground, the canes of the wild roses were tangled in heaps around the palings that separated the graveyard from the lawn. I could see the raw dark patch of earth where Jaspar Hayes was buried, and I averted my eyes.

Franklin had left with the viscount's servants, carrying a letter from me to Kittering. She intended to return to the village in Hampshire where she had been a girl rather than stay here in Cornwall. We had spoken for a long time the night before she left, and I'd learned much of her life and her son's, and of Lord Blake and his family. It was then I realized how much the two of us had in common.

I didn't tell her about the entwined roses and the drop of blood on my pillow at Lansmere, nor the mutilated bird Hayes had sent me in London. She had borne enough.

Still, as close as we had been for four years, and all we had shared these past four months, I was glad when she was gone. Her presence had been a constant reminder of Jaspar Hayes and I wanted to forget him as fast as I could. Forget him and get on with my life, whatever that life might be.

I found I'd reached the end of the garden.

Without thinking, I pushed through the gap in the hedge there and started down the path to my own private little glade.

I was sure I would be able to leave Trecarag in three days' time. I didn't know if I would find a ship sailing to London, but it didn't matter. I would take a room at an inn in Fowey and wait until there was one.

That reminded me I must be sure to have one of the maids accompany me and I reached into my pocket for the pencil and pad I was never without now, to make a note of it.

In the glade I sat down on the fallen log and tried not to think about all the times I had come here in the past to weep and bemoan my fate. I would never have to do so again, I told myself as I picked a long grass stem and scattered the seeds of it on the ground. In all probability, I would not return to Cornwall. Why should I? I smiled, just thinking of it.

"There you are. I expected I might find you here," a deep familiar voice said. I looked up to see Gareth Powell entering the glade.

It took a minute before I could say, "Why, what a surprise! I thought you well on your way to London by now, sir."

He didn't answer and he didn't smile. Instead, he reached me in two long strides and pulled me up into his arms.

"Now, Lucy, about that kiss," he said, his eyes blazing down into mine.

At first I felt nothing but sensation. How wonderful his mouth felt on mine — the thrill of having his hard body pressed tightly against me as his hands caressed my back — the warm, distinctive scent of his skin and the rough texture of his jacket under my fingers. When he lifted his head a few inches at last, I reveled in the broken words he murmured, stumbling over them in his haste to tell me of his passion. How he had loved me all along, but had wanted to give me time to recover from the ordeal I had suffered. How he had meant to escort his godmother to London and then go to Water House until he felt I could bear to see him as a man — a lover — a husband. And how he had not been able to be so noble and forbearing after all, but had galloped back to me as soon as Faith Abbott was safely aboard ship.

When he told me that, I felt a surge of the most intense joy I had ever known for I knew then he loved me. He really loved me.

"Tell me you will give me the chance to prove that marriage is not some kind of degrading trap; that love has nothing to do with the horrors you have known. It can be beautiful — an experience full of passion and fulfillment. I'll show you, Lucy," he said, his voice shaking a little. "I promise I'll show you. Trust me."

Forgetting all my avowals never to marry again as if I had never made them at all, I nodded, holding my breath until he crushed me in his arms again and kissed me till I was faint with wanting him.

When the coolness of late afternoon drove us

inside much later and we returned to the Hall, I knew exactly what he meant. And since we were both determined not to make love in a place where I had known such pain, I found myself able to leave Trecarag Hall very early the next morning after all.

You may be sure I did not look back.

The employees of G.K. Hall hope you have enjoyed this Large Print book. All our Large Print titles are designed for easy reading, and all our books are made to last. Other G.K. Hall books are available at your library, through selected bookstores, or directly from us.

For information about titles, please call:

(800) 257-5157

To share your comments, please write:

Publisher
G.K. Hall & Co.
P.O. Box 159
Thorndike, ME 04986

ACB-M
11-1-99